Excerpt from Evie's
Christmas Chocolate Kisses

I walked through the double doors and was overwhelmed by the sounds. Mostly from the people, "ooh-ing" and "aah-ing." I decided to move counterclockwise through the booths of animals, make notes on my hand-held computer, and then revisit the ones I liked best.

Well, in theory, that was a great plan, except the first booth wasn't full of animals, it was a really cute guy advertising a veterinary clinic. It was a good thing I wasn't shopping for a boyfriend because I would have adopted him on the spot. He had close-cut dark hair, blue eyes beneath slashing dark brows, high cheekbones, and beautifully shaped sensual mouth. How old? The late twenties? Maybe early thirties? He was dressed in dark jeans and a tight sweatshirt that revealed a lean muscular body.

"Hi," was all I could muster. His broad smile was captivating, and my girl parts did a swirl, flip, and tingle in all the right spots. Merry Christmas to me.

Evie's Christmas Chocolate Cookies

Sharon Kleve

CHAPTER ONE

Confection Connection was decorated for the holidays with a large holly wreath on the door, colorful lights hung around the windows, and poinsettias on all of the glass display cases. I never got tired of the sweet, sugar-filled scents that swirled around the bakery and especially during the holiday season. The bakery seemed to smell even better—more festive if that was possible.

The decadent scent of cupcakes, crisping croissants, and the distinct aroma of gooey pastry as it baked into delicious pans of hot cinnamon rolls, wrapped around me, like a warm blanket. I inhaled the delicious aroma once more, took a nibble of a chewy, chocolate kiss cookie and sighed in pleasure. Confection Connection was located in a trendy area of Boston, Massachusetts surrounded by boutiques, a flower shop, and a scrumptious Italian deli all decorated for the holidays.

There had been a steady stream of customers all day buying cakes, pies, holiday cookies, and freshly baked bread. The door chimed as another customer walked inside. I automatically smiled and looked up from the pastries case to see my latest failed relationship, Andrew Summerfield.

"Hi, Evie." He thrust a large bouquet of red roses into my hands. "You look beautiful."

I was grateful Caley Madden, my bakery assistant, was in the back mixing bread dough or she would take Andrew apart at the seams. She was as protective of me as a mamma bear of her cubs. I laid the roses on the counter without smelling the wonderful fragrance. I would do that after I kicked him out. I didn't want him to see the joy I felt from flowers even if they were from a total narcissistic jerk. He had an excessive need for admiration, a disregard for others' feelings— mine especially—and an inability to handle any criticism. "What are you doing here?"

"You aren't returning my phone calls."

His large ego couldn't accept that I dumped him. "I thought I was perfectly clear on the phone that I didn't want to see you any longer."

He smiled so wide his bleached white teeth almost blinded me. "I thought if I came by we could work out the misunderstanding."

When I learned of his cheating, it hurt, but not as bad as the knowledge, he was only seeing me because of my inheritance. His *other* girlfriend gladly informed me he was dating me to get access to my financial assets. My parents had left me their beautiful, turn-of-the-century home located three miles from the bakery.

Andrew was in commercial real estate and knew how much my home was worth. "No. It's over. There's nothing to talk about, no getting back together. Now, get out and stop calling me."

He stepped closer to the counter, reached out, and touched my hand. "I know I haven't said this before, but I love you, Evie Holmes."

My jaw dropped in shock. A couple of months ago, I would have melted into a puddle of happiness at his declaration, now I was able to see this for what it was—pure manipulation. "Caley is in the back. Would you like me to go get her? She'd be more than happy to show you to the door."

Andrew removed his hand and backed up. "I'll give you some time to think about our future together. I'll call next week, and we can go to dinner."

He had the gall to wink before he left.

I jumped when Caley leaned into my shoulder. "I thought you kicked Andrew to the curb last week?" She removed a cookie from the case and took a bite.

"I did. I told him to take a hike several times, but he brought flowers and said he'd call next week for a dinner date." I inhaled the lovely fragrance from the roses. "Should I have insisted he take the roses back?"

"No. Of course not. They are beautiful, but he doesn't know how to take no for an answer. If you had called me out, I could have educated him." Caley shook her finger at me.

Suzie and Brandy, the rest of the staff, giggled from the doorway. They loved a good piece of gossip.

"I can't believe he fooled me with his charming smiles and old fashioned courtesies. I would never have suspected he was dating another woman."

"Yeah well, sociopaths are great at deceiving people."

"Don't feel bad, he fooled us all," Suzie said.

"You have so much going for you." Caley motioned with her arm around the bakery and finished eating the cookie. "You're talented, generous, and smart. You'll find a guy who appreciates those qualities."

"I hope you're right. This time of year is hard enough with my parents being here. It would be nice to have someone to spend it with."

"He's out there somewhere." Caley hugged me tight and then took the roses to the back room.

But where? I asked myself.

Last year, three days before Christmas, the police called to tell me my parents were killed in a car accident. A semi-truck driver fell asleep at the wheel, crossed the centerline and hit them head-on.

The memories overwhelmed me and tears threatened to spill down my cheeks. I locked the bathroom door and I took a deep breath to calm myself.

I critically surveyed myself in the mirror. I had long, straight brunette hair, my body was on the slim side, and I was almost medium height, with blue eyes and fair skin. I might not be a ten, but I wasn't hard on the eyes either and a good person. I deserved better than Andrew. That was when I realized I looked just like my mother when she was my age and smiled—I would always have that.

I dabbed my eyes dry and went back to work at the one thing that would never disappoint me, Confection Connection.

CHAPTER TWO

Two weeks later.

Caley stood before me with her hands on her full hips and a concerned look on her pretty face.

"Evie, as your good friend and favorite employee, I'm ordering you to go home. We've got it all handled."

I wiped down the counters even though they were already spotless. Christmas was just around the corner, and we had countless holiday orders, but everything was under control—at the moment.

"Please, for the sake of the rest of the bakery staff, go home early and get a good night's sleep."

"What? Are they complaining about me?" I had been a little moody because of the upcoming anniversary of my parent's death.

"Complaining no, concerned yes. You haven't been your cheerful self for a couple of weeks. We all love you and want you to be happy."

"I know. I'll try and cheer up."

Caley wrapped her arm around my shoulders and squeezed. "You haven't had a day off forever, you're not exercising, or eating right. Basically, you are not taking care of yourself. Why don't you go for a run with your neighbor in the morning and come in late. We can handle the orders," she suggested.

"A run sounds wonderful." Gary, my neighbor, was always up for a run.

Suzie walked out of the backroom with a tray of gingerbread cookies and placed them in the glass case. "I've been thinking, maybe you should get a pet—something to love and cuddle. A dog would be great for you because you have a large fenced backyard."

If I got a dog, I could take it for walks in the park, or running when the mood struck, and we could keep each other company. "I hadn't thought about a pet. Maybe I will."

They both headed toward the back of the bakery.

Caley turned around at the last moment. "Oh, before I forget, my sweet hubby made me promise to ask you if you'd come over for Christmas Eve dinner."

"Is Bob going to be there, too?" I knew a setup when I saw one. The look on Caley's face confirmed my suspicions. John, Caley's husband, had been trying to set me up with his brother for several months.

She looked sheepish, and her cheeks turned pink. "Yeah, and he's even balder and more overweight than the last time we suggested you two meet."

"You know, it's not his looks." Caley looked skeptical. "Okay—if he's not taken, ask me again after the holidays."

"Don't worry, he won't be taken. We both know he's not the best catch." She chuckled. "Don't tell John I said that though."

"I won't. Just tell him I have other plans."

"Right, other plans my ass. You're going to mope around in that big house all by yourself."

"Maybe not. The idea of a pet is really sinking in. I'll look into it tomorrow."

"Good. Let me know if I can help. We have gotten all of our pets from shelters. We prefer mutts over pedigrees."

"Me too." I kissed Caley's cheek. "Thank you. You are so thoughtful."

"Back at you. Now, I need to get back to work. My boss is a slave driver."

"Yep. A real whip-cracker I am." We both giggled.

CHAPTER THREE

Beep, beep, beep, beep. My alarm clock blared. I had taken Caley's advice and slept in. Unfortunately, I had forgotten to turn my alarm off *and* to call my neighbor to see if he wanted to go for a run. I could go by myself but I wanted the company. Gary's phone rang several times before he answered.

"Hello?" He sounded sleepy.

"Hey, this is Evie. Are you up for a run this morning?"

"I'd love it. When can you be ready?" Gary sounded much more alert now.

"Ten minutes. I'll meet you out front." He was kind, cooked, cleaned, and was a sharp dresser. Too bad Gary had a partner named Scott, or I would have snagged him for myself a long time ago.

I quickly changed and met Gary in front of my house. We both stretched our muscles and jogged in place to warm up. "You ready?" I asked.

He took off running and laughed. "Come on, honey. Get your pretty butt in gear."

Three miles later, I was panting, out of breath, and still cold from frigid weather. The wind coming off the water chilled to the bone.

"Evie dear, do I need to call the medics?" Gary joked.

"No, I'm okay," was all I could muster.

"For your own good, we should run more often. When we get back, I'll blend you a refreshing kale, carrot, and avocado smoothie. I'll have you whipped into shape in no time." Gary nodded confidently.

In shape for what, I wanted to ask, but I couldn't utter a word.

Thirty minutes later, Gary forced a smoothie made of healthy crap down my throat before I could get out of his kitchen. It wasn't as bad as I thought it would be.

"Scott loves carrots and parsley, but I prefer fruit smoothies. Everyone is different." Gary shrugged.

"Thank you for the run and liquefied vegetables. If you'd tossed in one of my donuts from the bakery, it would have been perfect."

Gary cringed, and I laughed as I ran out the front door before he could punish me with another healthy smoothly.

My legs wobbled from overuse as I stripped off my clothes, filled the tub with warm water, and soaked until my wrinkles had wrinkles. I dried off, put on my mom's favorite lavender velour robe, sat on my bed, and thought about the holidays. I hadn't put up one single Christmas decoration in my home yet. They were all packed and stored in the attic.

The phone by the bed rang and jolted me out of the melancholy mood I was slipping into again.

"Did you get the email with the pet adoption link I sent last night?" Caley blurted.

"No. I haven't checked email today. What's it all about?"

"All the local shelters are bringing their animals to one location so you should have a wide variety of pets to choose from. It starts at 9:00 a.m. tomorrow morning and goes until 4:00 p.m. You should get there as early as possible—we'll handle the bakery."

"Okay, I promise I'll be the first one at the door. Now, do not get your hopes up. I'm not promising that I'll adopt anything. An animal is a big commitment, and I want to be sure it'll be a good fit." Who was I fooling? I wanted a dog more than anything.

Caley, Suzie, and Brandy baked shortbread cookies in the different shapes of dogs and piped icing in a variety of dog's names on each one. They were a hit with the customers.

I worked an extra-long to day to make up for sleeping in the day before, and the time I would be at the pet adoption facility tomorrow.

There were bagels in layered rows, topped with seeds and onions. In the glass case, sugar sparkled like snow on the cinnamon twists, and jelly donuts gleamed with translucent icing. Brown bread, in big round loaves, were layered on the bread shelves and a barrel in the corner held the slim baguettes. The bakery was ready for another busy day.

CHAPTER FOUR

I checked the link and knew exactly where the community center was located for the adoption event. They had photos of an assortment of available pets—I had an overwhelming need to adopt all of them.

The phone rang, as I was getting ready to leave. "Hello?"

"Hey Evie, I was hoping you'd already left," Caley sai

"If you thought I was already gone, why did you call my house phone and not my cell phone?" I teased.

"I don't know. You are still going aren't you?" she probed.

"Yes. I was on my way out the door, but what if I can't make up my mind and adopt all of them?" My house was large. I could have multiple pets if I wanted, but I worked long hours. This was going to be harder than I thought.

Caley laughed. "That's so you. They'll have people there who can explain the needs and care of each animal. Call me the minute you make up your mind. Better yet, take a picture and send it to me from your phone."

"Okay."

"Promise?"

"Yes. I promise." I laughed before hanging up.

The parking lot at the community center was packed full of cars, minivans, and trucks. There was even a Pepsi truck, a Doritos truck, and a couple pet food vendors. It was a Christmas bazaar full of pets instead of crafts.

I walked through the double doors and was overwhelmed by the sounds. Mostly from the people, "ooh-ing" and "aah-ing." I decided to move counterclockwise through the booths of animals, make notes on my hand-held computer, and then revisit the ones I liked best.

Well, in theory, that was a great plan, except the first booth wasn't full of animals, it was a really cute guy advertising a veterinary clinic. It was a good thing I wasn't shopping for a boyfriend because I would have adopted him on the spot. He had close-cut dark hair, blue eyes beneath slashing dark brows, high cheekbones, and beautifully shaped sensual mouth. How old? The late twenties? Maybe early thirties? He was dressed in dark jeans and a tight sweatshirt that revealed a lean muscular body.

"Hi," was all I could muster. His broad smile was captivating, and my girl parts did a swirl, flip, and tingle in all the right spots. Merry Christmas to me.

His smile was captivating as he extended his hand. "Hello. I'm Nick Tucker. I run the Tucker Emergency Animal Hospital on Beacon Hill. Can I answer any questions for you?"

Nick's hand was warm and gentle. He held on a little longer than customary, but I had no intention of pulling away first. There was no ring indentation on his finger, and his blue eyes twinkled when he smiled. "Yes.

I haven't had a pet since I was a child. I'm not sure what's best for me. Do you have a suggestion?"

"Do you have kids or a husband that have pet restrictions or preferences?"

"No. I don't have anyone." That sounded pathetic. "I mean, I don't have any restrictions. I have a large house with a fenced yard."

"That's good." He leaned forward and smiled again.

I might not have a pet yet, but I had just chosen my new veterinarian. It would be my lucky day if he made house calls.

"Why don't you look around for a while? Keep an open mind. Sometimes a pet finds you. If you still haven't found anything, I'll make a suggestion." He handed me a map and winked. "Take this, it shows the layout of the center. If you continue to your right, you'll find the cats and the smaller critters, like rabbits and chinchillas. Then finally, the dogs. They're my favorite."

"Thank you, I'll do that." I tried not to trip on the carpet as I walked away. I couldn't stop thinking about what it would be like to be cared for by a sexy veterinarian.

CHAPTER FIVE

I stroked and petted at least twenty cats and kittens but none of them completely bonded with me. They were all soft and playful, but not what I was looking for. There was a donation box where the cats and kittens were kept. My mom and dad had numerous cats over the years. It seemed fitting to donate five hundred dollars in their name.

A cranky chinchilla hissed at me, the rabbits backed into a corner when I tried to pet them, and the ferrets seemed a little too rambunctious for me. Another hundred dollars went into the donation box for the small critters.

Then, last but not least, the dogs and puppies. Nick said to keep an open mind, so that's what I did. There were definitely more dogs that needed homes than any other kind of pet. I wandered up and down the aisle. There was a crowd around one of the dogs. I couldn't get close enough to see what they were all looking at. I figured it must be a pretty impressive dog if it had that many admirers. Of course, I had to see what all the commotion was about. I got up on my tiptoes but still couldn't see anything.

Finally, a woman tried to move her son out of the way, but he kept staring at the dog. "Mom, why is that dog wearing a diaper?" the kid finally asked.

"I don't know. Bobby. Come on, let's go look at the rest of the dogs." She tugged her son's hand, and they walked over to a Springer Spaniel.

As I stared at the pathetic dog in the diaper, I realized no one wanted the dog—they were just gawking at him. The sign on the metal enclosure stated, *My name is Brewster. I am a mix of St. Bernard and Newfoundland. I need a loving home to call my own.*

My heart swelled for the dog, he looked so sad and all alone. He was very large, and he was slobbering everywhere. He should have a diaper around his neck. I turned to continue my search and looked down at Brewster again. When our eyes met, Brewster's eyes twinkled just like Nick's.

He raised his head up and out of the enclosure, and a glob of drool hit the top of my shoe and then he licked the goo off. I wanted to say, "gross," but instead I said, "Thank you." I was hooked. His fur was a reddish brown and soft as silk. Not caring about drool or dog hair, I leaned over the enclosure, wrapped my arms around Brewster's neck, and finally felt at peace.

Another glob of drool hit my shoe. He looked sad, as though that might be a deal breaker and I would leave him behind. I looked into Brewster's sad eyes and laughed. He pulled back his goofy lips and smiled.

That was when I heard Nick's voice. "Well Evie, it looks like you found your soul mate." He laughed, but I could tell it wasn't at my expense.

"Oh, I think I already love him. Is that possible?" If love at first sight was possible, it happened twice that day. Once with Nick, and the other with Brewster.

"Anything is possible. Brewster wouldn't have been my first choice for you, because he will be a lot of work in the beginning, but sometimes, when fate intervenes, it's easier to accept that some things are just meant to be."

"What do you mean by that?" I continued to stroke Brewster's head.

"Brewster's owners were killed in a car accident last month. He was hurt pretty badly, hence the diaper to protect his incisions. The state patrol brought him to my animal hospital, and I repaired some pretty substantial internal injuries. I didn't think he would make it, but he did."

"My parents were killed in a car accident right before Christmas last year. I thought it would be hard this year, but now, Brewster and I have each other."

"I'm sorry about your parents. I feel fortunate my parents are still alive and kicking. I have two brothers and one sister, all with kids and various animals. We all stay at my parents' ranch, Christmas through the New Year. It's always a zoo, but I love it."

"That sounds wonderful." Brewster drooled, and it dropped on my shoe again. I laughed. "Is there an instruction booklet that comes with him? Like how to turn off the drool?"

Nick stroked Brewster's head. "I'm afraid he doesn't come with an instruction booklet. The drooling is part of his breed. It helps to have lots of towels handy."

He was laughing at me again, and I was okay with it. "I can handle drool. Will he always have to wear a diaper?"

"No, it's not a bladder issue. He had multiple incisions, and this seemed like the best way to keep them clean and dry. I guess the shelter that took him in agreed with me. The instruction sheet you'll be given will have my contact information. He will need a follow-up appointment to remove his sutures in two weeks. Call my office and make an appointment when you have a chance."

That would give me another reason to see Nick. "I will. How long does he have to wear the diaper and are there any other health issues I should know about?"

"No, he's healthy, but his wounds will take a while to fully heal. Give it another week or two. He should cheer up now that he has a permanent home. I'm sure he misses his owners."

"I bet he does too."

"Well, it was a pleasure meeting you, Evie. I need to get back to my booth. If you have any questions about Brewster or me, call me or stop by."

We both chuckled. "I'll do that."

He walked away, and then stopped, and turned back. "Would you like to go out sometime?"

I nodded and then blurted, "Yes. That would be great." I handed him one of my business cards and wrote my cell phone number on the back.

He looked over the card. "Is this your bakery?"

"Yes. When I bring Brewster in for a checkup, I'll bring you something special from the bakery."

"I can't wait. How about tomorrow night for dinner?"

"Tomorrow would be great. I'm usually home by six o'clock."

Nick smiled. I bet he could seduce a statue with that full, sensual mouth. "I'll call you in the morning and get directions to your house. See you at six."

Wow! I adopted a dog and had a date. I couldn't imagine a better day. I filled out all the necessary paperwork, and paid the fee. They provided me with a leash for the collar and a free bag of food. I led Brewster out the door and toward my car. He moved cautiously and slow from his injuries, but relaxed, until we stopped in front of the rear door of my car and I opened it. He looked up at me, back at the car, and then backed away. He pulled at the leash and seemed to be shaking his head no. Then it hit me. He was terrified of being in a car. I wondered how they got him to the conference center. Maybe they sedated him.

I squatted in front of Brewster and then gently hugged him. "Brewster, I promise I won't let anything happen to you."

Woof-woof. Woof-woof. Woof-woof.

Luckily, two guys walked up and asked if I needed help. It took both of them to get Brewster into my car without hurting him. I snapped his picture and sent it to Caley. Then called her and asked if they could manage without me for the rest of the day and she said absolutely, yes.

Woof-woof. Woof-woof. Woof-woof.

"Back at you, big guy. We need to make a stop at the pet store and pick up a bunch of things for you. I'll be quick, and you can stay in the car."

Woof-woof. Woof-woof. Woof-woof.

The pet store had everything I needed and more. Brewster looked relieved to see me when I loaded everything into the back of my car.

CHAPTER SIX

As I pulled into the driveway, my cell phone rang and I assumed it was Caley wanting to know more about Brewster. I parked and answered phone without looking at the caller ID. "Hey, Caley. I just got home."

"Um, this isn't Caley," a sexy, familiar voice said.

"Are you sure?" I immediately recognized Nick's voice and teased him.

"Yep, I'm very sure." Nick chuckled.

There it was again. The roughness of his voice had me envisioning Nick exploring every inch of my body. If I didn't stop daydreaming, I would be drooling like Brewster.

"I called to see if you needed help with Brewster."

"We just got home, but we're doing well so far." I stroked Brewster's soft head.

"The more I thought about it, I decided to call now and not wait until tomorrow. If you're up for some company, I'd like to see you tonight, and not wait unit tomorrow. Is that all right?"

I felt my cheeks warm. "Yes. That would be great. I was going to make pasta. Do you like spaghetti?" I blurted.

"Spaghetti is my favorite. I'd love to. What time? Can I bring anything?"

"How about six o'clock? And no, you don't have to bring anything. I have a good supply of beer, wine, and soda. I'll make a salad, garlic bread, and I can whip up my favorite dessert, chocolate kiss cookies, too." I hadn't cooked anything savory for anyone, only myself, in over a year. I hoped I wouldn't disappoint Nick.

"I'm drooling like Brewster. Where do you live? Or am I going to have to follow the smell of spaghetti sauce?"

"Sorry, I'm usually more organized. My house is located in Madison Park, 21610 South Street. It's at the end of the block, on the left."

"Great. I'll see you tonight."

"Okay. Bye." He hung up at the same time as I did. My palms sweated, and I almost dropped the phone.

Brewster was eyeing the lawn. What did the instruction sheet say about him going to the bathroom? I pulled out the stack of papers given to me by the pet adoption agency and shuffled through them. Here we go: *Take off his covering when you let him outside, wipe his incisions clean before putting a clean covering back on.*

"Okay, Buddy, I'm going to help you to the ground." Brewster landed softly on all fours and sat back on his hind legs. We were going to be fine. "Brewster, come over here to the side of the house."

Once he was done, I led him to the front entry and opened the door. "Come on Brewster, come see your new home." His jowls pulled up in what appeared to be another smile. I took him into the bathroom, cleaned the incisions, and reapplied a clean diaper. After that, he waited patiently by the fireplace as I brought in his food, bed, and toys.

I placed his new bed next to the fireplace, and then tied a red bandana around his neck to hopefully catch some of his drool. I kissed the top of Brewster's sweet head and left him to explore the house. Time for me to get cooking.

I got a text from Caley. *He's a cutie. The next thing you know, you'll be dating.*

If she only knew....

The cookies were cooling on a rack and smelled wonderful, the sauce was flavorful, and bubbling on the stove, the bread was ready for the oven, and the salad to be tossed. I took a moment to look at myself in the hall mirror and was horrified. Speckles of sauce covered the front of my white blouse. Why in the world did I change before cooking?

I was headed upstairs to switch blouses when the doorbell rang. Not many people dropped by without calling first, except maybe my running buddy, Gary. I definitely had not expected Andrew to be standing on my doorstep. He looked the same, wearing his trademark black Armani suit, and crisp white shirt. It had been several weeks since he was in the bakery. He had called and left messages that I never returned. If nothing else, he was tenacious.

The first thing out of his superficial mouth was, "Evie, what's all over the front of your blouse?"

I rolled my eyes. "What are you doing here, Andrew?"

He ignored my question. "You look great, even in a dirty blouse. Can I come in?"

He was letting in cold air. The fastest way to get rid of him was listen to him and then kick him out again. I opened the door wider and motioned him in. "What can I do for you, Andrew?"

"You haven't returned any of my phones calls, so I came by to see when you are available to have dinner and talk about our future together." Andrew's eyes roamed around the room, taking in the Persian rugs, and hand painted vases my parents collected over the years. I was pretty sure he was calculating how much each item was worth.

Brewster lifted his head and barked. *Woof-woof. Woof-woof. Woof-woof.*

Andrew looked startled. I walked over to Brewster who sat alert on his new bed. I stroked his soft head, and he bumped his body against my leg. The bandana was soaked already, doing its job by absorbing Brewster's drool.

"Whose dog is that? It's getting hair all over your clothes," Andrew stated.

"This is Brewster, my new dog. You didn't answer my question. Why are you here?" I put my hands on my hips and scowled.

"I missed you, Evie. I want us to get back together. I thought we could go to the Bahamas for Christmas and get reacquainted." He smiled, but it looked calculated. He constantly looked around the house.

"I have no desire to go anywhere with you. It's over. It's been over for a while." I continued to stroke Brewster's soft fur.

Woof-woof. Woof-woof. Woof-woof.

"Would you please make that dog shut up!" Andrew yelled.

I heard the front door open and close softly. I forgot to lock it because I had hoped to get Andrew out of my house quickly. Nick stepped into the room and my irritation faded.

"I heard someone yelling, so I let myself in. Is everything okay, Evie?" He walked over and wrapped his arm around my shoulder, and I relaxed.

"Who the hell are you?" Andrew demanded.

"I'm Nick, a friend of Evie's. She asked you to leave." Nick had steel in his voice.

Brewster jumped up and bumped his head against Nick's leg. He reached down and stroked his ears, never taking his eyes off Andrew.

"Just friends?" Andrew sneered.

"That's none of your business. Just leave, stop calling, and never come by my home again, or I will call the authorities. Do you understand?"

All of a sudden, Nick tilted his head and then sniffed the air. "I think something's burning."

Nick was right. I'd left my sauce on the stove bubbling and had forgotten about it. Nick and I rushed into the kitchen to save dinner. But when I heard a yelp and a menacing growl, he and I made an about-face and rushed back to the living room. Brewster had Andrew backed against the front door.

"What did you do to my dog?" I yelled.

"He leaned against me. I nudged him with my foot, that's all." Andrew yelled back.

"Leave, before I let Brewster take a bite out of you." I moved Brewster away from the door, Nick opened it and motioned for Andrew to leave.

While I was bent over Brewster, checking to make sure he wasn't hurt, I heard that familiar voice murmur, "Now, that's one lucky dog." I looked up, Nick winked at me, and I smiled back.

Brewster was still near Andrew when he pulled his jowls up, shook his head vigorously, and drool sprayed all over his suit. Andrew made a sudden move toward Brewster, with murder in his eyes.

"Don't you even think about it." Nick opened the front door, and shoved him hard enough that Andrew stumbled on the concrete stoop and nearly fell on his face.

"Evie, I'll call next week and we'll talk." Andrew straightened his suit, as best he could, and walked stiffly to his car. He started the engine, and pulled out in front of another car. The driver blared the horn in obvious annoyance.

A snowflake fell from the sky, and then another one. They became larger by the minute. When I turned toward Nick to show him the snow, our bodies touched ever so slightly, and I wished for a sprig of mistletoe to appear. "It's snowing. I hope we have a white Christmas."

He moved in closer. "Me, too."

I could see the gold flecks in his blue eyes that made them appear to twinkle. The laugh lines in the corners made him even sexier, if that was possible. I heard a moan and hoped it wasn't me. Nick laughed. It was Brewster, feeling left out. We both reached down to pet his head and our fingers intertwined.

Nick's gaze dropped to my mouth for the briefest of seconds, and my stomach did an excited jittery roll. I wondered what the dark blond whiskers of his stubble would feel like against my skin, or how his lips would feel pressed to mine.

Nick rubbed his cheek near my ear. "You smell luscious." He lifted his head and sniffed again, but it wasn't me he was sniffing, it was the air again. "Evie, we forgot about the sauce."

"Oh no! My sauce—our dinner." We hurried back to the kitchen with Brewster on our heels. I grabbed a spoon to stir the sauce and see how bad the bottom was burnt, but Nick stopped me.

"Wait and let me taste the sauce on top. It might be okay. If you stir it, it'll incorporate the burnt flavor."

Nick had cooking skills. Always good to know. "Here's a spoon. Don't burn your mouth."

After a taste, Nick gave me a dazzling smile. "Wow, this is good and salvageable. Why don't you start the water boiling and I'll go get the wine? It's one of my favorite reds."

I put the bread in the oven, set the table, and removed the salad from the refrigerator. Nick appeared with Brewster in his wake, with crumbs on his whiskers. "Okay guys, what's up?"

"I bought Brewster some dog treats." Nick handed me the bottle of wine.

"Thank you for the wine, and the dog treats. I especially want to thank you for how you handled Andrew. I'm sorry you had to get involved in that situation. I haven't seen him in over a month."

"Why did he show up now?"

"I have a pretty good idea, but it's not worth mentioning. But, he cheated on me, and I broke it off."

"He's a jerk for hurting you." Nick leaned forward and caressed his lips across mine. "Am I moving too fast? I can stop if you want me to."

"No. I don't want you to stop." Heat flowed through my body, and I put my arms around his neck and kissed him back.

He caressed my face. His lips brushed mine, they were soft, until he deepened the kiss. He tasted like heaven, and I never wanted to let go.

He pulled away and chuckled. "Well. I need to stop."

"I'm glad you have restraint." We both laughed. "The water's boiling. I'm going to pour us a glass of wine," I said, a little out of breath.

After dinner, Nick and I sat on the floor and ate chocolate kiss cookies. Nick looked at Brewster's incisions, changed his dog diaper, and my sweet dog fell asleep on his new bed.

Nick took my hand in his. "You have a beautiful house. Why don't you have any decorations up?"

"Until now, I wasn't in the mood. My parent's death really shook me."

"I can understand that." He stroked my hand.

My heart felt lighter, not so sad all of a sudden. "Maybe it's you and Brewster, or maybe the snow falling, but I want to decorate."

"Then let's do it. Where are they?" Nick smiled, jumped up, and offered his hand to me.

"In the attic. Really? Are you sure?"

"Absolutely! Come on." He pulled me to my feet.

It took an hour to sort through all the boxes labeled Christmas. My parents kept all of our childhood ornaments. Nick found a box labeled *Grandma's antique ornaments* and opened it. I watched his face and knew we would be using those to decorate. "What did you find?"

"A box of really old, incredibly beautiful ornaments." Nick showed me the contents.

"Those were my great-grandmother's ornaments. I forgot about them. We haven't used them in years. In the corner is a couple of boxes that are labeled the same. I bet we'll find more decorations in those, too. I could decorate the whole house in an antique theme. What do you think?"

"I think it might take a couple of days, but we'll get it done." His eyes sparkled with joy even in the dimly lit attic. "If we don't get finished tonight, I'll bring pizza tomorrow night if you bake more cookies."

My body tingled with a warmth that I had never felt before. "I'd really like that."

We decorated the house for two hours before Nick had to leave.

"I have an early appointment in the morning. As much as I don't want to leave, I have to get a little sleep." Nick tried to cover a huge yawn.

I walked him to the door and handed him a plate full of cookies. "Caley, my bakery assistant, will never believe everything that happened today. I still cannot believe it. I adopted Brewster, I met you, we decorated the house, and it is snowing. Talk about a full day."

"There will be many more wonderful days together."

The goodnight kiss Nick planted on my lips tingled in delight. There was magic in those lips. "Drive careful." I watched Nick get in his car and drive away.

When it was time to go to sleep, I brought Brewster's bed upstairs and placed it by my bed, but he still woke me with his sad whimpers. After the third time, I took Brewster outside for a doggy break, and then helped him up on the bed, and the rest of the night, we both slept soundly.

CHAPTER SEVEN

Everything Brewster would need for the day was already loaded in the car. I waited until the last minute to take him outside. "Okay, Brewster. You're going to work with me today. The ride won't take long."

Woof-woof. Woof-woof. Woof-woof.

Brewster hesitated at the car door, but then let me help him into the passenger seat with little resistance. I petted him on the head. "You are such a good boy."

My cell phone rang as I clipped my seatbelt into place. It was Nick. My heart soared in excitement. "Hi," I said, slightly breathless.

"Good morning. I had a great time last night."

"So did I." *I haven't thought of anything else all morning.*

"How did last night go with Brewster? Did you get any sleep?" he asked.

"Not bad. Brewster ended up sleeping on the bed, but I think he was just getting used to a new home or maybe he slept with his previous owners."

"He's probably just scared. He'll get used to sleeping in his own bed eventually."

"That's good to know. Thank you for everything you did last night. I had fun." *Especially the kissing part.*

"Me, too. I forgot to ask what kind of pizza you like. I was going to order one from Henry's Pizzeria. I think it is the best pizza in town. "

"I love pepperoni and black olive, but I'll eat anything. Pizza is my favorite food group."

Nick laughed. "I feel the same way. I could eat it for breakfast, lunch, and dinner."

Woof-woof. Woof-woof. Woof-woof.

"I think Brewster wants out of the car. I should be going."

"Okay. I'll see you at six o'clock. Have a good day and if you need anything call me."

"I will. Thank you." We both hung up. I had been waiting my whole life to find such a special person. I was so happy, I sang along to a cheerful pop song on the radio. Brewster settled down on the seat next to me and seemed to be relaxed.

I parked behind Confection Connection, slipped the leash on Brewster's collar, and walked into the bakery with my dog by my side.

"Oh my gosh. He is beautiful." Caley immediately bent down and hugged Brewster around the neck.

Wait until she meets Nick.

Brewster licked Caley's cheek and she laughed. "I'm in love."

Suzie and Brandy came rushing into the backroom and took turns hugging Brewster. He looked happy about all of the attention—His tail flopped around like crazy and he licked anything that got close to his mouth. Suzie and Brandy giggled at his antics.

"I'm going to get Brewster's things out of the car and be right back." I got no response. They weren't paying attention to me, they were focused on Brewster, and that was exactly what he needed.

Brewster's bed fit nicely in the corner near the back door along with his food and water dish. He laid down after everyone went back to work. "I'll come check on you in a bit." He tucked his chin down and closed his eyes.

An hour had passed before Brewster needed to go outside. We circled the block several times, he did his business, and then he slowed down a little. "Time to go back."

We did that several more times throughout the morning. Around noon, I felt Nick's presence before he said anything. I looked up from the pastries case, and he was holding a colorful bouquet of daisies.

"Hi." His smile lit up the bakery.

"Hello." That funny little jolt tightened my stomach. I wasn't the least bit hungry, but my mouth began to water as if I hadn't eaten all day and had just caught the scent of some of the fresh-baked bread from the oven.

He handed me the flowers. "These are for cooking an amazing dinner last night. And I told my staff about the cookies you made, and they insisted I bring them some."

"Thank you. These are beautiful." I inhaled the fresh scent. "How many cookies do you want and what flavor?"

Caley, Suzie and Brandy, all stared in awe. Then Caley nudged me with her elbow. "You've been holding out on us. Who is this handsome man and where have you been keeping him?"

Suzie and Brandy giggled and Nick laughed.

"This is Nick Tucker. He's a veterinarian and I met him *yesterday* while I was looking for a pet." All three gathered at the counter, I guess to get a closer look at Nick. I pointed to each one as I introduced them. "This is Caley, Suzie, and Brandy. They are all my friends and amazing bakers."

"Nice to meet you," Nick said.

"You too," they replied in unison.

They were acting as if they had never seen a really cute guy before. "Would you like to come in the back and see Brewster?"

"Just for a moment. I only have a quick break before I have to get back—with treats—or I was told not to come back at all," he joked.

"I can get something ready for you. We have shortbread cookies shaped into Christmas trees with silver sprinkles and green frosting that are mouthwatering," Caley offered.

"That would be great. I'll take a dozen."

"I'll have them ready for you." Caley winked at Nick, and he winked back.

Brewster lifted his head and licked Nick's hand and then went back to sleep. "He sure is adjusting well."

"I'm glad." We leaned toward each other for a kiss, but Brandy walked into the room.

"Sorry. Here you go." She giggled, handed Nick the pastries box, and then left us alone.

"How much do I owe you?" Nick took out his wallet.

"Consider them payment for changing Brewster's diaper."

"You know I would do anything for Brewster and you." He tucked a strand of hair behind my ear.

"Thank you."

"I have to go. I'll see you tonight."

"Bye."

After Nick had left, they grilled me relentlessly for every little detail, including the confrontation with Andrew.

"I wish he would have flattened Andrew. I can't stand that guy." Caley punched a glob of dough with her fist.

"He won't be coming around any longer."

"Andrew doesn't seem like the kind of guy to give up easily. I wouldn't put it passed him to keep trying."

"Really? God. I hope not." We both shrugged.

The rest of the day was busy but went smoothly. I couldn't wait to get home, clean up, and get ready for Nick. It wouldn't take much longer to get the house fully decorated.

There was a knock at the door at exactly six o clock. I loved his punctuality. We both had on similar outfits—jeans and a sweatshirt.

Nick leaned down and kissed me softly on the lips. I wanted more. "Do you want to eat now? If not, I can put the pizza in the oven to keep it warm."

"Why don't you? I wouldn't mind sitting next to you on the couch for a while first."

"We can do that." I took the pizza into the kitchen and placed it in the oven, on low. "Would you like a beer or a glass of wine?" I called from the kitchen.

"A beer would be great."

I poured a glass of chardonnay for myself and grabbed a beer for Nick. When I came out of the kitchen, Brewster's paws were resting on Nick's feet. I sat next to Nick, handed him his beer, and he took my hand in his. It was warm, strong, and comforting.

"He sure has adjusted quickly, and his incisions look to be healing fine, too." He reached down and stroked Brewster's head. "You were meant to be together—I think we were meant to be together, too."

"It feels like we've known each other for much longer than a couple days."

"It sure does." Nick sounded sleepy.

"Do you want to reschedule decorating for another day? You sound like you could fall asleep any minute."

"No. I wouldn't miss decorating for the world. It was just a really busy day. We had three surgeries, plus a full schedule of appointments. I'll wake up after dinner." He hopped up and pulled me to my feet. "This is going to be fun."

"Okay."

We were finished within a couple of hours, and after taking Brewster for a walk, Nick wrapped his arm around my shoulder and we walked to his car.

"The house looks beautiful. I couldn't have done it without you. Thank you."

"I loved every minute of it. Would you be willing to help me decorate a small artificial tree at my house? That's about all I do because I'm not home much."

"Of course. Name the time, and I'll bring dessert."

"I can't imagine my nights without you." He leaned down and kissed me, it lasted longer than any other kiss. Then he pulled away and rested his forehead against mine. "How about tomorrow? Bring Brewster, he'll love the neighbor's dog. It's older, small, and loves to play with other dogs."

"Perfect. Six o'clock again?"

"Yes." Nick turned to leave, then grabbed me for another kiss, and blurted, "What are your plans for Christmas?"

"Nothing special. I close the bakery early on Christmas Eve, and we're closed on Christmas, so figured I'd stay home with Brewster."

"Come home with me. I want you to meet my crazy family. I know we just met, but it feels right, doesn't it?" he asked with uncertainty in his voice.

It did feel right. "Yes, it does. What about Brewster? I can't leave him alone."

"Oh, he'll be right at home at the ranch, I promise you."

"Yes! Brewster and I would love to spend Christmas with you and your family."

"Great. That's wonderful. See you tomorrow."

"Bye." We both waved as he drove away.

So much had changed in my life in such a short time. I had a wonderful dog, an incredible boyfriend, and would be spending Christmas with his family. I couldn't wait to tell Caley.

CHAPTER EIGHT

As the days got closer to Christmas, the bakery was busier than ever, but Nick and I managed to spend all of our free time together. Brewster was almost completely healed, and we even went for a morning run.

When I walked into the bakery, Caley rushed forward with her laptop in hand. "You've got to see this. Confection Connection was written up in *Boston Food Finds*, and we received an impressive Five Star rating. Nobody gets Five Star rating. The phone hasn't stopped ringing with orders. Suzie is in charge of the phones for now. Can I call my sister in to help with the phone so we can focus on baking?"

"Of course." I was stunned. *Boston Food Finds* has been known to make or break a business. "Do you know when the food critic came in? Or what they bought?"

"I guess it was last week sometime. They bought some Chocolate Kiss cookies and thought they were the best they'd ever eaten, and of course, they said the service was impeccable."

"Wow! That's great. Call Peggy and ask her if she can start right away."

"You got it, boss. Merry Christmas to Confection Connection."

"Thank you for sticking with me through everything. You are truly my best friend."

Caley hugged me and then wiped at her eyes. "Knock that off. We have work to do."

"Okay, boss," I joked.

Caley called her sister Peggy, and she agreed to start work immediately. She had helped in the past, so she knew how things worked. I could not wait to tell Nick.

He answered after the first ring. "Hi. How are you, beautiful?"

I wanted to say, *I was wonderfully in love with him*, but I didn't. "I have incredible news. Confection Connection was given a Five Star review in *Boston Food Finds*. I am so excited. This is like winning an Academy Award in the bakery industry. The phones haven't stopped ringing to place orders, but I had to call you. I wanted to tell you."

"Congratulations!" Nick shouted. Then got quiet before he said, "Evie?"

"Yes?" His hesitant tone worried me.

"I love you with all of my heart," he blurted.

My cell phone almost slipped from my fingers. "What?"

"I love you! God. I know this is the least romantic way to tell you. I planned a special, romantic dinner, but just now, the words just rose from my heart. I couldn't stop them."

"I love you, too. I think my heart is going to burst out of my chest. I can't believe how happy I am."

We both laughed.

"Me, too. At least you know now, that I won't ever be able to keep a secret from you." Nick admitted and then chuckled.

I could hear the bakery door opening and closing. It must be packed out front.

"Evie. We need help out here!" Caley yelled from the front.

"I'm sorry, but I have to go, or Caley will kill me. We've never been this busy."

"That's okay. We'll have a lifetime together."

"Yes, we will." I sighed in contentment.

"I'll come by after work or sooner if I can, and help," Nick stated.

"That would be great. Bye."

"Bye, Evie."

The stream of customers never slowed. Peggy answered the phones and helped customers, while Caley, Suzie, Brandy and I continued to bake. Peggy called a friend who said she could help over the next couple of days, too. If business continued at this pace, I could afford to hire Peggy full-time.

An hour before closing, the bakery slowed down enough for us to take a break. I hugged each one of my staff. "You guys are amazing. I can't believe how much we accomplished today."

Caley exaggerated wiping sweat from her brow. "I've never baked so many cookies in one day before today. I'm going to have nightmares about sugar and flour throwing me into a mixer."

We all grabbed our stomachs and laughed.

The doorbell chimed as Nick walked through the front door and I momentarily stopped breathing. I walked around the counter to greet Nick, and it took him six giant strides to get to me, but when he did, he swept me up into his arms and kissed me. I could hear everyone cheering. That's when he placed me back on the ground, and I looked up into his beautiful, loving blue eyes. "Hi there."

"Hi." He reached out and removed a smear of frosting from my cheek. "It looks like you survived the crazy day. What can I do to help? I'm very handy with a broom."

"Would you mind taking Brewster for a walk? He needs more attention than we've been able to give him today."

"That I can do."

After introducing Nick to everyone he hadn't met before, I took his hand and walked into the backroom. The minute Brewster spotted Nick he went bonkers, barking, circling his legs, and licking his hand as Nick petted him. "You have a friend for life in Brewster."

"He's a special dog who is very lucky to have you." Nick lifted my hand and kissed my knuckles.

I snapped the leash on Brewster's collar, and he got excited all over again. "We close soon, but I have several more hours of work to do, cleaning, baking, and reordering supplies. Would you mind taking Brewster home? He'd be happier with his own things."

"Not at all. I can stay with him until you get home."

"There's leftover lasagna and beer in the refrigerator." I hesitated, but then just said what had been on my mind for weeks. "If you want to drop by your place and get an overnight bag, you can stay over."

Just like when I first met Nick, his eyes sparkled. "I'd like that."

Woof-woof. Woof-woof. Woof-woof.

"I better take Brewster for his walk. I'll be back in a while." He stopped and captured my lips for a quick kiss. "I love you."

"I love you, too." It felt completely right to say the words I had never said to anyone else before.

Nick walked out the front door, turned, and smiled back at me. I would like to wake up next to that smile every day.

The lull was over and a stream of customers arrived all at once—most of them regulars. I went to the back to mix another batch of shortbread cookies and let Peggy take the orders.

Twenty-minutes later, I walked to the front counter and noticed Nick was talking to Andrew. *What was he doing here?* I wondered.

"What's going on?" I asked Caley.

"Nick was about to come in when Andrew showed up. Looks like they are having a *conversation*," Caley replied, never taking her eyes off them.

"I better go out there and see what's going on." I headed toward the door, but Nick saw me and shook his head back and forth.

"I guess he's going to handle it." Caley chuckled. *Woof-woof. Woof-woof. Woof-woof.*

Brewster's bark could be heard from outside the bakery.

"Brewster doesn't like Andrew any more than I do." Caley chuckled.

Brewster lunged at Andrew, who tripped but caught himself before he fell on his butt.

"Time to put an end to this, whatever *it* is." I walked out and stood between them. "Why are you here?"

Andrew's smile was forced and held no warmth. "I miss you." He reached into his jacket pocket, pulled out a velvet box, and got down on one knee. "Will you marry me, Evie?"

I started laughing so hard all of my staff and customers came outside to see what was going on. All along, Andrew had underestimated me. Once I got my breath back, I tapped my index finger against my lip. "Let me see if I have this right? You saw the write-up about the bakery, knew it would skyrocket business, and thought I would say yes to marrying you because *why*—?"

Some of the regular customers knew Andrew cheated on me and started to boo him. Nick had a hold of Brewster's leash, but my dog was still inching closer to Andrew.

Andrew stared down at Brewster. "I have a business degree and you don't. I could help expand Confection Connection into a chain of bakeries."

Andrew didn't look up when I turned to Nick and looked up into his beautiful, caring eyes. "I love you."

Andrew smiled but continued to watch Brewster. "Good! I knew you would come around. We can go to the courthouse tomorrow and get a marriage license." Without looking at me, Andrew opened the velvet box and shoved it toward me.

Nick nuzzled my neck. "He's really dense isn't he?"

"Yep." I breathed in his wonderful masculine scent and sighed.

Caley walked over and tapped my shoulder. "Would you like me to break the news to him?"

"By all means. Go ahead, I really don't care."

Caley walked over to Andrew, and stood toe-to-toe with him. "She wasn't talking to you, moron. She's in love with Nick."

Brewster growled and barked louder. *Woof-woof. Woof-woof. Woof-woof.*

Andrew looked at Nick and me and then frowned. "I can help make you rich. Can *he*?" Andrew nodded toward Nick.

"Nick has everything I need and more." It was as simple as that.

"Well—okay, fine. I guess you two deserve each other."

Andrew tried to make it sound like an insult. It was the complete opposite. When we didn't react to his ridiculous insult, he took a step back, and then walked off down the street.

Everyone cheered and then went back into the bakery.

When we were all alone outside, Nick lifted my chin and looked me in the eyes. "I didn't get to say it earlier, but I love you, too."

"This is the best Christmas ever." I hugged Nick around the waist.

"I agree, my love."

CHAPTER NINE

Almost one year later.

The door opened and closed at exactly 6:30 p.m. Nick was wonderfully predictable.

"Honey, I'm home!" he yelled from the front room.

Brewster sat at my feet sleeping, but when he heard Nick, he scrambled up and took off running to greet him.

Nick wrestled with Brewster, scrubbing his ears and chest, laughing the whole time. All the while, Brewster rumbled his contentment. I felt the same way when Nick touched me. He looked up and held my stare. His eyes closed slightly, and he smiled a lazy, sensual smile. He tucked his arms around my waist, and tickled my neck with his cold nose. Then he slowly inhaled.

"Yum. You smell wonderful. Good enough to eat." Nick kissed my neck and moved his lips lower to my collarbone. "Maybe we should skip dinner and go straight to dessert," he said, his voice husky.

I wholeheartedly agreed and raised my arms around his neck. "That's the best offer I've had all day."

Nick picked me up and started to carry me upstairs. I stopped him on the second step. "I better turn off the burners or we'll end up with burned sauce like we did last year." Nick smiled. It reached all the way to his eyes.

"It still tasted great."

Nick didn't put me down, he just turned around, and headed to the kitchen. I reached over and turned off the two burners and oven. Brewster followed us up the stairs, but not into the bedroom.

We made love slowly, like the first time we were together. Touching and stroking, all the while whispering our love for each other.

Our bodies were still entwined, and I could feel the rumbling from Nick's stomach. I laughed. "You're hungry. Let's go downstairs and get dinner warmed up."

"I'm going to take a shower first. I'll be right down."

"Okay." I leaned over and captured his lips one last time. "I'll see you in a minute."

I got dressed and found Brewster outside our bedroom door. He stretched and followed me downstairs. I turned everything back on and set the table.

Nick walked through the kitchen door. "It started to snow an hour ago. The news said we should have a white Christmas again this year."

He filled our glasses with wine and handed me one. His fingers closed around mine, and he caressed my hand.

"I can't believe it will be one year tomorrow that we had our first meal together," Nick said and kissed my cheek.

"I remember. I burned the spaghetti sauce and my jerk ex-boyfriend showed up. But after all that, we did find all those wonderful old ornaments together." I looked through the kitchen door at the Christmas tree we decorated. "I'm glad we put the tree up early this year. I love the smell of a fresh tree and the colorful lights are so pretty."

"So do I," Nick whispered and rested his forehead to mine.

He slid his mouth lower and gently kissed my lips. When he lifted his head, the love that he showed me every day, was evident in his warm eyes. "I love you. I love you with all my heart." My voice wavered.

"Oh, Evie. You're everything I've ever wanted." He paused and held me tighter. "I have a special present for you. I wanted to give it to you tomorrow, on our anniversary, but I don't want to wait any longer."

"You do. What is it?" Before Nick could answer, Brewster, paced between us and then headed toward the front door.

"Would you mind taking Brewster outside? Then you can have your present."

"Okay. I'll be right back." I grabbed Brewster's leash, snapped it on, and headed outside. We were only gone for maybe ten minutes at the most, but when we entered the house, it was lit with dozens of white candles. Two red cushions were positioned on the floor in front of the fireplace. A bottle of champagne with two red, crystal glasses sat on the coffee table in front of it.

Nick's broad shoulders were outlined in the doorway from the kitchen. "Oh, honey…" I was speechless. I walked over and hugged him tightly. "Everything looks so pretty. How did you do all this in just a few minutes?"

"I can move fast when it's important." Nick chuckled.

I continued to look around in awe, and then spotted a small, gold box sitting next to the champagne glasses. The lights blinked on the Christmas tree, soft music played from the speakers, and I had never been happier. Nick took my hand, helped me down to the cushion, and then handed me a glass of champagne.

He picked up his glass and clicked it to mine. "I love you, Evie."

"I love you, too. With all my heart."

Nick took the small box from the table and placed it in my hand. "I wanted to wait and give this to you somewhere really unique, like on the top of a mountain peak or in a really fancy restaurant over a romantic dinner, but in the end being here seemed right. Plus, I've never been a patient guy, and I didn't want to wait."

His eyes twinkled, and my heart melted all over again. My hands shook and I was afraid Nick could hear my heart beating in my chest with excitement and anticipation. I snuggled closer to him. I breathed in his warmth and citrus scent. He took my free hand and kissed my knuckles.

My throat felt dry so I took a sip from my glass and then removed the paper from the box and under the paper was a red velvet box. My breath hitched. My hands shook as I lifted the lid and saw a beautiful, sparkling diamond ring that lay nestled in the box.

"I want to spend the rest of our lives together." Nick slipped the diamond ring on my finger. "Will you marry me, Evie?"

I hugged Nick around his neck and squeezed. "Yes, yes yes!"

Woof-woof. Woof-woof. Woof-woof.

Brewster danced around us, spraying slobber everywhere. We both laughed at our dog. "We're a package deal you know, slobber and all."

"I can handle the slobber." Nick scrubbed Brewster behind the ear.

"I can't imagine a more wonderful Christmas."

"Me either, my love. Merry Christmas!"

CHOCOLATE KISS COOOKIE RECIPE

Ingredients:
1 ¼ cup softened butter
2 cups white sugar
2 eggs
2 teaspoons vanilla extract
2 ½ cups all-purpose flour
3/4 cup unsweetened cocoa powder
1 teaspoon baking soda
55 milk chocolate kisses unwrapped

Directions:
1. Preheat oven to 350 degrees F (175 degrees C).
2. In large bowl mix butter and sugar till fluffy, add eggs and vanilla mix well. Sift together flour, cocoa, baking soda, and salt, and add to creamed mixture.
3. Roll dough into balls about 1 inch in diameter then roll in white sugar. Place balls on ungreased cookie sheet and bake for 8 to 10 minutes. Place unwrapped chocolate kiss in the center of each cookie while still hot. Let cool and enjoy!

Analeigh's Christmas Cupcakes

Jennifer Conner

Chapter One

"This is it," Analeigh said to herself as she looked at her reflection in the shop's door. Frowning, she rubbed a smear of bright pink lipstick off her front tooth. "Merry Christmas to me."

Excitement rushed through her bloodstream, as she fished the key from the bottom of her purse to lock the door. This was her first big job for her newly formed cupcake company, *"Let Them Eat Cake."* The wedding couldn't have come at a better time. With the publicity the event would garner and Christmas rush gearing up, it could mean a push in holiday sales and parties. A friend of a friend referred her for the job, but what really helped was that the mother-of-the-groom was the head food critic for Seattle's *Local Best Food* online magazine. Everything had to be perfect. If the magazine wrote about the wedding her business could skyrocket.

Analeigh opened the back hatch of the older SUV and surveyed the straight line of opaque plastic containers arranged in straight lines. The bride and groom picked four flavors for their Christmas-themed wedding: gingerbread cupcakes, banana crème pie cupcakes that looked like Christmas trees, tiramisu ones with red frosting Santa hats, and chocolate bourbon pecan pie with maple bacon. The last cupcakes weren't very 'Christmassy' but they were the groom's choice.

She lovingly laid a hand on one of the containers. Analeigh put tender loving care along with blood sweat and tears into each little cake. Everything was there that she needed. She'd checked, double-checked, and then checked again. Finally, assuring herself that she hadn't forgotten anything she slammed the hatch and headed around to the driver's door. She tossed her purse on the seat, slid in, started the car, and slowly backed out of the alley.

It was fifteen minutes to the wedding venue. Analeigh knew this because she'd taken a test drive out there the previous night. It was hours before even the stated delivery time. Her cupcakes would be arranged on the reception tables for the wedding party and florist to see as the rest of the event was set up. *Early is always better than late*, she thought.

She slowed and stopped at the first stoplight. Even though it was still morning the headlights in her rearview mirror caught her eye.

The car's not stopping. THE CAR'S NOT STOPPING!

Her smile flipped and her eyes widened, as her heart lodged in her throat. It wasn't her life that flashed before her eyes, more like all the things she'd worked so hard to accomplish. In a second this could be the beginning and the end of getting her dreams fully off the ground. She pushed harder on the brake with both feet and prayed she wouldn't be thrown into the intersection.

For a split second, her mind raced as she desperately thought what she could do. Should she speed forward? *No.* There were cars flying through the busy intersection in front of her. A woman to her left waited at a crosswalk. *Not that way.* Analeigh tensed her shoulders, gripped the steering wheel, and closed her eyes.

The impact of the collision filled the car with sounds of crushing plastic, metal, and broken taillights. Her car lurched forward spilling the contents of her purse to the floor. When the car stilled Analeigh forced her eyes open, and turned to look at the other car. The driver suddenly backed up, hooked a U-turn and sped off.

Anger replaced fear. Analeigh yanked open her door, jumped out, and yelled at the disappearing car, "Come back here, you… you jerk! You hit my car! What are you doing!" Rain pelted her in the face.

A few bystanders already had cell phones in their hands, she assumed to call 911.

She looked down at the crumpled and bent bumper. Panic washed over her like a wave. "No, no, no!" She wrenched at the jimmied back hatch. Giving up, she hurried around to throw open the side door. The impact of the crash broke the ties holding the sturdy plastic cupcake carriers in place. They were tossed haphazardly on top of each other in the back of the car.

Analeigh stumbled back, sat hard on the curb, and hugged her knees.

A middle-aged man placed his briefcase on the pavement and crouched beside her. "Are you hurt?" he asked as concern etched his face.

Analeigh shook her head.

He continued as he looked in the direction of where the car sped off. "That was an obvious hit-and-run. He can go to jail for that."

"Did anyone get his license plate number?" Analeigh asked and then watched the bystanders shake their heads.

An older woman stood next to the man and grasped the front of her coat. Her chest heaved. Analeigh pulled herself to a standing position and laid a hand on the woman's arm. "I should be asking if you're okay? You look pale."

The woman's milky blue eyes met hers. "Heavens. I was waiting at the crosswalk. That car slammed right into you." She made a grand gesture with her hand and then shook her head. "In my ninety years, I've never seen anything like that."

Looking back at the toppled cupcakes trays, Analeigh realized there were more important things in life than her crunched cupcakes. She'd just been in a car accident. There were many worst-case scenarios which could have played out in those few seconds. Other than stiffness in her neck and a growing headache, she was fine and so was the elderly woman.

Everything was great—except possibly her ruined business she'd worked so hard to start. If she couldn't deliver the cupcakes to the wedding, she was dead meat. The wedding coordinator would make a fifteenth-century torture chamber seem like a luxury spa when she was done with her. Weddings didn't allow for 'do-overs.'

Analeigh had to blame something. "Damn car," she swore at it. The ugly gray SUV attracted bad luck like superglue to her fingertips. It was the only thing she'd gotten when she and her boyfriend broke up. Analeigh swore the car was cursed like her and Todd's relationship. Since the breakup, she'd nearly hit two deer, three possums, and a cow. She kicked the tire and recoiled as pain lanced up her leg. A police car arrived with its flashing red and blue lights reflected on the rain-soaked pavement.

****

The officer took down the information about the crash, first from her, and then the witnesses.

"I called a tow-truck," the policeman said. "The bumper's pushed against the back tires, so you won't be able to drive it home."

Analeigh bobbed her head in acknowledgment. She considered herself a nice person, but right now, as she watched the officer write down the details of the hit and run, she felt anything but *nice*. She hoped the guy that hit her was caught... and then tasered... and then landed face first in a mud puddle...and then tasered again until he flopped around like a fish.

She pulled her thoughts back, as she watched the officer ask the older woman if she remembered any additional details.

"We'll do our best to find the car that hit you. Probably didn't have insurance, or was high on something. A lime green Pinto that has front-end damage? Frankly, it shouldn't be hard to track down. They'll check the traffic cameras for a license plate." The policeman shook his head. "I swear, people lose their minds when it rains."

The paramedics arrived, checked her out, and gave her the option of being taken in for a complete check-up. Analeigh declined and took a few aspirin she had in her purse. Her cupcakes took a much bigger hit than her.

After the ambulance left, she opted to wait inside her car for the tow. If she broke down in hysterical tears, fewer people would see her. Rain began to fall harder from the sky. The droplets splattered against the windshield like tiny ink blots.

How could this be happening? She didn't give a rat about Todd's car, but if she was going to be hit, couldn't it have happened an hour from now so she could have delivered her cupcakes?

Knuckles rapped on the driver's side window making Analeigh jump. She pushed the button to lower the window.

"Hi, ma'am. I'm Danny from Above All Towing. Sorry, it took me so long. Are you Anaeigh?"

"That's me."

"Looks like you got into a fender bender."

"*I* didn't get into anything, someone got into it for me." She sniffed at tears but refused to let them fall.

"That's usually the case with a bumper that looks like yours." He flashed a sympathetic smile and pushed his baseball cap higher on his forehead. A chunk of dark hair tumbled down his forehead. "You okay?" He asked the same question as the others. She guessed this was what you did in a situation like hers.

"Never been better," she bit out.

"Sorry, stupid question. If you want to grab your bag and get out of the car, I can pull it onto the flatbed."

Analeigh opened her door. When she stood her head swam, and she reached for the side of the car.

A large, sturdy hand grasped her upper arm. "Whoa, there." Danny glanced toward the police car.

"I think it's nerves. The paramedics checked and I don't have a concussion."

"Is there anyone you can call? They can pick you up, or I can drop you at home."

She shook her head. "Nope. No husband or boyfriend to swoop in and save me."

"I was thinking along the lines of a friend or family." His gaze flicked to her hand, she assumed to see if she wore a ring. A smile quirked up one side of his mouth. "I'm sure you can handle everything on your own, but it's nice to know that you're single."

"I'd call my aunt, but she's out of town for the weekend."

Danny opened the side door of the tow truck, reached under the seat and pulled out a blanket. "It's clean, I promise. I washed it yesterday." He wound it over her shoulders and tugged it closed in the front. His gaze met hers. "You sure you're okay?"

"I'm fine."

"Why don't you sit here in the front of my truck and I'll get your car ready to tow?"

****

Analeigh watched Danny as he quickly hooked and jostled her car to get it up on the bed of the truck. She cringed when part of the bumper fell off, but there wasn't much she could do about it. The driver door creaked when he opened it, his tall body silhouetted in the frame. "I'd feel better if I could drop you somewhere. Who knows when you could get a cab out here, and if you don't want to call someone…"

"You can drop me at my shop. It's about a mile from here." Analeigh pulled the blanket tight and stared out the window, as she tried to formulate what she'd say to the bride. Dread clogged her throat as she drank water from a bottle the paramedics gave her.

She'd work through this…somehow…she would make it through. She always had.

When they arrived at Let Them Eat Cake, he pulled the tow truck up in front and cut the engine. "You own this place? I love your cupcakes. I know you've only been open for a month, but I try and come here at least every other day. I live down the block."

She cocked an eyebrow. "Really? I don't remember seeing you."

He laughed. "I'm not always in greasy overalls. This is my disguise so you wouldn't know that I'm the guy with the cupcake 'problem.' " Your lemon peel cupcakes with Key lime frosting. Well, they are better than se..." his words trailed off. Pink tipped the outer edges of his ears.

"Those are my favorite too. They are better than..." Analeigh grinned.

"When I come in, there's a redhead, an older woman. I think she said her name is Macey?"

"She's my aunt and a Godsend. She comes in and helps when she can."

"I noticed that the cargo area of your car was filled with cupcake containers. Were you on your way to a delivery?"

"Yes, a wedding." She sighed. "I know you're probably on the clock, but I have a huge favor to ask. If you'll help, I promise that I'll pay you for your time. In the back of my crunched car are three-hundred cupcakes. I was on my way to the Benton Hotel for a one-o'clock reception. If there are any of them I can save I need to now, or I'll have to call the bride and groom and then jump off a bridge before the bride and her mother arrive to kill me."

"Let's get the carriers to your shop so you can assess the damage. I'm done for the night...morning, whatever time it is. I lose track sometimes. I've been working the night shift to get some money for college. There's no charge. Don't be silly. I'm all yours."

Mine? Oh my. Nice guys like Danny were like uncovering a chunk of gold buried on a public beach with a metal detector. It was near to impossible to find.

Danny jumped out of the truck and came around to her side. He offered his hand, and she slid out. His hands were firm and warm at her waist as she stepped down. He looked down into her eyes. "I just wanted to make sure that you're stable on your feet. No falling over on my watch."

"I'm fine." Danny was a thin needle of bright light in the day, and he was cuter than sin. Also, she was a sucker for dimples, and this man had *great* ones.

Danny waited for her to open the front door, and followed her inside. She flipped on the overhead lights and wove her way around the counter to the back kitchen. The white walls had trim boards painted in stripes of bright pink, yellow, and lime shone back. The undecorated Christmas tree stood in the corner reminding her of one more thing she needed to do. Analeigh found an old chandelier in the dumpster behind the shop and DIY'd it back to life. It now hung from the ceiling in the middle of the shop in its sparkly crystal glory. Her favorite piece.

"The place looks empty when it's not filled with cupcakes." He ran a hand over the glass case.

"I agree. I'm usually in the back slaving away. I don't get out here much. So, is this what the front of the store looks like?" Analeigh kidded.

"That explains why I didn't recognize you from my semi-daily impulse buys here."

"I guess I need to come out of the back more often."

"I guess you do." The dimples in his cheeks formed again as he grinned. *Dang.* His eyes were a fascinating color of golden brown. They had an interesting slant like a cat's that held a possible hint of Pan-Pacific descendants. "Before we do anything, I have a few things I'm going to insist on." He held up a finger. "First, you are going to sit down on that stool, and then second drink some water, and let your body's nerves calm down. I'm going to change out of this grease-monkey outfit. *You* are going to stay right *there* while I carry in the cupcake containers."

"I can help."

"If you move… or argue, I am going to drive off with the cupcakes. You will never see them again."

"Where's your cupcake ransom note?" She tried to frown. It wasn't working.

"Don't push me, lady." He jingled the tow truck keys in his hand and said in a tone of a thirties gangster movie, "One more word and the cupcakes get it."

"The cupcakes already 'got it' from that idiot that rear-ended me. Their little cupcake guts are smeared all over the back of the car."

"Sit." He pointed to the stool again. "Do you have bottled water?"

She started to stand, but hearing a gruff sound from him, sat back and tipped her head toward the refrigerator.

He opened the door, pulled out a pitcher, and filled an empty glass that he handed to her. "Stay."

"I'm not a Golden Retriever."

"I know. I have one. Betsy listens pretty good. I'll be right back."

"Pushy...man," Analeigh mumbled under her breath. But, she was happy Danny was there. His silly, light-hearted ribbing eased the stress bubbling through her. She still had no idea what she would do about the wedding and knew how she would feel if someone called at the last minute with problems.

Danny reappeared through the door with a pile of clean clothes on his arm. "Bathroom?"

Chapter Two

Analeigh rolled the glass of water between the palms of her hands. She had five hours.

"I borrowed a grocery bag from the back for my dirty clothes. I hope you don't mind." Her gaze flicked over him. He'd changed into a pair of jeans and a navy V-neck T-shirt. The work overalls had hidden the muscles that his T-shirt accentuated. She licked her suddenly dry lips. He'd run water over his head, and his sandy brown hair glistened dark, slicked back from his strong face.

Double dang. He'd cleaned up well. She really needed to get out front more if she was missing customers as cute as Danny. "Did you find everything you needed to clean up?" she asked.

"You have me at a disadvantage. I usually scrub off all the night's grease and grime with some toxic chemicals back at the tow base before heading home. All you have in your bathroom is frou-frou stuff. He came closer, and her heart did a flip. He leaned in and gave her a grin. "Now I smell like vanilla beans. Probably not very manly."

She inhaled. Not a good idea. He smelled good. *Really good.* Analeigh couldn't remember the soap in the bathroom smelling like that on her. *Vanilla.* One of her favorite things. She was a baker after all. But add *man* and vanilla. *Yum.*

"Did I miss any grease anywhere?" he asked. He tipped his chin up toward the ceiling.]

"Just one that I can see." She picked up a tissue and rubbed at a small black streak of grease under his ear.

Danny took the tissue from her hand. His fingers were warm against hers. "Thanks. Should I call you Ms. Russell?"

"No. Analeigh. You can leave the formality for the ransom note."

"Analeigh." Her name sounded sexy as it rolled off his tongue. "I'll remember that. I'm going to bring in the containers, and we can go from there. Are you sure that you're okay?"

"I'm fine. No, I'm not fine. I mean, it's someone's wedding. You don't get to have do overs. What am I going to tell the bride and groom...the whole family?" She covered her face.

"Before this doomsday scenario goes further, I'm going to bring in the containers, and you can start an evaluation of what is damaged beyond serving. Let's not get ahead of ourselves." He placed a hand on her shoulder and gave it a squeeze.

She was, she knew it, but he had no idea how much she'd put behind this job's success.

Analeigh watched his quick and easy gait as he walked away. In stacks of two, he carried the cupcake containers in and piled them on the stainless-steel counters.

"That's the last one." He brushed off his hands.

She rose to her feet and popped the lid off the first container. White streaks of frosting smeared the lid and dotted the sides of the containers. Analeigh sighed and shook her head. "This just… stinks." She slumped back on the stool. "I'm never going to be able to re-bake and decorate three-hundred cupcakes. My big break has turned into a *big* disaster."

Danny lifted the lid and peered inside once again. He took out one of the cupcakes, inspected it, and then placed it on the counter. He drew back the lid and completely opened the tray. "How many do you think you can bake, get cooled, and frosted in, say, three hours?"

"I don't understand. I can't bake three-hundred cupcakes and deliver them to the wedding in time."

"That's not what I asked. How many *can* you bake?"

She shrugged a shoulder. "A hundred or so."

He held up the first cupcake he'd placed on the counter. "The only thing that is wrong with this cupcake is the frosting's damaged. If we carefully scrape it off and re-frost it, no one will know."

She took another from him and surveyed the tiny cake. He was right, the cupcake was undamaged.

"You can do it. We can get them back before anyone suspects that there was a problem."

"What is this *we*? You didn't sign on for this mess. You probably want to go home, pop a beer, and watch some football."

"I'm not the kind of guy that leaves people out on the limb. I'm off work, and I'm *offering* my help. I don't want you to have to make that call to the bride anymore than you do."

"I can pay you."

He waved a dismissive hand. "Don't worry about it." He lifted the second container. "Let's take the rest out of the carriers. I'll put the undamaged ones in a save pile and then the rest in a road kill pile. If two-hundred are salvageable, then we're in."

She'd gotten through tough situations before. She'd left her old career behind for her baking passion, she couldn't give up now.

He opened one of the lids and frowned. "What flavor is this one?"

"Gingerbread."

"This whole tray took a pretty big hit. Why don't you start with these?"

Analeigh gave a quick nod. "Those are actually the easiest to decorate. No special additions." She pulled out the industrial metal mixing bowl and attached it to the KitchenAid. Grabbing a hair-tie from the shelf, she whipped her shoulder-length black hair into a bun, then threw on an apron over her torso and tied it behind her neck.

"You start baking, and I'll work on damage control and cleaning up the containers," he said.

As she dumped ingredients in the bowl, she watched Danny carefully take each of the cupcakes, one by one, and inspect them with painstaking thoroughness. The save pile was much larger than the road kill pile.

He'd been right.

When he finished, he scooped the ones that couldn't be saved onto a tray. "I can drop these off at the homeless shelter if you don't mind. They will love them." Danny ate a few bites here and there. He closed his eyes as he held up the battered chunk, "Which cupcake is this?"

"It's the bacon bourbon."

Danny sighed, licked his fingers of the last remnants, and then rewashed his hands. "I don't remember seeing these in your cases."

"It's a new flavor I'm trying out."

"You don't need to *try* it out anymore. You have my word. You need to put some of these bad boys out for sale. I've brought in a few of the guys from work and gotten them hooked. Anything with bacon would be a deal sealer." He grinned making his dimples stand out.

"I'm happy you like them." Analeigh felt the heat rise in her cheeks. The compliments were embarrassing but nice all the same.

"This is sad," he commented, as he shook another half dozen cupcakes into the trash barrel. "I feel like I should play taps or something. They were too young to die."

Taking a baker's spatula from the holder, he carefully scraped off the damaged frosting of the ones he saved and flipped it in the bin. Then he lined up the undamaged cakes into perfect rows. "Okay, these are the ones you can work with. There are one-hundred and seventy-five. Good news or bad?" he asked.

"I think I can make it work. I have a few trays that I baked for extras over on that tiered cooling rack." She counted in her head. "That would give us three-hundred and three."

"Whoo-hoo." Danny pumped his fist in the air.

"This is really nice of you to stay and help. You've been working all night. You can take off. I'll be fine."

"How are you going to mix, bake, and decorate at the same time?"

"Well… I'm not sure. I'll do what I can."

He looked at her for a long moment. "I didn't see another car out there, so I assume that your car's totaled. Even if you get the cupcakes ready, how are you going to get them to the wedding if you don't have transportation?"

"Rental car?"

"And take the chance they may all be rented for the weekend?"

She hadn't thought of that. "What are you, my voice of reason?"

He let out a chuckle and propped a hip on the stainless-steel counter. "I could be. Also, my skills are a little rusty, but my mom worked in a bakery at a local grocery store. I worked with her on weekends when I was younger."

"This isn't just a tall tale? You wanted to be a baker too?"

"No. I don't know what my plans were then." Danny shook his head. "She was happy to have me help and show me what she did. I got money to go snowboarding with my friends."

"What did you help her with?"

"Mainly, the frosting. Just like this." He waved a hand at the completed cakes. "She'd make up the frosting bag, and I'd decorate them. I think that's probably where my cupcake 'problem' started."

"This is all too coincidental. Are you my guardian angel?"

"You caught me. But, tonight, I left my wings out in the tow truck." He pulled his phone out of his jeans. "Before I forget, I'm going to call the guys at the shop and have them bring my car over when they get off shift.

That way we will have something to drive to the wedding."

Analeigh nodded. Could things really be working out from this horrible day? She tapped the batter into the pans and then slipped the first batch in the ovens to bake. Out of the refrigerator, she pulled out the ingredients and tossed them into the free mixer. Retrieving a frosting bag from the cupboard, she filled it with the creamy mixture.

When Danny completed his call, he popped the phone back in his pocket. She picked up one of the cakes. "Start on the outside with a spiral and end the frosting in the middle in a peak.

He concentrated on her every move. When she was done with the demonstration he said, "Let me see if I can remember what the heck I did back in my mom's bakery." He took the bag and then stopped. "Before I start, is there any way I can get a strong cup of coffee? I've been awake a long time and need some caffeine."

"Of...sure. Sorry. I should have asked you before. Would you like regular coffee or I also have an espresso machine. I can do up to a quad shot with that."

"That should do it." He grinned again. "After the cupcake sugar and caffine, I might still be awake and want to come over and paint the outside of your shop. I probably won't sleep for a week."

"I'll make it three shots."

Chapter Three

As Analeigh pulled the cakes out and slid them onto the counter and placed a large next to them to speed the cooling. She pulled her hair out of its ponytail after she eyed her reflection in the oven doors. With the flyaway mess on her head, of course, she was near the cutest guy she'd been with in months, and she looked like she'd stepped out of a wind tunnel.

But he wasn't watching her. His gaze was glued to his work. Danny's concentration made her grin. Lines furrowed his brow, and his tongue stuck out the side of his mouth as he moved from cake to cake. He started, then stopped. "Do you have to watch me? Jeez, you're making me nervous. You're a pro, and I'm an amateur."

"You are doing fantastic! Come on bucky, show me what you got, Mister *Ace of Cakes*."

His hand clenched on the bag as he began to squeeze the frosting. When he was finished, he set the cake back on the counter. "That's fifty. Can you fill another bag of frosting for me?"

"I can do better than that. Now that all the cakes are in the oven, I can help decorate."

Analeigh put on some upbeat music and then came to stand beside him. He hummed and bobbed his head along with the beat.

She eyed his current creation. "You're doing great, but if you tip the bag a little straighter, you'll get a cleaner line. Keep the tip about an eighth of an inch from the cake."

"Keep me from a life of cupcake kidnapping and make me an honest man." He steepled his hands. "Am I hired?"

"You'll let me pay you?" she asked again, still feeling guilty.

"Tell you what, how about a free cupcake a day for a month?"

"You drive a hard bargain."

"My way or the highway, missy." He chuckled.

Analeigh's smile matched his. "But, free cupcakes for *two* months…or really, anything you want. Do you want more than that?"

"I would eat a dozen a day, but I don't think I could work out enough to burn that many calories. I'd be roly-poly tons of fun." He put an arm up behind his back. "But, here, if you twist my arm, I'll take the one a day. Two months of Let Them Eat Cake cupcakes, that's half a car payment. Maybe, I'll steal all your secrets and start my own rival company, 'Cupcakes and a tow.'"

"I guess I'll have to take my chances and trust you." She sighed dramatically.

"And then maybe go out with me when all this is done?"

Analeigh kept her mouth from dropping open. When she regained her composure, she answered, "You decided to drop that in?"

"I was on a roll. I thought it wouldn't hurt to ask." He shrugged. "Not today, but you know, another night after I get some sleep and a proper shower and you haven't been in a car accident?"

They worked side by side for the next few hours as she watched the time tick by. If she hurried, they could make it. She'd been expecting a terrible stress filled afternoon, but it somehow had magically turned into the most fun she'd had in months. A cute guy singing along with 80s pop bands and decorating cupcakes next to her? Was she dreaming? Every time he bent to lower a tray on a rack, she cocked her head to the side to check out his rear end. She had to say, his butt was even better than his skills with a frosting bag.

As she baked and cooled more cakes, Danny washed and dried the carriers, then restacked the finished cakes in the containers.

"How did you get into the tow truck business?" Analeigh asked.

"I went to college and got a degree in business. My grandfather started the business, and my father took over from him."

"And, you'll take over from your dad. Third-generation?"

"I have already. My dad's health hasn't been the best. He went through a round of chemo treatments. He's okay now, but can't work as many hours as he once did. We're lucky that we have a great staff of hard workers. Every kid has dreams of doing something else, but I like working in the family business. I love my dad, and it means a lot to him to pass the business to me. What about you? How did you become the queen of cupcakes?"

"I got a degree in computer programming."

"That sounds like two different career paths."

"Tell me about it. I worked in computers for about four years and made some money, but lost something called 'passion.' So, I took the money and started this business. I love walking through the door every morning. I put too many hopes into this job today. It wasn't the end of the world. I could have come up with something to piece together for their wedding cake. And overall, this day could have been much worse."

"You're right."

"I could have been hurt in the accident." She rubbed at her neck.

He set the frosting bag on the counter, washed his hands, and then came up behind her. He gently pulled her ponytail to the side and then began to rub her neck with his thumbs.

"Don't tell me that you have training as a masseur, too." She looked over her shoulder.

"Nope. But, who doesn't like a neck rub ?" He pressed his thumbs in deep. "You should take something for stiff muscles and then go see your doctor or chiropractor tomorrow. They can make sure there is nothing knocked out of place."

"There was an elderly lady waiting at the cross walk… I… could have run her over." She hadn't allowed the memories of the early morning to seep in before that moment. Analeigh swiveled on the stool to face him.

He touched her cheek. "It's going to be okay. No one was hurt, and you're going to save the wedding job. As I said, I've had to tow some bad accidents. You weren't involved in one of them." He brushed a thumb over her cheek. "I tried to convince you, I'm here to save the day."

"I believe you. Seriously. Where did you come from? Am I dreaming all of this?"

"I sure hope not. All I've wanted to do since the moment I saw you was kiss you. Can I?" His voice dropped, luring her into his orbit.

She nodded. Their breaths filled the scant space between them and merged soundlessly. He took a thumb, raised her chin, and then dropped his head until their lips met. His kiss was tender and soft, a total antithesis to the steely muscles of his chest. She sighed and melted into him.

He broke the kiss and placed his forehead against hers. "I could do that all day... and I'm going to keep that as a future plan. But right now, we have work to do."

"Work...oh yeah...cupcakes. What am I supposed to be doing?" Her mind had been wiped clean of anything but the memory of his mouth pressed to hers.

Danny's coworkers arrived with his car and its keys. Analeigh boxed a dozen cupcakes from the back as a thank you.

"Wow!" The first man took the box and grinned. He eyed Danny who had frosting on his shirt.

"You taking up a new profession?"

"Nope," Danny replied. "Just helping out a friend who needs some help."

The second man piped in. "You never said that you knew the owner of this place."

"I do," was all he said.

His friend held up his hand. "Point taken.

Danny frowned, as his gaze flicked to Analeigh. "Truth be told, I only met Analeigh today when she was in an accident. I stayed because she needed some help."

"You don't need to make excuses, Dan. You're always there when people need you. That's what makes you one of the 'good guys.' "

The second guy lifted the lid and took a swipe of the frosting with his finger. "Danny keeps telling us how great this place is. They will love these back at base— that is if I don't eat them all first."

"Thanks guys. And I will see you tomorrow." Danny walked them out.

She and Danny finished decorating the final cakes with the special touches. Danny carefully took the newly filled carriers out and secured them in the back of his truck. When he came back in, he asked, "All done?"

She nodded, took the apron off and threw it over the stool. "Showtime."

The elegant banquet room was abuzz with the hotel's catering staff who were busy stocking the tables with last minute touches to the linens and china.

The frantic wedding coordinator pounced on Analeigh when she came through the door. "Oh. My. God! There you are! I thought you said you were going to be here to set up hours ago."

Analeigh steeled her spine. "The contract stated I would arrive at three. It's three o'clock. right now. I know I mentioned that I might be here early, but I wanted to make sure everything was perfect."

The woman paused before saying, "My heart nearly stopped. I thought something was—"

"As you can see. Everything's fine, ma'am." Danny cut the woman off, and gave her a lady-killing smile "Ms. Russell had a little car trouble. You know how temperamental cars can be."

The woman turned her attention to Danny. Her stance softened, and she batted her eyes his direction. "I sure do, that alternator thingy went out on mine last week, and I had to walk a mile in heels for help ." She waved a hand. "Well, never mind all that. The cake table is over there. Hey. Hey! That bouquet doesn't go there!"

she yelled at one of the catering staff setting a table arrangement and flew off in the other direction.

"Flirt," Analeigh whispered.

"You gotta do what you gotta do. I distracted her, didn't I? Let me get the carriers from the truck and you can start setting up the table."

"Don't trip." She grinned.

"Don't even say that." He shook his head as he disappeared out the door. Analeigh went to work decorating the cake table with small white and red flowers and ivy.

As Danny brought in one container after the other, she lifted out the tiny cakes with tongs and placed them gingerly on tiered serving trays. Finally, she placed the final touch of silver flakes and red hearts over the cupcake's frosting.

Danny stayed with her as they stepped back to examine the table. A short time later, guests began to filter into the reception and the band began to play. The bride and groom were introduced and entered the room to a round of applause and hoots.

The bride's mother headed over to meet Analeigh at the table. "Oh, Analeigh. You did exactly what we wanted. It's perfect! My daughter and new son-in-law will love it. You'll see nothing but a good write up in my magazine. I can't believe how much time this must have taken."

"The easiest day of my life," Analeigh said under her breath, and smiled at Danny.

Analeigh and Danny sat off in a corner of the room.

"Are you ready to go?" Danny asked.

"Just a few more minutes. I want to see the bride and groom's reaction to their cupcakes."

Soon the DJ made the announcement and the newly married couple headed to the cake table. Everyone laughed when the bride and groom turned and smashed cake in the maid-of-honor and best-man's face.

The best man took his finger, wiped off the frosting, and stuck it in his mouth. "I would be upset if this didn't taste so good!"

Everyone laughed. Flashes fired. The couple looked happy. It was perfect.

"Okay, we can go now," Analeigh finally agreed.

They exited out into the back hall before she stopped and turned to face Danny. "There is no one to thank but you for this success. I couldn't have done it on my own. I owe you everything." She looked at the closed door as music filtered from inside the hall.

"If you owe me everything, how about owing me a dance?"

"I think that could work." She smiled up at him. "It's the Christmas season and I feel like I'm getting an early present."

Danny reached for her hand and spun her around on her toes. Then, he pulled her close. Their bodies swayed to the music. She'd only known him a few hours, but in his arms, it felt right. *Perfect.*

When the song ended he slid a hand in her hair and pulled her in for a kiss. She sizzled from head to toe as his lips glided and slipped over hers. He caught her lower lip and tugged it gently between his teeth.

Besides frosting cupcakes, this man was the Ace of Kissing, too. Her knees threatened to buckle, but he held her up for more.

When he finally pulled away, his lips were parted and his breathing was as ragged as hers.

"If you want to keep your working relationship with the wedding party professional, we'd better find somewhere else to take this. How about we drive to your place and you can get a bathing suit. My apartment complex has a hot tub to soak in and then I'll take us to brunch."

"My apartment has a hot tub, too."

"Fine. I'll get my trunks, and soak in your tub. But, I get to buy brunch."

"Pushy man."

He kissed the tip of her nose. "Only if I know what I want. The voice of reason, remember?"

"What does soaking in my apartment's hot tub versus yours have anything to do with reason?"

"It has… well, nothing. Are we going to stand here all afternoon? I'm starving, and you have a stiff neck. You can soak, and I can eat."

Analeigh pulled him in for another kiss. "See, I knew you would find a good reason to offer me."

"Hope this is only the beginning of a great Christmas season." As he tugged her by the hand out the door, she knew that sometimes out of bad came good. Her good was a six-foot two-man, full of nothing but surprises and promises.

Chapter Four

"Morning, Danny," Hailey said cheerfully as he hurried through the front doors of Analeigh's shop. Danny was glad he'd left his house a few minutes early. Any reason to spend a few more minutes with Analeigh.

"Morning," he answered back as he bypassed the front counter and headed toward the back of the shop. He'd spent much of his free time there, and he didn't need to wait to be escorted to the back any longer. Music played as it always did and the air was filled with the luscious aromas of fresh-baked goods. Analeigh stood at the counter swaying her rear end to the tunes and stirring something in the large bowl in front of her.

He quietly came up behind her and nuzzled her on the neck.

"Guess who?" he whispered.

"How many guesses do I get?"

Danny spun her around. "Only one. Can I start my morning with a kiss?" When she nodded, he kissed her deep and long. Stepping back, he grinned. "If that's the way you're going to play it this morning and be a smart aleck, then I guess you don't want to see this." He waved the magazine in his hand.

"What's that?" Analeigh asked, as she wiped flour off her hands.

"I looked online to see when the newest edition of the magazine would hit the newsstands. If the wedding you did was featured, it should be this issue."

"Did you look?" Nervous energy flitted across her face. He loved how dedicated she was to her business. He'd acquired the tow company through his family, but she gave up one career and put everything on the line to pursue her dreams.

"No. I bought it and thought you should see it first."

He unrolled the magazine and handed it to her. She took it, flattened it on the counter and then turned to the first few pages. Slowly she flipped through it, and sucked in a deep breath as her eyes scanned the words.

Her gaze rose to meet his. "This is the best write-up ever written. Marnie loved the cupcakes for her daughter's wedding and said that they were the best she'd eaten in a long time."

Danny took the magazine and read the article. He grabbed her and spun her around as they celebrated. "What did I tell you! And, you see that she mentioned the bacon bourbon cupcakes? I told you that you needed to add them to your lineup."

She grinned, turned, and lifted one of the cakes she'd just finished frosting.

"Is this what I think it is?" he asked.

Analeigh swiped off a finger full of frosting and wiped it along his bottom lip. He tasted the sugary sweetness first and then the salt of the bacon. She kissed him sweetly, and he felt another piece of his heart slide to her's. He and Analeigh had only known each other a few weeks, he had to wait awhile longer before he told her how he felt. He'd told someone before that he loved her, but it had only been words.

This time he wanted to make sure.

Analeigh must have sensed his hesitation and stepped away. "I'd better get back to work, and if I remember your schedule"—she pointed to the clock—"so do you."

"You're right. I just wanted to bring over the magazine."

She smiled. "Christmas Eve is tomorrow. Are we still going to spend it together?"

"I can't wait." And that was the truth. He had to decide if Christmas was the time to tell Analeigh how deeply he'd fallen in love with her.

"How about a cup of your favorite hot chocolate and a cupcake for the road?" she asked.

"Will you let me pay?" Danny reached for his wallet.

"You're still on the freebies. Don't even think about it, buddy."

****

The afternoon flew by. Analeigh's feet weren't touching the ground. The shop's phone rang off the hook with upcoming orders for the New Year. She had been right about the article boosting her business.

He brought me a magazine. How sweet is that? But Danny knew that it meant more to her than if he'd brought a dozen roses. Danny conjured up everything she hadn't had with Brian. Danny thought of things that were important to her...not him, first. This was a new sensation, all she could think of was the next time she could spend time with Danny. He'd texted her and said that he would stop by after work.

She didn't have to wait long. Hands came around her eyes. "Guess who? I've missed you."

She started to smile but then froze. These weren't Danny's hands. They were too smooth and not work-hardened. She drew the hands away and turned. "Brian, what are you doing here?"

"After you left CompStream I couldn't find you." He still looked the same. Slicked back blond hair and a worn polo shirt. "I thought you would at least let someone at your old stomping grounds know where you went."

"Why would you want to find me? *You* left *me*, remember?"

"Everyone is allowed at least one mistake, right?" He shrugged. "I saw the article in the Seattle magazine today about your deli."

"It's a cupcake bakery."

"Bakery, deli, same thing." His wolfish grin spread. "How do you stay so sexy eating all this sugar? You know it's bad for you."

Anger pounded through her veins. "Again…is there a reason that you're here?"

"I knew when I found you I had to come right away and that this was my second chance to make things right."

A few months ago, she probably wouldn't have thought twice and would have considered his offer. But even in that time and through the tears and anger she realized that Brian had never given her that toe-curling, take your breath away kind of experience she was looking for. Now was different.

"I'm not interested in making things *right*. I'm really busy, and I don't have time to talk."

His smile was forced. "Come on, Analeigh. What we had was great."

"No. It wasn't. I thought so at the time, but after you left me, I was able to think about it. You weren't the man for me. I was more in love with the idea of love than with you."

"You're wrong. I should have said it before." He paused for a long moment and then said. "I love you, Analeigh, and I want you back."

Before she could step away from the bakery workspace, Brian stepped closer. He trapped her against the stainless-steel island and pulled her to him. She let out a startled squeak of protest, but then his mouth was on hers. Hard. She struggled beneath him, but he wouldn't let her go. Her brain raced as she tried to figure out how to escape.

Analeigh thought she saw someone in the kitchen doorway but couldn't see around Brian's large shoulders. Hailey knew who Brian was and would bop him with a pan…but, then no one came. She wanted to cry out but couldn't with his mouth sealed to hers like he was trying to give her mouth-to-mouth resuscitation.

As her mother always said, if you want things done right, then do it yourself.

She drew her knee up. She really wanted to kick Brian where it would hurt the most, but she didn't have enough room. Finally, she settled for stomping down hard on his left foot. Glad she'd worn boots that day, she ground her heel down hard.

"Ouch!" Brian cried out and jumped backward.

While he looked down at his foot, Analeigh took the opportunity to haul back her hand and slap him hard. The crack reverberated in the quiet room. Brian hopped on one leg as he held a hand to his cheek.

"You have no right to treat me or any woman like that. I didn't give you permission to kiss me much less even be here. We'd been together for a year when you came home and told me you'd met a Hooter's waitress who was the new love of your life. What gave you the idea I would take you back into my life?"

"Analeigh…" he whined.

"Don't Analeigh me. You…you jerk. You made your decision, and I never truly loved you. Get out!"

Hailey came from the front of the shop after probably hearing raised voices. She held a phone in her hands. "Are you okay, Analeigh? Do I need to call the police?"

Brian held up his hand. "Don't bother, I'm leaving. For good…this time." He glared at Analeigh. "Last chance, sweetheart. You don't know what you're missing."

"I'm not missing anything. Leave." She pointed to the open delivery door.

She pointed at the door. Brian shrugged and headed out the ajar door. Had someone else been there?

Hailey's eyes were wide. "I didn't see Brian walk in, did he walk in the back door? I saw Danny come in but didn't see Brian or red flags would have gone up."

"Danny was here?"

"A few minutes ago. He'd barely walked back here, and then he left in a hurry. Did Danny say anything to Brian?"

"I didn't see Danny." But then the pieces fell into place. *He saw Brian kissing me.*

"I'm so sorry. If I'd known Brian was back here I would have come back sooner. I know you didn't want to see him again." A tear streaked down Hailey's cheek.

Analeigh walked closer and hugged her friend. "It's not your fault, and I'm fine. But, I've decided that I need to keep the back door closed for better security and not leave it open when I need ventilation. It's too dangerous for anyone to just walk in when I'm alone in the back."

Now, she needed to get ahold of Danny and explain things.

****

Danny pulled into the driveway of his condo and turned off the engine. He slapped his hands on the steering wheel.

I love you Analeigh, and I want you back. Analeigh's ex-boyfriend's words binged around in his head like echoes in a valley. 'I love you' was supposed to come from his mouth, not someone else's. Had he waited too long?

"Damn…" he cursed into the air. Just when he thought he'd found that special someone. Analeigh told him about her old boyfriend, Brian, and Danny recognized him from a vacation photo she'd shown him. But she said it was over. Why was she standing in the middle of her shop kissing him? She'd said he didn't even know where she was. Had she changed her mind? Had she called him? A million questions with zero answers.

Blood pounded in Danny's ears. He looked out the windshield at the sky. The weather pattern shifted, and now they were predicting six to eight inches of snow in the Seattle area for Christmas. For everyone else, it meant a white Christmas with festive lights and merriment. Snow for a tow company meant twelve plus hour shifts, no merriment, and the only lights would be the ones from his truck.

He should go and talk to Analeigh. But, he needed to clear his head first.

Maybe it was a sign. If he wasn't meant to be with Analeigh, then he could fill his day with work. Not his first choice, but considering how much his heart hurt, it might be the best.

His cell phone rang, and a picture of Analeigh popped onto the screen. He wanted to talk to her, but he didn't want to hear bad news. He hit Ignore, slipped the phone back in his pocket and headed out into the cold wind.

He'd have a few beers, some leftover Chinese food, and a few hours of sleep.

All he really wanted was Analeigh.

Chapter Five

Analeigh called Danny's cell phone over and over, but he never picked up. How could she explain his misunderstanding if she couldn't reach him?

Candice, the dispatcher at the shop, finally answered, "No Business like Tow Business, how can I help you."

"Candice, this is Analeigh. Could you get a message to Danny and tell him I have to talk to him?"

"I can tell him, honey, but since the snow started at 3:00 a.m. he's been pulling people out of ditches. All the trucks are out, even the old ones." There was beeping in the background.

"But it's Christmas Eve." She paused. "I know, that's silly."

Candice let out a sharp laugh. "Tell Old Man Winter that. Looks like all of us will be spending Christmas here at the shop. Wouldn't be the first time. Hey, honey. I gotta go."

The line went dead, and Analeigh stared at the phone. No one should have to work on Christmas. At least there was something she could do to make it a little brighter.

****

Danny was so tired he could hardly see straight. Sliding out of the driver's seat of his truck he slammed the door closed and pocketed the keys. Everything felt as if it was moving in slow motion. He knew there were more people out in the snow needing help, but he would have to get some shut-eye or he would be as dangerous out on the road as the people who couldn't drive in the snow.

Some of his plans worked. He'd kept himself busy, but the part about not thinking of Analeigh was a joke. She had been on his mind every second. He wasn't ready to give her up.

He would go over there now and talk to her. He looked back at his truck and frowned. When he talked to her, he wanted to be coherent, and if he did it now he wouldn't be.

He'd start with returning her call and set up a time to talk about things. *Talk about them.* Danny knew, even as tired as he was, he would have to call her before he went to bed or he would never sleep.

He walked through the door of his company and stomped snow off his work boots. He slipped a hand into his pocket, pulled out his phone and hit Analeigh's number. He heard it ring…in front of him.

Danny looked up and found Analeigh standing in front of him her phone in her hand. Her soft hair fell around her shoulders and the sight of her sucked the breath from his lungs. He wanted to run to her and pull her into his arms.

"Should I answer it?" she asked with a slight smile.

He pushed the End Call button and dropped the phone on the counter. "I didn't expect to see you here…tonight." He fought to keep his voice level when it was filled with so many emotions.

"Where else would I be? I thought we were going to spend tonight together." She took a step toward him, but he turned to shuck out of his coat and hang it on the hook. She stopped and frowned. "Talk to me, Danny. I can take a guess, but I want to hear it from you."

He looked at the ceiling for a moment to gather his thoughts. "I was *planning* on spending Christmas Eve together, but I showed up at your shop. It was kind of a 'holiday' breaker."

"I thought I saw someone in the doorway." Analeigh's mouth went into a thin line. "What exactly did you see?"

"You want details? I saw you kissing Brian, your ex." The man's name left a bitter taste in his mouth after saying it. "He had you pinned against your baking counter." Danny grabbed a water bottle and downed half of it.

"I guess you came to my rescue once, but twice?"

"What are you talking about."

Analeigh took a step closer, but this time he didn't shy away, even though half of him wanted to run out and jump in his truck. He didn't want to hear that she was leaving him.

"What did you hear us say?"

"All I heard him say was that he loved you and he wanted you back."

"But, you never heard me answer his question did you? You're a big jealous dummy." She took another step and placed a hand on his chest. "If you had stayed around for another ten seconds you would have seen how things turned out. No one grabs me without my permission."

"You didn't want him to kiss you?"

"No. I didn't want Brian to *kiss* me. I don't want anything to do with him, and I would have been happy to have never seen him again. Things have been over with Brian for a long time. I always put more into it than he did. When he walked out that night, I was angry, but I found I wasn't really heartbroken. If I had wanted him back in my life, I would have gotten in touch with him."

"You said he didn't know where you were. You didn't call him?"

"No. I didn't." She sighed. "He must have found me through the article in the magazine. Remember, there was a picture of me and the *address* of the shop. That's why he showed up. I didn't want him to kiss me and I was trying to get him to stop."

"He was forcing himself on you, and I walked away." All he felt was sick. Disgusted with himself. "I should have stopped him…helped…I don't even know what to say." He closed his eyes and stepped away from her.

"You don't need to say anything. Especially, that you're sorry. I can take care of myself. I stomped on his foot, slapped him, and told him to get out of my shop."

"I missed all of that, too?"

"Yeah. You missed that too."

Just then, Karl, his coworker, came into the room. He slurped something from a big bowl. "I have to tell you Analeigh, you are a total lifesaver. This soup is fan-tas-tic!"

She took Danny's hand and led him into the other room. All his drivers were huddled around tables which were decorated in red and green striped tablecloths. Small fake trees were adorned with shiny bulbs and blinking lights sat on top of them. Smells of spicy warm food and baked goods filled the air and made his mouth water.

"You did all this? For us?" Danny asked as he listened to his friends laugh and eat.

"To be honest, I did this for *you*. I have a hard time cooking in small batches, and I decided that everyone deserves a little Christmas. I figured if you were out in the snow for hours on end, so were all your employees. Analeigh smiled as she walked to the Crockpots that held hot soup and chili. She dished out a heaping bowl of beans and handed it to Danny.

"I'll eat this later." He set the bowl on a table.

One of the drivers tipped his head toward the others. "Let's give them a little privacy," He said, as he pushed his chair back. Danny was suddenly happy that his company had more than one room.

Danny looked around. "Where did you get all this stuff? It's like a winter wonderland in here."

"When I locked up the shop, I dropped by my mom and dad's house. My dad has a bunch of decorations from his office, and I asked if I could borrow them. Then I gathered things I could throw in the pots to make soup and chili. I had some extra cupcakes and threw those in too. You'd said that when it snowed, it was a nightmare for the tow company."

Danny laughed. "You're right about that. I've been out since three o'clock this morning. I came back knowing I needed some sleep."

She looked around. "Sorry. I'd better let you get something to eat and go to bed."

"Suddenly, I'm not very tired." He shook his head. "I still can't believe you did all this."

"I said I was going to spend Christmas Eve with you. When I make a promise, I stick with it. I think you do too. Like the day of the accident when you promised me that things would get better. I believed you."

"Things have gotten much better since that day." He sat in a chair and pulled her onto his lap. He tucked a loose strand of hair behind her ear. "And it all has to do with meeting you. The first time I saw you sitting on the curb, I thought you were the most beautiful woman I'd ever seen."

"You did?" She looked shocked.

"Yes, I did. But, I couldn't very well hit on you, you'd just been in a car accident." He grinned. "Since then I've found out that you are smart and funny and a real bulldog when it comes to your business." His heart sped up as he pulled in a breath. *It's now or never.* "The first time I saw you sitting on the curb…I think I fell in love with you."

"I love you too," Analeigh blew out the words on a breath. "I'm so happy you said something. I've been torn up not knowing if you felt the same way. I have a baseline now. This is how I know things are different than they were with Brian. The things I am feeling are different. Deeper."

Danny reached into his pocket and pulled out a little box. When her eyes widened, he laughed. "Don't freak out, it's not an engagement ring…yet." He kissed her on the tip of the nose.

She opened the lid to reveal a chain and a charm. Analeigh lifted it out. "It's a little gold cupcake."

"I saw this in a window downtown and knew that I had to get it for you for Christmas." He took it out of the box, pulled her hair aside and clasped it closed. Then he drew a finger down the pulse in her neck. Leaning in, he inhaled. "You always smell like freshly baked cupcakes. I love that smell."

She handed him a similar box. Opening it, he found a leather strip with a pair of silver wings.

"I thought you could hang this in the window of your tow truck. They're guardian angel wings. You helped me, but I know that you help lots of people through bad days. If you hadn't been there that day to help and encourage me, I would have thrown in the towel. You told me to believe and keep going. Now business is booming, and I've fallen in love with an amazing man."

Analeigh slid a small box across the table and opened the top. She pulled out one cupcake.

"This is a special cake I made just for you. It's hot chocolate, with marshmallow topped frosting and a miniature candy cane. I'm calling it the Danny Special."

He bit into the cupcake and closed his eyes in bliss. "This is amazing. But you missed my favorite ingredient."

"What's that?" she asked.

"You." He pressed the cake's frosting to her mouth and then kissed her. Danny poured out all the love he felt as he let the kiss go on. The frosting was sweet, but not as sweet as Analeigh's lips.

She wrapped her arms around his neck. "I'm happy it's a white Christmas because being snowed in with you makes it the best Christmas ever. I love you."

"I love you too."

Analeigh's Christmas Cupcakes Recipe

Bourbon Bacon Cupcakes

Serves 16

Ingredients:

1/2 cup Crispy bacon
3 Eggs
4   Tbsp Maple syrup
1   box Betty Crocker yellow cake mix
1/2 cups Powdered sugar
1/2 cup Vegetable oil
1   cup Butter, unsalted
2   oz Cream cheese
1   tbsp Bourbon
1   cup Water

DIRECTIONS:

Prepare cake mix according to directions using the eggs, water and oil.

Add 2 tablespoons of maple syrup.

Fold in one cup of the bacon crumbles.

Use a muffin scoop and fill a muffin pan (prepared with cupcake liners) 2/3 of the way up with batter.

Bake at 325°F for 18-20 minutes until slightly golden brown on top.

When done, remove from oven, place on wire rack and let cool.

While cupcakes are cooling, prepare frosting.

Using a stand mixer (or a bowl and electric mixer) add the cream cheese and butter together and cream until light and fluffy, about 3 minutes.

Add bourbon, 2 tablespoons of maple syrup and 1 cup of powdered sugar and beat on low speed. Once powdered sugar is incorporated beat on medium speed.

Continue to add powdered sugar one cup at a time until you reach desired frosting consistency.

Pipe frosting onto cupcake (or just with knife).

Add the remaining 1/2 cup bacon crumbles on top of each cupcake for garnish.

Chrissy's Christmas Sugar Cookies

Angela Ford

Chapter One

"Is it true what they say about you?"

She came to a sudden halt with that comment. Intrigued, she turned to find the most beautiful man she'd ever laid eyes on. She raised an eyebrow, and smiled.

"Yes, if it's good." She laughed, and then apologized. "I'm sorry." Chrissy was known for her quick comebacks but usually with people she knew. This man was a stranger, but one she'd like to make a friend. "She set the coffee pot down, wiped her hands on her apron and extended one hand. "Christine Spencer. Welcome to Sugar 'N' Spice."

His firm handshake, along with his tailored suit and tie, told her he was all about business. She wondered what he was doing in Troy. No man in her small community dressed the way he did, except the bank manager and mayor. Even then, their suits were not of the same quality of the man's who stood before her.

"Nicholas Reed. I heard you serve the best coffee in town. I'd like a cup of your best."

She'd like to give him her best. But she knew he meant her coffee. "Our specialty coffee of the day is cinnamon spice with a twist."

His grin told her he enjoyed flirting. He seemed eager to entice her interest, but not desperate with his chosen words. "Perfect. I enjoy a good twist."

She silently laughed. He'd captured her interest. She could play the game. And better.

Her hand motioned above the filled trays of all the sweets one's heart could desire. "May I interest you in a little sugar?"

He chuckled. "What would you suggest?"

His playful tone continued the flirtatious game. She played along for fun.

"How much sugar can you take?" she asked and waited for his reply, with her most serious expression. But his response threw her off -guard.

"I can take all the sugar you can dish out."

Chrissy swallowed hard. *This man is good. Maybe even slightly better than me.* She let the corners of her mouth curve, slowly and seductively.

"I'll surprise you. Please take a seat. I'll bring it to you." She spoke professionally, but the thoughts that raced through her mind, were not. He smiled and thanked her. She watched his confident stroll to the back-corner table.

"He's yummy."

Chrissy laughed and turned to her faithful friend, Beth. Her best friend since grade school always had her back. She'd been the one to convince Chrissy to open her own shop. Everyone in town craved Chrissy's sweets.

"Isn't he? Any idea who he is?" Chrissy softly spoke and walked over to the sweet trays.

Beth followed and leaned in to whisper, "Dressed like that? Maybe he's with the company who wants to buy the old Delbert farm."

Chrissy laughed. "That's last year's rumor. There's been no talk of that since May."

Beth shrugged and began to prepare the cinnamon coffee. "Those things take time."

Chrissy prayed no one wanted to buy the farm. She'd always wanted to, but couldn't afford it. Mrs. Delbert had been Chrissy's grandmother's best friend. Chrissy spent her younger years exploring the farm while her grandma and Mrs. Delbert had tea and gossiped. Chrissy hated the thought of someone else buying it. Especially someone who might tear down all those memories.

Beth peeked around Chrissy in the mysterious man's direction.

Chrissy tapped her arm. "It's not polite to drool."

Beth took her focus back to Chrissy. "I may be happily married, but I can look."

Chrissy laughed. "Shall I ask Mike about that?"

Beth tossed her a glare. "He knows I only have eyes for him," she said and then leaned in closer. "I'm looking because I have my best friend's interests at heart."

"Yeah, yeah." *Now help me decide what to serve him.*

Beth pointed to the tray that held her famous sugar cookies. "He said he could handle all the sugar you could give him." Beth tilted her head. "Give him a *Chrissy*. Sugar on sugar." Beth winked.

Chrissy planned to use Beth's exact words. Her sugar cookies were so popular everyone in town called them *The Chrissy*.

Beth handed her the spiced coffee, with a demand. "Go get him, *sugar*." Beth stressed her last word, and then giggled.

Chrissy focused on her plan to win the attention of Mr. Mysterious. Her grandma always said the way to a man's heart was through his stomach. She silently laughed at the thought as she made her way to his table.

"Sugar and spice." She set the cup and plate on his table, "Hope my reputation stands."

Chrissy stood so close, her hip brushed against his shoulder.

"Smells wonderful." He thanked her politely, with the compliment.

"Sure does."

He looked up at her. She felt the sudden flush fill her. *Did I just say that aloud?*

She wondered how she'd cover that remark. She'd meant his cologne but she wasn't so bold to admit it. He chuckled, and then saved her. "Confident and sweet. I like that."

He had class. She liked that about him. "Enjoy, Mr. Reed." She turned to leave but his hand reached out for hers. Chrissy stopped.

"Please, call me Nick."

Those eyes melted her heart. His touch ignited feelings she hadn't experienced for a long time.

"Hope you enjoy *The Chrissy*, Nick."

He smiled and she felt another rush of heat race through her. This man had an effect on her that made her thoughts speak aloud. She laughed and pointed to the sugar cookie. "The town named it, *The Chrissy*."

"Oh," he said and took a bite. "Hmmm. I believe my new favorite sugar cookie is Chrissy." His seductive tone told her she'd successfully gained his attention.

Chrissy smiled. She fanned herself as she headed toward Beth. Mr. Mysterious had her attention.

*****

Nick finished his sugar and spice, as she'd referred to it. He knew firsthand, she'd be competition. The investors he'd booked for a tour of the Delbert Farm had possible plans for a strip mall. The ones they'd put in small towns always included a well-known coffee franchise. He had hoped *Sugar 'N' Spice* wouldn't have been so damn satisfying. Nick's company made millions finding locations for his investors. He never enjoyed the affect it had on local business owners, but it was business. He also hadn't expected a beautiful, confident woman to be the competition. Nick never believed in fate until he set eyes on Chrissy. She was the perfect woman for him. This deal would destroy any possibility of him getting to know her better. He made his way to the counter.

"Your reputation stands."

Chrissy smiled. "Thank you. Please come again for more sugar."

Nick chuckled. He loved her confidence, and her comebacks. She played the same game he did. Maybe even better than him. He walked out of her shop, but she wouldn't be leaving his thoughts anytime soon.

Nick stopped outside the shop, and turned. He'd quickly glanced at the shop's holiday display before he'd entered. But after meeting Chrissy, he stood in amazement of the winter wonderland before him. She'd spent time and effort with her holiday decorations. The Sugar Plum Fairy and Nutcracker dolls stood beside a decorated tree in the window display. The train that moved around the tree had "Holiday Express" written on it, with Santa on top of the caboose. Across the top of the display read, "Have a Sweet Holiday."

Nick smiled as he took notice of the sugar cookies used instead of tree ornaments. Between the tree and the train, were plates of all the sweets one's heart could desire. But his eyes drifted back to the Chrissy sugar cookies. His heart desired that sweet.

Chapter Two

"What do you mean, I can't have the dance at the Delbert farm?" Chrissy held her stance, and her glare. "I can't cancel. It's a Troy tradition! You're the mayor, you know that." She looked over the mayor's shoulder briefly when she saw Nick Reed enter her shop.

"I didn't say you had to cancel the dance, Chrissy, just have it somewhere else."

Her attention drifted back to the argument. "But —"

"No buts, Chrissy. The investors are in town next week and want to view the property."

Chrissy grabbed the cup from his hand. "Well then, you better find me a place to have the dance."

"What about my coffee?"

His expression was priceless. Chrissy held back laughter, and held her ground.

"No time for coffee breaks today, Mayor. You need to find a place that can house the dance."

He attempted to argue. "But you're the town's event coordinator."

She motioned for him to go. "I'm not fixing this. You allowed investors in, you find a place for the dance," Chrissy demanded, and then added, "And soon. I need time to plan and decorate. Now go." She snickered at the sound of his frustrated mumbling as he stood and walked toward the door. Nick Reed held the door open as the man grumbled and nodded on his way out.

"I always thought mayors received more respect in their towns."

Chrissy sighed at Nick's comment.

"Not when he's your dad. He expects his daughter will fix the problem so he won't look bad to the residents of this town."

Nick bowed his head and confessed, "That would be my fault, not his. I'm sorry, but the investors wanted a viewing before the holidays."

Great, she thought. The one good-looking and charming man to roll into town, is the man who was going to ruin her holiday tradition. And the man who just might put her out of business. She'd heard the rumors last May of a strip mall, with a possible coffee franchise, moving into town. She sighed with frustration, not sure if it was the last-minute plan to house the Christmas dance, or the lost chance to win the attention of Mr. Reed.

"You're the reason I can't hold the dance at the Delbert farm?" She felt her blood boil. Yesterday she wanted to do nothing but flirt with this man. Today, she wanted to throw him out of her shop.

"The investors can only come next week."

His calm tone and short explanation only confirmed what she'd thought the day before–*he's all about business*.

"That doesn't help me. Or the town." Frustrated, she turned to walk away.

"I'd like another *Chrissy* and a cup of your best."

His flirtatious tone did nothing for her like it had the day before. It only heightened her anger. Chrissy called out to her friend, "Beth, can you help the customer?" Saddened at the thought she no longer wanted to gain his interest, she continued to walk toward her back office. Anger took control of her emotional state. Angry with her dad, and Nick, she couldn't hold the annual Christmas dance at the farm.

****

"I really screwed things up."

Beth nodded in agreement with Nick's comment and began to prepare his coffee. "Yeah, you did."

Desperate to regain Chrissy's interest, Nick asked Beth for her advice. "Do you think there's a way I can fix things?"

Beth handed him a cup of the day's specialty. "Peppermint mocha, to start." She smiled, and then added, "I'd offer you a Chrissy, but I don't think it's the Chrissy you want."

The hidden question in her comment made him laugh. "That much I know. But I don't believe there's a chance she'll even speak to me now."

Beth smiled. "Unless you can make the Christmas dance happen at the farm."

Nick stood quietly for a moment. He took a sip of the mocha, and lifted the cup in the air.

"This is good."

Beth smiled. "She is the best in town. No matter what competition you bring into town, people here are loyal. They love Chrissy. You'll lose." Beth tilted her head slightly. "And I don't mean just in business."

Nick knew she was right. The confident woman who'd captured his interest would be the toughest competition he'd ever met. He'd dealt with small towns many times. Some had been difficult, but he never got personal. His focus always remained professional. But this time was different. He'd never met anyone like Chrissy. She had a spark about her. One he didn't want to put out. For the first time in his life, he put his heart before business. He raised an eyebrow.

"I have an idea." Beth smiled, and lifted the portion of the counter that allowed him access to her side. She pointed in the direction to find Chrissy. Nick stepped in beside her and then followed her instructions, "First right at the end."

He knocked lightly on the door that read, "Office."

"Not now, Beth."

Nick leaned forward slightly and rested his forehead against the door. Any other day, he would have turned and walked away. He had looks, money, success, and a handful of women to choose from at any given time, but he wanted to get to know Christine Spencer better. To him, she was the perfect woman—beauty, brains, and a great sense of humor. He attempted to plea for her forgiveness. "It's Nick. I am sorry. May I come in?"

He stumbled slightly when the door opened. The passion in her eyes wasn't what he'd hoped for. She appeared completely annoyed he'd knocked on her door.

"Seriously. Haven't you done enough?" Her glare screamed answer me.

"I'm sorry you're upset. It's business."

Chrissy huffed. "Well, your business is upsetting mine. Please leave." She turned toward her desk. Her abrupt drop into her chair told him she didn't want to talk to him. Not now, and possibly not ever.

Nick took a deep breath, and then closed the door. She looked up. The rage in her eyes told him to run, fast. But determination, or stubbornness, kept him in her office. He surrendered his hands in the air. "Five minutes. Give me five minutes to pitch a proposition."

Chrissy leaned back in her chair and crossed her arms. "Proposition for what?"

Great. He at least had her attention. Hopefully, he'd buy some time so she'd get to know the Nicholas Reed she'd met yesterday. Nick blew out a puff of air, and then reached for the chair in front of her desk. "May I?"

Chrissy nodded, "Five minutes." She looked at her watch. He felt the pressure start. Nick took a seat. Cool, calm, and collectively he pitched.

"Yesterday, we both seemed interested." He placed his hand over his heart. "Or, am I wrong to assume that?" He waited for a response or gesture for him to continue.

Chrissy shrugged.

Good enough. At least it wasn't a *no.* "Today, business entered the equation and created an upset on both sides here." Nick motioned between them.

Chrissy nodded

"I have the authority to fix this." He paused for her reaction.

Chrissy released her arms from their fold, and moved her chair in toward her desk. "Why would you fix *this*?" She stressed the last word.

Nick lifted his forearms to her desk, and then leaned closer. "I'd like to get to know you better."

Chrissy let out a short laugh. "Yeah, okay. So, for a date with you, I'd have the farm back for the dance?"

Nick smiled. She no longer appeared as angry with him as she had moments before. That alone confirmed she was at least interested in his proposition. His answer would confirm whether it was just to have the dance at the farm, or to get to know him better.

"Not one date." He watched her eyes widen, and then continued. "The dance is next week. I want one date every night for the next week, including the dance. Then, if you're not interested, you've had the farm for your dance. And, I've had the chance to prove I'm not just about business." Nick raised an eyebrow. "Still interested?"

Chrissy sat quiet for a moment, and then stood. and extended her hand. "Deal."

He smiled at her gesture. The one simple word gave him hope. Hope that in seven days neither of them would be everything but business. He stood and shook her hand. "I'll pick you up tonight at eight o'clock." Nick's hand rested on the doorknob when she cleared her throat. He turned his head slightly. "Time not good?"

Chrissy shook her head. "Would you like my address? You know, to pick me up at eight?" She laughed.

Nick smiled. "Not necessary. I'm a businessman. I've done my research."

Chrissy looked angry again. "You've stalked me?"

Nick laughed, "No, it's a small town. Barb, at the motel, told me."

Chrissy nodded and laughed, "Too small, sometimes. See you at eight."

Chapter Three

"Thanks, Beth." Nick grinned as he passed Beth.

She finished pouring a coffee for a customer, and looked up. "You're welcome. Have a good day," she called out, but Nick had already exited the shop. Curious to know why he thanked her, she knew who could answer that question. "So?" Beth stood at the opened door, coffee pot still in hand.

Chrissy looked up. "So, what?"

"Don't give me that, Miss Spencer. You're smiling. Mr. Mysterious smiled on his way out of the shop."

Chrissy laughed. "Miss Spencer. You only use my proper name when you want something."

"I do." Beth smiled, and continued, "I want to know what happened to make you both smile."

Chrissy came around from her desk and stopped for a moment beside Beth. "I made a deal so I can still hold the dance at the Delbert farm."

Chrissy continued to the front of the shop. Beth followed. "Deal? What deal?"

Chrissy briefly turned her head. "I have to date him for a week and go to the dance with him."

Beth met Chrissy at the counter. Mr. Peters had just taken a seat on one of the stools.

"Morning, Joe." Beth smiled. "Coffee?" He nodded and Beth reached for a cup. Her focus went back to Chrissy. "That's it? You get him and the farm? That's a win-win."

"My coffee?"

Beth turned to the anxious man, waiting for his coffee. "Sorry, Joe." She poured him a cup, and then set the coffee pot back on its warmer. Chrissy handed Joe his usual delicacy to go with his coffee. But only one. Mrs. Peters had asked the girls to give him only one, and a small one. She'd been watching his sugar levels.

"Thanks, Chrissy. Don't tell the Missus." He winked.

Chrissy smiled, "Our little secret, Joe."

Beth silently laughed. He had no idea he was eating a low-fat, healthy alternative. But it was for his own good. "I can't believe you're going on a date with Mr. Mysterious. You go girl!" Beth stood in awe. She was happy for her best friend. Chrissy hadn't dated in two years. And that attempt was a disaster. A friend of her husband, from a nearby town, invited them to a dance. Beth thought it would be good for Chrissy to get out. She hadn't dated since college. And there wasn't a large selection to choose from in Troy.

"Chrissy has a date?" Joe piped up.

Chrissy turned to him. "Don't start that gossip around town."

Her stern look at Joe made Beth laugh. She turned to her friend. "Sorry."

"It's not a date. It's the deal I made to secure the farm for the dance."

Beth laughed. "Yeah, okay." She knew she wouldn't get any more from her friend until she was ready. She could wait. But not long.

****

"We can reschedule after the holidays. Let me know what date works."

Nick ended his call. He knew he could possibly lose the investors by rescheduling. But it was a risk he was willing to take. *I must be crazy.* Nicholas Reed never rescheduled a deal. But Christine Spencer was worth the risk. He'd never met someone like her. Nick wondered if she could be *the one.* He wasn't even sure what that meant. His mother had always told him he'd know the first time he met her. It was one deal. He'd made his millions. If he screwed this one up, he'd make more. But for once he wanted to put his heart ahead of making money.

"Hi Barb, I need your help. "Nick found the motel owner in her office. He wanted to impress Chrissy and needed help with it.

"Sure, Mr. Reed. What can I help you with?" She gestured for him to take a seat.

"I have a date. A very special one. You know this town better than I."

Barb's interest sparked. "Who is the special lady?"

Nick chuckled. *Small towns.*

Barb took her glasses off and set them on her desk. "I know the town and everyone in it. It will help if I know who she is. Then I'll know how to direct you, according to her likes and dislikes."

Nick smiled. "Christine Spencer."

"Ah, our Chrissy." Barb grinned. "Sweet thing she is. Probably why she makes the best sweets in town." Barb leaned back for a photo on her desk and handed it to Nick.

"That's Chrissy's mom. Sheila and I were best friends. She left us at too young of an age." Barb paused. "She had the biggest heart but one that couldn't keep up with her. Chrissy was so young to lose her mom."

The news Barb shared saddened him. He couldn't imagine losing his mom. She'd always been his rock. He listened as Barb continued to share.

"She was only ten when her mom passed. But her grandmother, Agnes; Carrie Delbert, and I helped her dad raise her. Her grandmother passed not long after Chrissy's mom. Agnes and Carrie had been best friends. Chrissy spent a lot of time at the Delbert farm. Carrie groomed Chrissy as the town's event coordinator. Especially for the annual Christmas dance at the farm."

Nick now knew why the farm was so important to Chrissy. There were memories he was about to destroy if he made the deal and his investors put a strip mall on the farm property.

"Why didn't Chrissy put an offer on the farm?"

Barb looked at him and sighed. "Not like she didn't try."

She took the photo from Nick and placed it back on her desk.

"She fought her father, and her uncle on it when the rumors first began to fly back in May of the farm going up for sale."

Nick's curiosity piqued. "They wouldn't help her out?"

Barb shook her head. "The mayor and the bank manager—her father and uncle, the two in town who could help her— both told her it was too much for her to take on."

Nick laughed. "I've only known her since yesterday but from what I see, she's a determined and successful businesswoman."

Barb agreed. "That my girl is." She looked at Nick and seemed upset. "Our mayor, Chrissy's dad, always tried to shelter her. But she's a feisty one. Always argued with him. He wants her to settle down and have a family. He's a little old-fashioned, just like his brother." Barb patted Nick's hand. "But those old-coots don't know Chrissy the way I do, and her grandmother and Carrie Delbert did."

"So, if she could get the financing, she'd like to buy the Delbert farm?" Nick's mind raced with all the information Barb had presented.

"Yes, in a heartbeat. I'd be the first one to cheer for her." Barb clapped her hands. "How did you land a date with Chrissy when you're the one about to kill her dream?"

Nick chuckled. "I made a deal with her."

Barb tilted her head, obviously waiting for further explanation.

"She agreed to a date—well, a week's worth of dates including the dance. In return, I hold off the investors coming to town until after the holidays."

"Smart business man," Barb said, and then added, "One with a heart."

Nick smiled. "Will you help me then?"

Barb nodded. "If my girl agreed to the deal, then she's either interested in you, or keeping the farm within her grasp. I'm hoping for both."

Chapter Four

"What are you going to wear tonight?"

Chrissy locked the front door and turned to Beth. She hadn't talked to Beth all day about Nick. Her friend had respect but Chrissy knew Beth's patience would only last so long.

"I have no idea. I don't even know what we're doing, or where we're going."

Chrissy blew the loose piece of hair that had fallen onto her face. "Guess I should have asked."

"I don't think you really care. As long as you're with Mr. Mysterious." Beth laughed as she closed the cash register. "Balanced," she proudly added.

"He's no longer Mr. Mysterious. Stop calling him that." Chrissy demanded.

She flipped off the lights, leaving the few above the counter. "Ready?"

Beth nodded and grabbed her purse. She met Chrissy and walked toward the back door. "Well, you have a good couple of hours to figure out what to wear."

Chrissy looked at her watch. It showed 5:11 p.m. They always closed shop around 5:00 p.m. The townsfolk usually stopped coming by late afternoon—except for the odd one who wanted to pick up sweets on their way home from work. Chrissy baked fresh daily and sold the remains at half-price at the end of the day. She held the door for Beth. "See you in the morning."

Beth nodded. "Always." She hugged her friend good-bye. "Go get him, *sugar!*" Beth winked and laughed as she made her way to her car.

Chrissy waved good-bye. She loved her friend and knew Beth wanted to hear her share the excitement she felt about the date. But Chrissy fought to remain professional. She wanted the farm, at least for the Christmas dance. She didn't want to admit, even to herself, that she wanted Nick.

Chrissy stood in front of her empty closet. She looked back at the pile on her bed.

"I don't even know where I'm going. How the hell am I supposed to know what to wear?" Lue meowed. Chrissy laughed at her cat's reply. She picked up her cherished pet when she heard the doorbell. She looked at the clock on her bedside table. It was only one minute after seven o'clock. "Don't tell me he's early." Chrissy carried Lue in her arms to the door. "Oh, thank God!"

Beth smiled. "Don't worry, you still have time." She leaned in and kissed Lue on the head. "Is your mama in a panic not knowing what to wear?" Lue meowed again. Beth laughed.

"Auntie Beth is here to the rescue." She held up a garment bag in one hand and a canvas tote in the other. "I have the solution."

Chrissy thanked Beth, "You are the best friend ever!"

Beth's eyes moved up and down Chrissy, "Well you can't go out in your pink robe." She headed up the stairs and demanded her friend follow. "Come on girl, we must get you dressed."

Chrissy climbed the staircase behind Beth. "But I don't know where I'm going, so I don't know how I should dress."

"I do." Beth stopped at the top of the stairs and smiled.

"How come that doesn't surprise me?" Chrissy laughed, and then grabbed Beth's arm.

"Wait. You didn't call Nick, did you?"

Beth took Chrissy's hand and led the way to her friend's bedroom. "No, of course not. I did the next best thing." She chuckled. "I called Barb at the motel. She knows everything."

"And?" Chrissy stopped at her bedroom door.

"Barb says he asked for her help. So, I know how to dress you. I'm not giving anymore up."

Beth's stare told her she wouldn't get it out of her either. Chrissy surrendered, her arms in the air. "Okay. I trust you."

"Of course, you do. I'm your bestie." Beth laid the garment bag on top of the pile of clothes on Chrissy's bed. She unzipped the bag and held up the emerald green dress she bought for the Christmas dance.

"I can't wear that. What will you wear for the dance?" Chrissy knew Beth bought it that summer when they went on a shopping spree in San Francisco.

"You bought two. I'm going to wear one of yours," Beth sternly announced.

Chrissy nodded. "Then you get to pick which one and I'll wear the other." Chrissy held the dress against her in front of her free-standing Victorian floor mirror that had belonged to her grandmother. She swung back and forth as she felt the smooth silk between her fingers. "This will look better on me anyway." She laughed.

Beth swatted Chrissy on the arm. "Don't push it girl."

Chrissy looked at Beth's reflection. "Is tonight's date this fancy though?" Beth turned around and opened the bag, pulling out the matching shoes. "Yes, and don't ask for more information."

Beth helped Chrissy finish her hair and makeup. The doorbell rang just as Beth zipped up the back of the dress. "I believe that would be your date."

Chrissy took a deep breath. "Okay, I'm ready." She walked out of the bedroom and stopped at the top of the stairs. "Are you coming?"

Beth laughed. "You're on your own, big girl." Then she added she'd wait and lock up after Chrissy left, calling out as Chrissy made her way down the stairs, "I want details in the morning."

Chrissy opened the door to find Nick dressed in black tie attire. He held a single red rose in his hand. His smile took her breath away. The same feeling she'd had when she first laid eyes on him, flowed through her again. All the anger and frustration she'd had earlier in the day disappeared. Perhaps the deal of dates for the dance at the farm, wouldn't be so bad after all. At least she'd get through this Christmas before she had to deal with the loss of the Delbert farm.

"Stunning."

Nick lifted her hand to his lips for a gentle kiss. Chrissy's heart beat faster and she took a deep breath. "You, as well." He handed her the rose and extended his arm into a loop, "Are you ready to get to know the real Nicholas Reed?"

Chrissy smiled and then nodded. She slid her arm around his. "I am."

He motioned toward his parked Bugatti. Chrissy knew her cars. She drove a '67 Mustang that was her mom's. But Nick's car was a little more expensive than her car.

"You own a Black Bess?"

Nick opened the passenger door for her. "You continue to impress me."

He closed the door once she was seated and she looked up at him.

"Veyron Grand Sport Vitesse with a hundred-eighty-four-horsepower."

Nick smiled. "You simply amaze me."

Confident she'd further impressed him, she smiled as she watched him walk around the front of his car. She admired the rich black paint with 24-carat gold accents on the outside, and then the interior combination of beige, brown, and red leather.

Nick started the ignition. It purred better than her cat.

"There's only like three of these, which would have cost you a couple of million," Chrissy commented as he slowly started down her street.

"Two -point-nine-seven, to be exact."

Chrissy almost choked trying to repeat the numbers in her head. If she had that much money, she'd buy the Delbert farm, not a car.

Chrissy wondered why Nick pulled into the Delbert farm. "What are we doing here?"

He pulled up to the barn. The one where Chrissy held the annual Christmas dance.

"I thought it would be the perfect place for our first date. It *is* the place that brought us together." He held her door open and extended his hand to help her out. Rich and charming. She thought. Too bad he was the one about to destroy her chance of holding onto the farm.

"It's also the place that will never keep us together." She hadn't meant to be sarcastic but she couldn't help it. She needed to remind herself that no matter how handsome and charming he appeared; he was the man to steal her farm and not her heart.

"Let's just live this week out. Forget about business."

Damn he was smooth. It only made it difficult to not like him.

"But we are in the middle of a business deal—dates for the farm to hold the dance,"

Chrissy reminded him. Her hands motioned in the air between her and the barn. His next words made her forget.

"It's not business to me." His smile that followed, weakened her. Nick opened the barn doors and Chrissy's jaw dropped. She admired the magic before her. Tiny white lights lit up the barn inside. She looked down to step inside onto a red carpet. It led to the middle of the barn floor where a table for two had been setup. Low romantic music played throughout the barn as he led her down the red carpet. Nick reached for the bottle of champagne. He poured her a glass and then one for himself.

"Here's to our first date, and hopefully many more."

Chrissy tapped her glass against his. She knew they'd have at least six more dates. Or did he mean more than that?

Chapter Five

"Well?"

Chrissy laughed at Beth's greeting the next morning. Beth stood at the shop's back entrance, apparently waiting for details of the night before.

"Good morning to you too." Chrissy unlocked the door and held it open for her.

Beth sighed loudly. "Well, it's good if last night led you to the morning."

Chrissy turned to her friend and rolled her eyes. "It wasn't that kind of a date." She stopped at her office and tossed her purse on her desk. Beth did the same and then followed Chrissy down the hall. She flipped the lights on along her way. She heard another loud sigh come from Beth.

"Shall I remind you of last night's request for details?" Beth reached for their aprons once in the kitchenhand tossed Chrissy's at her.

"Whoa! A little cranky this morning, are we?" Chrissy chuckled as she turned on the ovens. She reached down for the bowls to set on the counter but Beth grabbed them.

"Okay, enough torture. It's bad enough I have to be awake at this ungodly hour, are you going to tell me how last night went?"

Chrissy took the bowls from Beth. "Start baking and I'll start talking." She raised an eyebrow at her friend, and they both laughed.

Beth started with both the baking and the questions. "Did he have the barn setup like Barb described to me?"

Chrissy smiled. "It was beautiful."

"And?"

Chrissy looked up from the bowl, "Well if Barb told you everything, why do you want me to repeat it?"

Beth gave her a look she knew too well. "Not that stuff. I mean the good stuff. What was he like? How did it feel being with him?" Beth sighed.

Chrissy knew her friend was a romantic. She gave in to her demands.

"Nick was a complete gentleman. He's very charming, easy to talk to, and a great dancer."

Beth's eyes widened. "And hot as hell!" Chrissy laughed but had to agree.

"He's a great guy. If he wasn't the man that planned to demolish the Delbert farm, I could be interested. But he is. So, I'm keeping it business."

Beth's expression turned sad.

"Don't be like that. It just wasn't meant to be. There's no way I could look at him and not remember what he did to my dream." When Beth went quiet, Chrissy pulled the dough from the bowl, and reached for the rolling pin. "Is that the last one?"

Beth turned to check for baking trays. "Yep, set the timer."

Chrissy gave her a thumbs-up. "Coffee?" She poured their coffees when she noticed the bulletin board. "Oh, crap. I totally forgot."

"Forgot what?" Beth came up behind her.

Chrissy pointed to the board. She had a half-a-dozen school kids coming after school today.

"I thought that was next week. It's Mike's parents' anniversary. I'm having them for dinner." Beth took a seat beside Chrissy.

"We moved it. Remember, it was originally booked the day before the dance? But we have to decorate."

Beth nodded, and then looked at Chrissy. "Unless, you ask Nick to come bake with six ten-year-old kids." She laughed. "That would be a great second date."

Chrissy snorted. The sudden picture in her mind of Nick in a kitchen with kids made her laugh. She turned to Beth. "If he wants to get to know the real me, he should spend some time in my kitchen." She reached for the phone.

Beth laughed. "I wasn't serious."

Chrissy paused before she picked up the phone. "I am. Perhaps after he bakes with six kids, he can take them for a ride in his Veyron Grand Sport Vitesse." She laughed, and then added, "With sticky hands."

"The man drives one of those?" Beth asked excitedly. "Doesn't that cost a couple of mill?"

"Two, point-nine-seven, to be exact," Chrissy confirmed.

"Holy crap! I thought he had money but he must be loaded." Beth grabbed the phone from Chrissy. "So, he's a hot, rich, and charming gentleman?"

She knew where her friend was going with this information. "Doesn't change a thing."

Chrissy grabbed the phone back. "Morning, Barb. Can you patch me through to Nick Reed's room?" After what seemed like a hundred questions from Barb, she got connected. "Hi Nick, hope I didn't wake you."

"Good morning. No, you didn't, but I wouldn't mind if you had."

Chrissy rolled her eyes. Beth slapped her arm and she gave her friend the death-glare.

"I have an idea for date number two, unless you've already made plans."

"Not yet. What do you have in mind?"

Chrissy smiled. "I forgot I have six kids coming after school to bake for their Christmas bake sale. It would run into the evening, so I thought perhaps you'd like to join us."

"Not the usual kind of date, but I'm up for it." He laughed. "What time?"

"Any time after four o'clock. The shop gets quiet then."

"I'll see you then."

Chrissy ended her call, and turned to Beth. "Done. Now you can go home to your in-laws."

Beth laughed and checked on the trays in the ovens. "Think I'd rather spend the evening with the kids."

****

At precisely 4:01 p.m. Nick entered the shop. Chrissy looked up at the clock.

"You said, any time after four." He smiled, then added. "Where do you want me?"

Beth cleared her throat behind Chrissy. Nick knew instantly his question had come out the way he'd intended. Chrissy ignored them both.

"Would you like a coffee? We should be able to close the shop by 4:30 when the kids arrive."

Nick took a seat at the counter. "Love one. What's the special today?"

"Gingerbread Latte."

"I'll take that with Chrissy—" Nick cleared his throat. He'd made his point, then politely corrected, "The sugar cookie."

Chrissy ignored him again and reached for a cookie. "Beth will make your coffee. I have a few things to do in my office."

Beth smiled at him and shrugged. Chrissy's calm demeanor told him he still had work to do to win her heart. He watched her walk down the hallway and close her door.

"She's determined she's not interested. But I know her better than she knows herself."

Beth handed him the coffee. Her few chosen words gave him hope.

The shop remained quiet for about ten minutes after the last customers left. Then the sound of chatter and laughter came through the front door. Nick turned to see a herd of happy children enter. Beth met them and was bombarded with a group hug.

"Where's Chrissy?" one girl piped up.

Nick turned when he heard her voice. "I'm right here, honey. Are we ready to bake?"

Chrissy's tone held excitement. He only wished she'd have that much excitement when he walked through her front door. But he was determined to work on that. He stood when Chrissy began the introductions.

"Kids, this is Mr. Reed. He's visiting and would like to bake with us today. Can we give him a big Troy welcome?"

Nick barely heard Chrissy announce each child's name as he received a loud group hug.

Beth announced she'd lock up the shop. Nick followed the crowd to the kitchen. He rolled the sleeves of his shirt up and Chrissy tossed him an apron. He knew what she was up to. Baking with all these kids was supposed to scare him away. But what Chrissy didn't know was he was an expert in the kitchen. He'd baked with his mom since he was a child, and about to prove to Chrissy that this second date wouldn't turn out the way she expected it to.

"So, what are we baking?" Nick asked the kids with excitement.

The little girl who'd asked for Chrissy, walked up to him, and took his hand. "Gingerbread men, Santa cookies, and of course, Chrissy's sugar cookies." She led Nick over to the counter and stood close to him.

Chrissy passed by him and leaned in. "I believe there might be a little crush happening here."

Nick grinned and whispered back, "I've been waiting to hear you say that."

Chrissy nudged him. "I meant Abbey."

Nick chuckled. "I'll continue to wait, then." Chrissy flashed him a look that yelled out *never*. Not that it would stop him. He smiled.

All trays were in the ovens by five-thirty when he heard a knock at the front door.

"Want me to get that?"

Chrissy smiled. "Sure, if you want to splurge for the pizzas."

He laughed as he headed for the front door. Her determination for him *not* to be interested in her wasn't working. Nick graciously left the kitchen and reached for his wallet.

Nick opened the pizza boxes as many little hands reached for a slice. The kitchen was filled with the noise of kids laughing and talking while they ate. He handed a slice to Chrissy.

She took a seat on the stool beside him.

"Thanks." She took a bite and then complimented him. "I'm impressed with your capabilities in the kitchen. I didn't know you could bake."

Nick winked. "There are many qualities you don't know about." Chrissy laughed and took another bite. He waited for her comeback when the shop's phone rang. "Want me to get that?"

"Another capability?"

Nick laughed as he reached for the phone. "One of many. "Sugar 'N' Spice, Nick speaking."

"Very professional. I might lose my job."

Beth's words gave Nick an idea for date number three. "Thank you, Beth. But I'm sure you're much better than me." He looked at Chrissy who rolled her eyes.

"How's it going with all those kids? Sounds crazy in there."

Chrissy held her hand out for the phone but Nick ignored her. He stood and walked to the other end of the kitchen to hear Beth better. "Great bunch of kids. And I believe my hidden talent in the kitchen is impressing *our boss.*"

Beth laughed. "Good to hear. She'll come around, Nick. Trust me."

"Hope you're right. How's it going at your end?"

"My in-laws should be coming through my door any minute. Save me." Beth's laugh told him she'd rather be at the shop with a half-a-dozen kids. It sounded like she'd need a vacation after tonight. His idea was perfect.

"Hey, Beth; how about a day off to recover from the in-laws?"

"That would be wonderful, but I don't think *our boss* would like that." He liked that she used *our boss* in her response.

"Well, I was thinking a perfect third date could be my assistance at the shop tomorrow."

Beth cleared her throat. "Seriously? You want to work at the shop all day?"

"Yep." Nick's quick response awaited Beth's thoughts.

"Personally, I'd love it. And it would give you two more time together. Can't speak for Chrissy. Good luck there." Beth laughed.

"Consider yourself on vacation tomorrow. Unless *our boss* says no." He laughed. "I'll call back if I'm unlucky."

"Thanks, Nick. Good luck."

Nick set the phone back and turned to find Chrissy standing with her hands on her hips.

"Using my best friend won't help change my mind."

Her stern words went in one ear, and out the other. "I'm serious. Our third date can be me working at the shop all day tomorrow with you. You're the boss. I'm at your beck-and-call."

Chrissy sucked in a big breath. "Fine. Six o'clock sharp." Nick smiled, his plan to prove those sparks were real was working. "Come on, it's time to create magic with icing and sprinkles."

"What every man wants to hear from a beautiful woman." He heard her laughter as she moved across the kitchen.

Chapter Six

Chrissy heard the alarm, and rolled over. The big bright red numbers read, *5:00*.

She smiled, knowing she'd work Nick's butt off today at the shop. He'd been on her mind when she went to bed. She fought those thoughts of him, and tossed and turned all night. Tired, yet eager to get to the shop, she threw the blanket off her. Chrissy's feet hit the hardwood and carried her to the shower.

****

"Good morning, beautiful." Nick opened the car door for her, and then held out his hand.

She took the proffered hand and placed hers in his. Once upright in front of him, she spoke. "You're a morning person." She stepped around him and walked toward the shop door. "Another fine quality to add to your list." Chrissy unlocked the door and held it open for him. "Ready to be slave-driven?"

Nick smiled. "Every man's desire."

She laughed at his response. He was quick with the comebacks which made their time together more fun. At least her part of the trade was interesting. She continued to deny the fact this his sweet smile and touch ignited feelings she chose not to admit.

****

He set down the brown bag he held in his arm on the kitchen counter. Chrissy peeked inside. "What's all this?"

"A romantic breakfast for two." Nick itemized and announced each item he pulled from the bag and set on the counter. "Two breakfasts, two orange juice, two candles, candlestick holders, a lighter, and a mistletoe." He turned to Chrissy. "Where shall I hang it?"

She grumbled, "Not near me."

Nick ignored her comment. "I'll hang it later." He smiled. "Leave it as a surprise."

"You and your damn surprises." Chrissy walked to the ovens and turned them on. She reached for the baking bowls but he stopped her.

"Please, have some breakfast first." He tilted his head. "It's the most important meal of the day."

His facial expression was priceless. She had to laugh. "Okay, but only a few minutes. There's work to be done. We open in an hour."

Nick promised he'd eat fast, and work faster. He lit the candles, and then pulled out the kitchen stool for her to sit. He placed the Styrofoam container in front of her, and opened it.

"Barb's Big Breakfast," she announced.

Nick sat across from her and opened his. "She makes an awesome breakfast."

He finished five minutes later.

"Did you taste it?"

He looked at her shocked expression. "Every single bite." He took the napkin from his lap and wiped his mouth. He then downed his orange juice like he was doing a shot of tequila. Nick looked over to Chrissy's half-eaten breakfast. "Already ate? Or not a big breakfast person?"

"I don't like mornings, but I like to bake." She closed the lid, and then looked up at him. "Would you like to finish mine?"

He rubbed his belly. "No thanks, I'm stuffed." He reached into his pocket and pulled out the mistletoe. "You could help me work it off?" He winked. Her stern expression made him put it back in his pocket. "Maybe later." Nick disposed of the Styrofoam containers and blew out the candles. Once he cleared the counter, he asked where she wanted him to start.

"Do you know how to work a cash register?"

He nodded.

"Great. You'll find the float in the safe in my office. It's already opened." Chrissy reached for the baking bowls once more. Nick headed to the office and heard her call out. "Once you get that ready to go, turn on the front lights and come help me bake."

He whispered, "At your beck-and-call."

"What?" she called out from the kitchen.

"Be there in a couple of minutes." He spoke louder. Nick finished his duties and reached for the mistletoe in his pocket. He hung it above the cash register. "Chrissy, can you come help me?" He heard her mumbling something about him stating he knew what to do. He stood with his back against the cash register, and smiled.

"What's wrong?"

"Nothing. There's something else needed that's important for the day."

Chrissy raised an eyebrow. "Nick, we open in forty-five minutes, which gives us about fifteen minutes to prepare. What's so important that can't wait?"

"This." He placed his hands on her face and looked up at the mistletoe.

"You can't be serious." Her words carried hesitation but her body did not move from his hold. He moistened his lips and slowly placed them on hers. The feel of her softness against him only enhanced the feelings he already felt. He deepened the kiss and felt her body relax against his. He released from the kiss and his hold. Nick looked up at the mistletoe.

"I found the perfect spot. Where we first met." He smiled proudly. "Now, we can work."

He left her standing with a dazed look on her face, and called out from the kitchen.

"Come on girl, we've got fifteen minutes to prepare."

Nick leaned against the counter in the kitchen. Exhaustion wasn't even the word to describe how he felt. This job wasn't easy. He'd been on his feet non-stop for four hours.

Chrissy came around the corner. "Not as easy as it looks."

"You got that right."

She grabbed a stool. "Take five. The lunch rush won't start for a half-hour."

"How do you do this every day?"

Chrissy smiled. "Not every day. I close after lunch on Saturdays until Monday morning. Only a sixty-two-hour week."

Nick watched her clean off the counter and start to prepare the croissants they'd baked earlier. "You never stop. You amaze me."

Chrissy looked up and smiled. "Our lunch customers will be hungry. Today's special for lunch is potato soup with ham and cheese croissants." She set all ingredients on the table and then reached for the knife. She set it on the table. "Whenever you're ready." Chrissy walked over to the stove and removed the lid from the big pot. She opened the refrigerator and pulled out what he assumed was potato soup. He took a deep breath and dragged his aching body over to the counter and picked up the knife.

When the last customer left at 4:20 that afternoon, he hauled the stool from the kitchen and placed it in front of the cash register. He locked the front door and turned off the lights, leaving the counter lights on. Nick plumped himself on the stool with a sigh. He turned when he heard her come up behind him.

"Would you like to work for me full-time?"

He shook his head. "I hope you pay Beth well."

"Not good enough. She knows I'd give her more if I could. I only opened last winter after the holidays. It was Beth who convinced me and then stuck with me."

Nick smiled. "She's a true friend."

"Yes, she is. We don't do it for the money."

Nick kicked off his shoes. "You do it for the agony of pain it causes." He lifted his foot to his knee and rubbed it. Chrissy laughed. "No, silly. For pure enjoyment. We love to bake, and we love people."

"What about financial reward?" Nick was curious. He knew about the Delbert farm, and the fact she wanted to buy it. Her uncle and her father were against it, as Barb mentioned. He understood why. He'd read her financial statements when he researched his competition in town.

"Not important. I do what I love."

"What about the farm? You want it for personal reasons?"

Chrissy sighed. "Yeah, its more personal. A lot of memories there. But I'd love to remodel the older barn into a bake shop."

"You want to build a franchise? Make Sugar 'N' Spice, a chain?"

Chrissy shook her head. "No, I'd just like to bake more there. Then I could give this part to Beth to run."

Nick understood now. Money wasn't important to her. But this town, the people, the farm, and Beth were. He wondered if he could help make her dream come true. More so, he'd like to belong to the list that was important to her.

"Enough of the dreaming. Let's get back to reality and close shop." Chrissy headed back to the kitchen.

Nick turned to balance the cash.

"Chrissy, can you come here?"

She appeared within seconds, "What's wrong?"

He hadn't moved from his stool, he wanted her by the cash register. Once he felt her presence, he swiveled and stood. Nick's lips quickly met hers. This time he filled the kiss with more passion and desire than he had that morning. He didn't feel her fight his gentle hold.

"Nothing. I just wanted to end the day the way it began."

Chapter Seven

"Good morning, Nick."

Nick smiled, and then joined her on the patio for breakfast. "Good morning, Barb."

She poured a cup of coffee and handed it to him. "Sleep well?"

He'd slept like a baby. The day before at Chrissy's shop had exhausted him. "I did, thank you. And you?" Nick took a gulp of his coffee, and then picked up his fork to delve into the best breakfast in town. He took a few bites as Barb described her usual restless sleep. Her humor and stories entertained him as he ate.

"Enough about me, how was your day as an employee of my darling Chrissy?"

Nick chuckled. "Extremely busy. She worked me to the bone. But well worth it."

Barb smiled. "She's always been a determined girl and a hard-worker." She paused a moment and then added, "And a little stubborn."

Nick laughed and nodded. But he was determined and stubborn too.

"So, any idea for date number four?"

He told Barb he'd like to plan a romantic dinner on the beach. She offered her assistance and he accepted quickly. Having Barb on his side made it easier in his attempt to impress Chrissy. He mentioned he had to take a trip back to the city for some business but would be back later in the day. Barb promised she'd help arrange this romantic dinner. Nick mentioned a couple of things he'd like, but his questions directed more toward Chrissy's likes. As usual, Barb knew what additions she'd add for Chrissy. He knew he was in good-hands with Barb.

"Thanks Barb." He pointed at his empty plate. "And for the best breakfast."

"Good morning, Mr. Reed. Welcome back."

Nick stopped outside his office. "Good morning Sharon. I'm just here for the morning, can you get Martin on the line for me?"

His assistant agreed to get Nick's lawyer on the phone, and then bring in his coffee.

He smiled, and thanked her. She'd been with him since he opened his office five years before. She knew the business better than he did some days.

Nick opened the door to his corner office with a view of the city skyline. He set his briefcase on his desk, and then stood at the window and enjoyed his view. Thoughts of Chrissy raced through him. He would have loved to be with her instead of his office. He'd had so much fun working with her and getting to know her better. Each moment he spent with her, his feelings grew deeper. He couldn't explain it. For the past five years of success he'd thought nothing besides business. Now, all he could think of was Chrissy and being with her in Troy. His thoughts were interrupted with Sharon's entrance.

"Martin is on line one." Nick turned and nodded. Sharon handed him the cup she held. "Your coffee."

"Thanks, Sharon." Nick returned to the view of the city and lifted the cup to his lips. He heard Sharon close the door and he turned to his desk. Nick hit the flashing light, and pressed the speaker button.

"Martin, I need you to draw up a contract of purchase for the Delbert farm."

"Thought you rescheduled the buyers."

"New buyer. Her name is Christine Spencer."

"Never heard of her."

Nick silently chuckled. He assumed Martin's mind drifted through the list of buyers they'd dealt with over the years.

"She's a Troy resident. The Delbert property is of high importance to her. I'd like to make her an offer to buy it through my financing. Can you draw up the papers? A moment of silence filled the air. Nick smiled. He pictured an image in his mind of Martin's jaw dropping.

"Still there, Martin?"

Nick heard the man clear his throat. "Still here. Are you sure? Who is this Miss Spencer?"

"The most beautiful, confident woman with a sense of humor better than mine."

"So, you want to give money to a woman you've slept with?"

Nick didn't like Martin's response. But he'd known him a long time. He wasn't just his lawyer but a good friend. "Haven't slept with her. But that's none of your business." Nick laughed.

"I'll prepare the contract and send it to Sharon within the hour."

"Thanks, Martin." Nick pressed the button to end the call. He returned to the view before him. Chrissy deserved to own the farm. Her father and uncle didn't think so. Nick understood their concern and their love for her. He knew she could manage the farm, the bakery, and much more. He believed in her. Nick also understood the hidden concern in Martin's tone. There had only been two women in Nick's life he'd generously helped —his mother, and Sharon. He wasn't sure where things were going with Chrissy. He hoped she felt the same as he did. But he wasn't going to make this offer to win over her heart. He knew it was the right move.

Nick pressed her doorbell at seven-thirty that evening. He'd text her earlier to dress casually for date number four. He kept the remainder of their date a surprise. Her continued sarcastic comments about his damn surprises only made him more determined to keep it that way. He waited in blue jeans and a white cable knit wool sweater. Chrissy opened the door and took his breath away. She smiled. "Hi Nick." Her sweet and simple greeting warmed him. The bold wine-color ribbed sweater she wore enhanced her blonde curls that fell around her shoulders. But the fitted denims flattered her every curve, and his every desire. He cleared his throat.

"Evening gorgeous, ready for your next surprise?" He curved the corners of his mouth to a seductive grin.

Chrissy laughed, "I can't wait." He extended his arm for her, and led her down the front steps. She stopped. Horse and carriage?" She turned to him.

Nick smiled. "Not as fast as my *Black Bess*. But this way, I get to focus on my date."

He heard her chuckle as he helped her step up into the carriage.

"Hi Bob." Chrissy acknowledged the man at the reins.

Nick had a lovely chat with Bob on the way to Chrissy's. Barb mentioned Chrissy always loved a holiday ride on Bob's carriage with her grandmother and Mrs. Delbert. Nick was thankful to have Barb help with the extra details. He only had three more dates to impress the woman he was falling in love with. By the time their seventh date would arrive, the night of the dance, he hoped she'd feel the same.

"Evening, Chrissy." Bob waited for Nick to settle in beside Chrissy. "Ready?"

Nick nodded, and then Bob turned and pulled the reins. His attention quickly returned to the beautiful woman at his side.

"Barb introduced you to Bob? "she drilled him.

He laughed. "Yes, she did. She's been a great help this week. Sharing the little details of your likes and dislikes has helped prepare my surprises."

"And what surprise is on the menu tonight?"

"Besides the mussels I've flown in from the Atlantic, and the bottle of Chardonnay I grabbed while in the city earlier today..." Nick paused. "You'll have to wait."

Chrissy laughed. "I can wait." Nick wasn't sure how to take her tone. He wondered if she'd meant it sarcastically or if his surprises had begun to do what he hoped, intrigue her. The expression on her face as Bob turned toward the beach at the end of town confirmed the latter. Her eyes widened, her jaw dropped, and then her hand reached out for his. "You did all this for me?"

Her excitement told him not too many, if anyone, had ever done something special for her. Chrissy seemed to be the one in town that did for everyone else. Nick felt good inside. He'd been the one to show her how special she really was. The romantic dinner on the beach he'd planned, appeared to be a great start to winning her heart. He hoped.

Bob pulled on the reins to stop at the edge of the boardwalk. Nick stepped down first, and then offered assistance to Chrissy. She stepped down from the carriage, still holding Nick's hand. He led her across the boardwalk where the private table for two sat on the sand. Rose petals led the path to the table. Candles were lit, wine had been poured, and their waiter stood patiently to serve them.

"I must admit." Chrissy turned to Nick. "I'm impressed."

He smiled. Success had been confirmed. He pulled out her chair and offered her to take a seat. At that moment, a violin began to play not far from the table.

"Dinner music included." Chrissy smiled.

Nick moved around to his seat across from her. His hand motioned toward the silver dome before her. She lifted it gently to discover the steaming mussels he'd had flown in earlier. Her pleased smile assured him Barb had been right. Mussels were a special treat she shared with her grandmother.

"Barb? "she asked.

He chuckled. "Guilty." And then he added, "Guilty for the simple desire to please you."

Chrissy smiled and tilted her wine glass toward the center of the table. Nick followed her lead and lifted his glass to meet hers. "Thank you, Nick. No one has ever gone to these extremes for me."

He met her stare and felt something different. He wondered if she'd begun to have feelings for him. "How about a dance before we eat?" Nick stood, and extended his hand. Chrissy didn't argue and placed her hand in his. He pulled her in close. His senses drove him wild as he rested his face against her hair. The sweet scent of berries filled the air. He stepped back and leaned closer to her lips. Their softness he could no longer resist. The sound of a horn honking in the near distance interrupted his kiss. Their focus turned toward the boardwalk. Headlights shone brightly. Nick's hand rested above his eyes. "Who's that?"

Chrissy stepped forward. "I think it's Mike's truck." She turned back to Nick. "Beth's husband."

She'd been correct. He heard Beth's voice call out. She ran across the boardwalk. "Chrissy. The Delbert farms. There's a fire."

Chrissy raced toward Beth. She stopped for a moment and turned to Nick. "Are you coming?"

Nick followed her to Mike's truck.

Chapter Eight

Mike's truck -tires squealed as he turned the bend in the road. The smoke-filled sky hovered above the edge of the trees. She gasped in horror of the thought of what she was about to see. Memories flashed through her mind. Beth's hand squeezed hers as they inched closer. Smoke filled the air with a bright glint of orange between the trees. Sirens echoed in the distance. A single tear had fallen on her cheek. Her eyes welled with fluid. Chrissy fought back the tears. She prayed the firefighters of her small town would be able to control the fire. Mike pulled into the Delbert gravel road lined with trees. Chrissy held onto Beth's hand tightly as she peeked through the trees, frantically searching for hope. Hope that there'd been some salvage to the farm. Then she spotted the town's fire trucks, half a dozen volunteer vehicles, and her dad. Mike stopped as Chrissy opened the passenger door and ran into her father's arms.

Over her dad's shoulder she watched the blaze and heard the loud crackle of the flames. In the distance, the town's firefighters fought hard against the fire. The barn glowed orange against the smoke-filled night's darkness. She knew there'd be no hope to save it. The barn had been taken over by the fire. Chrissy felt a gentle touch on her back. Her dad released her from his hold. She turned to find Nick. He stood quiet. But his expression told her he felt her pain. The farm meant everything to her. It held so many memories for her. Beth ran into Chrissy's arms.

"Oh, honey. I'm so sorry." She held Chrissy tight in her embrace. "I know how much this place means to you."

Chrissy's pain released. She could no longer hold back the tears. Beth rubbed her back to comfort her. Chrissy heard Bill's voice behind her and turned to Troy's fire chief.

"I'm sorry, Chrissy. We can't save the barn. But we have it under control."

Thankfully, they'd be able to save the house, and the main barn. They were far enough away she was told. But the old barn had always been her first view of the property. The one she'd always hoped to make her bake shop. That dream disappeared as the flames engulfed its structure. She heard Bill continue.

"My guess is the wiring and electrical systems caused it. They are humid and have elevated levels of corrosive gases such as hydrogen sulfide and ammonia."

"So, no one started it? "Chrissy stumbled her question through sobs.

Bill shook his head. "It's been left unattended. It could simply be corrosion and rodents chewing on the wiring. Most likely cause of an old barn in my experience."

Bill made it sound like it wasn't a big deal. Just an old barn. Chrissy was thankful it wasn't the main barn where they held the dance, or the farmhouse. She knew it could be worse. Still, the old barn at the front of the property had always been her favorite. It was the perfect place for her bake shop. Not that her dream was possible. Her father and uncle had made certain of it. Nick planned to support their effort to keep her from buying the farm. She loved her father and uncle. She knew they wanted the best for her. But they never believed she could run both a bakery and a farm. They wanted her to fall in love, settle down, and raise a family. No wonder they liked Nick. He was their savior. Sell the farm, and settle her down. She wondered how she could have feelings for Nick. He was no better than her father or uncle. Bill was right. Maintenance of the farm hadn't been kept up since Mrs. Delbert's death. It had been left, unattended to. Chrissy turned to her father. Anger took over.

"If you had only let me take over its care, this may not have happened. But no, you and Uncle Tom didn't believe in me. That I could handle the farm. You just let it sit and deteriorate. Waiting for some outsider to come in and take it away from me." Chrissy quickly glanced between her father and Nick.

"Chrissy, I—"

"Don't. Just don't, Dad. You've never believed in me." Chrissy stormed off. She heard him plead in the distance.

"Chrissy, I just want the best for you. I hate seeing you work so hard, endlessly. I want you to be happy."

She stopped and turned. "Then you should have listened to what would have made me happy." Chrissy passed by Mike. "Can you take me home? "He nodded. She climbed into his truck and slammed the door.

Beth opened the door a minute later and climbed in beside Chrissy. Mike started the ignition. "What about Nick?"

Chrissy turned her head in the direction of her father and Nick. "Leave him with my father. The two of them never wanted me to have the farm. Nick can get a ride from him."

Chrissy took the next day off. The first ever. Beth promised to run the shop single-handedly. She needed time to mourn. Not just for the fire that destroyed her dream, but for the reality that she'd never own the farm. Chrissy picked up the picture of her and her dad. She loved her dad. She knew he only wanted the best for her. He'd shown up late the night before to apologize. He never wanted her to think he never believed in her, he just wanted life to be easier for her. They agreed to disagree as they always had. A cup of coffee and a few laughs and then he'd said good-night.

The doorbell startled her thoughts. She opened the door to Nick.

"What the hell are you doing here?"

"May I come in?"

Chrissy shook her head. "I need time alone. I've had enough bad news lately. I don't need to be reminded that you are the one to completely destroy my dreams." She began to close the door, but Nick's hand stopped her. He waved a paper in his hand.

"I've cancelled the investors. I'd like to purchase the farm—"

Chrissy slammed the door, and then locked it. "Seriously," she said aloud as she made her way back to her couch. "He wants to buy the farm? Like that news is good?" Chrissy sunk into the cushions of the couch, and then cried.

Chapter Nine

"What are you doing here?"

Barb stepped up beside Nick, "We're here to decorate."

Chrissy wasn't about to argue with the woman who would attempt to convince her to listen to Nick. She knew Barb only had his point-of-view. Today wasn't the day to hash it out.

"Fine. "Chrissy pivoted on one foot and reached for a box from Beth's truck.

"I think you should listen to what he has to say." Beth leaned in against Chrissy's shoulder.

"I've heard enough." Chrissy carried the box toward the barn, determined not to look at him as she passed by. There were enough Troy residents around to help her avoid him.

"As magical as always."

Chrissy smiled and hopped up beside Beth on the back-end of the truck.

"We did a fantastic job. Looks great. "She sat in admiration of the hard work put in to decorate the barn for the Christmas dance.

"Even with the disaster down the road. We didn't let it stop us."

Beth's head turned in the direction of the burned down old barn. "Did you hear that Bill found a few cigarette butts outside the barn? Wonder if someone had been smoking in the barn or near it that evening?"

Chrissy had spoken to Bill that morning. "Yeah, he mentioned it. I don't imagine our small town will investigate it any further. According to Bill, it's been reported as a misfortune. No one really owns this place so there wouldn't be any insurance claim filed."

"True." Beth sighed. "Still, a shame."

She knew her friend meant it was a shame for Chrissy. But both knew it wasn't Chrissy's property to worry about. That was more of a shame.

"Probably teenagers smoking in the barn. Remember, we used to do it."

Beth laughed. "The good ol' days."

Chrissy felt a nudge at her arm and looked down. Beth tapped the bottle of wine against her.

"Traditional glass of wine after decorating?"

Chrissy smiled. "Of course." She watched the last few helpers walk to their cars and waved.

"Damn!"

Chrissy heard Beth curse but turned the opposite way when she heard his voice.

"Is there a problem, ladies?"

Chrissy frowned. "Yes, you're still here." She felt the nudge from Beth but ignored her friend.

"I forgot the corkscrew. Don't happen to have one on you, do you Nick?"

He shook his head. "Sorry." Chrissy watched his focus drift to the farmhouse. "But, perhaps there's one in Mrs. Delbert's kitchen."

Chrissy laughed. "Yes, let's break in and steal a corkscrew. Come on Beth, let's have wine at my place." She wiggled off the back-end of the truck.

Nick reached in his pocket and pulled out his keys. He removed a key from the ring, and hand it to

Chrissy. "No need to break in. Enjoy your wine. You can leave the key at Barb's." Nick sadly turned and walked away.

"You broke his heart."

Chrissy turned to Beth with a sarcastic, "Please, don't."

Beth shrugged. "Okay, I won't tell you how stubborn and stupid you're being. It's not hard to see that man has deep feelings for you." Chrissy flashed Beth a look to make her stop. Beth waved her arms in the air. "Fine. I won't say anymore." She grabbed the key from Chrissy and headed toward the house. "Are you coming?" Beth called out.

Chrissy stood for a moment and watched Nick get in Barb's car. A sudden sadness hit her. She knew she felt the same way he did. But he was the man who would destroy the farm and the memories she held dearly in her heart. His plan to buy the farm himself didn't change the fact that he still stole *her* farm. His idea to rebuild the old barn that burned down for her bake shop was generous. But she couldn't be bought. Her stubbornness and determination to make it on her own stood in the way of her feelings for him. She turned to follow Beth.

"Found it." Chrissy held the corkscrew in her hand and turned to Beth.

"I found something better. "Beth looked up from the paper she held in her hands.

"What's that?"

Beth handed her the paper. "Mrs. Delbert's will. I don't think Nick will be buying the farm."

Chrissy grabbed the paper and quickly read it. She looked up at Beth. "She left me the farm." Her eyes lit up. Her dream had come true. Her memories would not be destroyed by Nick or anyone else.

"Read further down," Beth instructed and walked out of the kitchen.

"Where are you going?"

Beth continued walking. "Read. You'll know where to find me."

Chrissy met Beth in the attic. Mrs. Delbert explained in her will that she only gave a portion of her savings to Chrissy's uncle at the bank. She kept the remainder in the attic in the trunk by the window. Beth slowly opened the trunk to a wedding dress with a note attached.

My dearest Chrissy,

I leave you not only the farm, and enough savings to build that bake shop you always talked about, but my wedding dress. I was never blessed with children of my own. You were my only blessing. I loved you like you were my own. I hope someday you'll put aside your ambitions to fall in love. I will always love you,

Bess

xoxo.

Tears fell upon her cheeks as she read the last word and looked at Beth.

"She's right you know." Beth smiled. She said no more, but Chrissy knew what she meant.

"I look fabulous in this red dress. I'm glad I let you wear the emerald one."

Beth spun in a circle around Chrissy. She laughed. "Good thing I bought two that day."

Chrissy turned in front of the mirror to get a look at the backside of her white lace dress. It hugged every curve she had. The silk lining beneath the lace felt heavenly against her skin. She slipped into her white, three-inch heels, and turned to Beth. "Ready?"

The doorbell rang at the same time and Beth laughed. "I do love a punctual man." She led the way down Chrissy's staircase. She'd agreed to get ready with Chrissy and told Mike to pick them up at her place. "Still wish you'd kept your date for tonight."

Chrissy followed her down the stairs. "Why? I own the farm. There was no need."

Beth stopped before she opened the front door. "For pleasure, I meant, not business."

Chrissy stepped around Beth without acknowledgement of her friend's comment, and opened the door. "Hi, Mike. We're ready." She walked past him.

"Everything okay?" Chrissy heard Mike ask Beth. But all she heard come out of Beth was a loud huff. She giggled as she made her way to Mike's car.

Chrissy made her way around the magically-lit barn. She kept busy with a tray of sweets she offered as she mingled. Chrissy made her way through the crowd and stopped suddenly at the sound of his voice.

"I believe you owe me a dance."

Chrissy turned quickly. "I owe you nothing."

"We made a deal."

Chrissy laughed. "That deal ended when I inherited the farm."

Nick sighed. He reached for the tray in her hands, and then set it aside on the table. "I wasn't trying to buy you. I only wanted to help make your dream come true.

It wasn't a gift. It was a loan. If you'd just let me finish the other night." He stood quietly.

Chrissy's eyes met his. He seemed sincere. "You wanted to give me a loan? I thought you meant you wanted to buy it."

He nodded. "Yes. I mean yes for the loan. I knew you'd be good for it. You just needed someone to believe in you. I've been there. Someone took a chance on me once."

Chrissy lowered her head. "I feel terrible. I thought you were—"

Nick interrupted. "I would have felt the same way. I should have started the conversation differently." His finger reached for her chin and tilted her head up. His eyes met hers. "I've never met anyone like you before. I still want to get to know you better."

Chrissy smiled. "To be honest, Nick, I'd like to get to know you better too. But, no more business deals. Let's stick to pleasure."

He nodded. "Agreed."

She felt his hands rest on her face. His eyes lifted and she followed his focus. "Did you hang that mistletoe there?"

Nick laughed. "Guilty."

Chrissy lowered her focus and met his stare. He stepped in closer and placed his lips against hers. She remembered the first day they met. The day he stirred her emotions and made her wonder if love was possible.

Nick released from the kiss and reached for her hand. "May I have this dance?"

Chrissy smiled, and then placed her hand in his.

"I have to warn you. I may want more than a dance."

Thank you for reading *Chrissy's Christmas Sugar Cookies*. I wish you a happy and safe holiday season. Enjoy Chrissy's Christmas Sugar Cookies (recipe below).

Chrissy's Christmas Sugar Cookies

Ingredients:

- 1 cup granulated sugar
- 1 cup butter, softened (2 sticks)
- 2 tsp vanilla
- 1 cup powdered sugar
- 1 cup oil
- 2 eggs
- 5 cups flour
- ½ tsp salt
- 1 tsp baking soda
- 1 tsp cream of tarter
- Red and green colored sugar

Directions:

Preheat oven to 350. Cream granulated sugar, butter, and vanilla. Add powdered sugar, oil, and eggs.

Sift together (in a separate bowl) flour, salt, baking soda and cream of tarter. Slowly add to above, mixing until just combined. It's best to add about a cup of dry ingredient mixture at a time, mixing after each addition. Form rounded teaspoonfuls into balls and place on ungreased cookie sheets.

Tip: Using a moistened paper towel wet the bottom of a glass, dip in colored sugar (re-dipping for each cookie) and flatten ball of dough. You may need to apply the moistened paper towel every so often, to keep glass wet and easily able to pick up sugar crystals. Bake at 350 degrees for 11-13 minutes or until edges turn slightly brown. Remove immediately from cookie sheet and cool on wire rack. Makes 6 dozen Christmas Sugar Cookies. That's a whole lot of delicious cookies to share with friends, family, neighbors, Santa... whoever could use a Christmas pick-me-up.

Amy's Christmas Casserole

Tammy Tate

Chapter One

The cafe didn't open for another fifteen minutes. Christmas was four weeks off and Matt had Christmas carols coming from the cafe's overhead speakers. Amy glanced over the delivery man's shoulder at a window overlooking the street. Past the tinsel, wreaths and Merry Christmas written in artificial snow, she watched a red pickup truck stop in front of the cafe. A man she'd never seen before, crawled out of the passenger's seat wearing dark shades and sporting a short military-style haircut.

After a brief conversation with the driver, the stranger pulled a black nylon duffle bag out of the bed of the truck right before it sped away.

"I ordered four cases of chicken," Amy mumbled to the delivery guy over "Jingle Bells." "Not two."

"Sorry, Miss Olson," the delivery man said. "My invoice says two."

Amy glanced at the bold number two in the quantity column he was pointing at and said, "Well, that's not right."

After implementing her famous chicken Dorito casserole into the lunch special, she needed a minimum of four boxes. This wouldn't last a week. Much less, two.

Scratching his sandy blond head, the man looked genuinely concerned. Was it her mix-up or his company's?

As a last-ditch effort to get two more boxes, Amy asked "Do you have extra on your truck—"

Once again, the man shook his head and replied, "Sorry, Miss Olson. I don't."

At the risk of sounding Scrooge-like four weeks before Christmas, Amy decided to save her sarcasm for customer service. Not that it mattered. Deliveries were every two weeks and since Sawyer Creek's family-owned grocery didn't sell by the bulk, she'd have to drive into San Antonio to get more.

Amy hated big cities. Especially, this time of the year. That's why she left San Antonio four years prior. Buying the cafe in Sawyer Creek was supposed to be a new beginning. A new chapter in her life that didn't include a man in a black ski mask preying on innocent women.

The thought of making the seventy-four-mile trip back, wasn't appealing. But, then again, neither was turning away hungry customers.

Still curious about the stranger, Amy once again craned her neck to see past the delivery guy's shoulder. She wrinkled her brow when she saw him walking toward Mitchel's Gas Station at a steady pace.

Amy jumped when Matt, her cook of four years, burst through the kitchen doors pushing a noisy cart.

After loading the last box, Matt frowned. "I thought you ordered four cases?"

"Don't get me started," Amy said scribbling her name on the delivery ticket so he could go.

While taking the carbon copy he shoved at her, Amy noted the time. It was 5:45 a.m. Matt escorted the man to the door and let him out. But before he could close it again, Sarah rushed past him wrapped in a winter coat over her beige waitress uniform. Like always, she smiled, as she padded to the back to put her things away and prepare for the morning rush.

Amy eased to the glass enclosure overlooking the street and was surprised to see the man talking with the station's tow truck driver.

That was odd. He didn't even have a car. *Or did he?*

Once more, a loud crash caused Amy to cringe as Matt plowed through the doors to the freezer. Amy hissed. Her first instinct was to tell him to knock it off, but it was his last week and she couldn't bring herself to scold him. Amy understood that he had to move to Chicago to take care of his ailing mom, but it didn't mean she had to like it.

Along with placing an ad in Sawyer Creek's tiny paper, she posted a "Help Wanted" sign in the window of the cafe. It was Monday. And still no applicants. If she didn't find a replacement soon, she'd have to slave over the grill like the old days.

Luckily, a few weeks after opening the café she began serving chicken Dorito casserole and business picked up allowing her ample funds to hire a cook, two waitresses and counter help. When growing up, it was something her grandmother served with traditional Christmas dishes. It was a hit then and still was.

Matt whistled while he worked. He arrived early. Unlike Sue Ellen, who couldn't get to work on time to save her life.

Matt cleaned windows. *Who did that?*

Another ten minutes slipped by. Since Sue Ellen still hadn't arrived, Amy took the liberty of unlocking, the door. She grinned when she saw Sue Ellen running along the sidewalk, waving a black apron.

"Sorry, Miss Olson," Sue Ellen said, charging into the cafe. "My alarm didn't go off!"

It was the same excuse she used yesterday. Amy thought of giving her an alarm clock for Christmas this year instead of the usual smoked ham.

Anyone else would have fired the girl by now. But not Amy. The customers loved Sue Ellen. Amy hoped one day she'd come around, but so far that hadn't happened.

A cloud hovered around Mayor McNeil's mouth as he paced along the sidewalk, staring down at his wristwatch. Amy opened the door to let him in. The brisk December air rushed in as he limped inside.

A few years back, he'd suffered multiple leg fractures from a seven-car pileup on San Antonio's freeway. With the morning temperature dropping, he was favoring it more than usual.

Smiling, Amy said, "Good morning, Mayor McNeil."

The mayor stopped blowing warm breath onto his hands and allowed them to drop to his sides. "I take it Sue Ellen is late again?" he asked, removing his coat and draping it over his arm.

Amy defended his niece like she was her own kin. "It's okay, Mayor McNeil. Sue Ellen had a *situation*."

The wealthy mayor, who owned half of Sawyer Creek, pursed his purple thin lips making the frown lines around his mouth appear deeper. Shaking his head, he limped away to his favorite table with a newspaper tucked under his arm.

Since it was Sue Ellen's section and she hadn't come from the back, Sarah graciously fetched his coffee.

Black. Just the way he liked it. Mayor McNeil gave her an appreciative nod over the one-page menu that he should have memorized by heart.

A bell jingled from the top of the door as Sheriff Martin and Deputy Barnes arrived and took a seat at the counter for their morning coffee, biscuits and gravy. The sheriff handed the waitress behind the counter a white envelope. She removed the Christmas card inside and taped it to the wall with the others.

Mr. and Mrs. Miller passed the "Seat Yourself" sign while going to their favorite corner booth. Amy went over to say good morning and Mr. Miller, also known as Santa, blinked up from behind silver-rimmed glasses and handed her a red envelope that read "Merry Christmas" on the front. A white beard framed the lower portion of his face.

Amy thanked him for the card and said, "I need to add something to my Christmas list this year. A cook."

Santa's bushy white beard brushed the front of the flannel shirt covering his jolly midsection. "Matt still leaving?" he asked.

Amy sighed. "Yeah. I need a replacement. *Fast*." With the café filling up, she mumbled, Excuse me..."

Amy handed the Christmas card to Mindy to put with the others and went to see what was keeping Sue Ellen. She skidded to a stop in the hallway to avoid a collision.

While she pinned her hair up, Sue Ellen kept her head down.

Sensing there was something wrong other than being late, Amy grasped the nineteen-year-old girl's arm. "Sue Ellen—"

The girl interrupted, "I know, Miss Olson. I'm sorry. I'll try to do better."

Amy lifted the girl's chin. She frowned when she noticed Sue Ellen's eyes were bloodshot and puffy as if she'd been up during the night crying. There wasn't time to take her to her office for a private talk, so Amy vowed to get with her later when things quieted down.

As she followed Sue Ellen to the front, Amy overheard Mindy telling Sheriff Martin about her mom who'd come down with a nasty cold.

The sheriff gave her a compassionate nod and then paused when Deputy Barnes nudged his shoulder. A hushed exchange took place between them. Staring through the window, the sheriff nodded and the deputy stepped outside and wove through the traffic to where the stranger was bent over, studying the front page of the *San Antonio Times*.

With Sawyer Creek's crime nearly non-existent, it was no secret the sheriff didn't take kindly to strangers. He preferred barking dogs and loud music. "Less paperwork," he said.

As the deputy approached the drifter, he straightened up, towering over the officer's hat a good six inches. He pulled his wallet out, removed an ID and handed it to him.

Amy's jaw dropped when the deputy stepped back, laughing as if someone had tickled his funny bone. She would have given anything to know what that was.

Chapter Two

Amy drove into the parking lot of Cody's Bar & Grill. She braked for a couple jogging to their car to get out of the wind. A Ford Mustang vacated a spot by the door and Amy wasted no time pulling her Volkswagen Beetle into it.

The second the car door opened, a north wind nipped at her face and cheeks. Tucking her chin into her chest, she hugged her body and hurried inside to get warm.

In the doorway, Amy paused while her eyes adjusted to the dim interior as Whitney Houston belted a love song from the jukebox. A sweet and spicy aroma came from bowls of pinecones that Connie, the bar owner's daughter, had sprayed with cinnamon oil and placed around the bar.

From across the room, Logan, her friend and favorite bartender, waved from behind a horseshoe-shaped bar, reminding her of an over-sized elf in a red and white Santa hat.

"Working late?" Logan asked watching her climb onto a barstool.

"Yeah. Paperwork!" Amy shouted, then removed a shoe to massage her toes.

Years of working in a bar environment served Logan well. He was a master at reading lips.

After giving her a nod, Logan took a beer to Mr. Morgan, who owned the hardware store across the street, and currently sat at the end of the counter. He kept a running tab and paid it come rain or shine on Fridays. A year ago, Mr. Morgan's wife left him, and since then, he'd always stopped on his way home.

Muscles flexed in Logan's arm while he wiped down the counter. The over-sized armholes of his shirt, exposed his well-defined chest. The shirt looked new. Just like Logan to cut off the sleeves.

Tilting his head sideways, Logan grinned. The same one that drove most of the girls in Sawyer Creek bat shit crazy, but not Amy. "What'll it be?" he asked.

Still upset over the cafe's botched delivery, she replied, "Rum and Coke. And, make it a double."

Shaking his head, Logan filled a glass with ice, Coke and two shots of rum. He stirred it with a plastic candy cane swizzle stick and placed it in front of her on a cardboard disk that bore the bar's logo. Resting a thick, tattooed arm, with the words "Born To Be Bad," at the edge of the counter, he asked, "You still looking for a cook?"

"Yeah," Amy said, chuckling. "You want the job?"

"No. But, I know somebody that's interested. Henry Cobb. He just moved in the trailer next door to me."

"Can he cook?" Amy asked.

"He said he used to work at a fancy restaurant on San Antonio's Riverwalk."

"Why on earth would he move here?"

Logan winked. "Maybe the same reason you did."

Amy rolled her eyes before taking a drink of what tasted like watered down gasoline, and then made a twisted face as it made its way to her stomach. She heard the sound of laughter erupt throughout the room and sighed when she saw that it was from Allen. Judging by the cash under a nearby beer bottle, it looked like he was waging a week's worth of salary on a game of pool.

Amy belched and then covered her mouth as the burger she'd forced down before leaving the cafe, rose in her throat. For the past week, the locals had been sniffling and sneezing. Living in a close-knit community meant it was only a matter of time before someone passed it on to her.

Logan frowned from the other side of the counter. "You okay?"

Thinking maybe she should go home and take a hot bath, Amy glanced at the door wondering if she could slide past Sawyer's Creek biggest playboy without being seen.

She imagined Allen intercepting her on the way out, her passing out in his arms and come tomorrow, Sawyer Creek's residents having a new rumor to circulate.

"Amy!"

"What!" she hissed, turning back to Logan who was snapping his fingers in front of her face.

"I asked if you're okay."

"I'm fine," she repeated.

Talk about timing.

The jukebox was in-between songs and her voice carried, turning heads, including Allen's. For someone who appeared to be losing a ton of cash, she was surprised he smiled.

Yay me, she thought watching him retire his pool stick to a rack on the wall and sidestep an artificial Christmas tree to advance in her direction.

Leaning across the counter, Logan whispered, "Here comes trouble."

Amy inched closer while staring into his chocolate brown eyes. She mouthed, "Save me, Logan."

Logan's eyes twinkled like the Christmas lights flashing from the ceiling over his head. "I tried that three years ago, remember?"

After moving to Sawyer Creek, Logan had asked her out. Not wanting a romantic relationship, she declined. Logan backed off and they had become friends. A year later, she confided in him about the attack in San Antonio, yet the idea of any man touching her still sent her into a full-blown panic.

Even now, Amy's heart raced when she turned around to find Allen holding a strand of her hair between his forefinger and thumb.

"Hey, beautiful," he said, lifting it to take a whiff. "I hear you need a cook."

"You heard right, Allen," she said mentally counting to ten as her shrink had encouraged.

"Does it come with benefits?" he asked.

Amy tensed when Allen's shirt brushed her shoulder as he sat on a stool to her left.

She jumped when Logan's powerful fist banged on the bar. "Don't you have somewhere to go, Allen?"

Allen rose to his feet, pinning his shoulders back, adding another inch to his already six-foot-three stature. "Look, the lady needs a cook," Allen said. "I was just trying to help."

The two men locked gazes. Allen was taller, but Logan was thicker and outweighed him by a hundred pounds. Logan's thin lips were barely visible through his brown beard. He said, "Leave her alone."

Allen gave him a one finger salute with his middle finger and then charged out of the door as if he were five, shouting, "Screw you, Logan," before disappearing into the parking lot.

The night air rushed in, evaporating nervous beads of sweat that had accumulated on Amy's upper lip. She sneezed and Logan set a tissue box on the counter next to her.

"Thanks," she said, using one to dab her forehead and face.

"Be right back," Logan said, and headed toward a dispute that had erupted on the dance floor.

With Allen gone, Amy stood up to leave. Her cell phone vibrated in her back pocket.

She shouted into the phone over the music, "Hello!"

"Amy, it's Marty."

"Hey, Sheriff. What's up?"

"The alarm went off at the cafe. I walked the premises. The only thing I found out of place was a shovel against the back door."

"Did the alarm shut off?"

"Yeah. But, I'll hang around if you want me check inside."

It was the first time the alarm had gone off since she'd had it installed four years ago. Not to mention, it was after midnight and the sheriff was slated to go home.

"Nah," she said convinced it was the wind. "Go home to your wife."

"Suit yourself," the sheriff said. "Call dispatch if you change your mind. Deputy Barnes will be on duty."

"Thanks, Sheriff."

After hanging up, Amy tried to remember why she'd gotten the alarm in the first place. The locals seldom locked any of their doors. Then she remembered the free installation the alarm company offered and after the attack, it gave her peace of mind at a time when she desperately needed it.

Logan leaned across the counter. "Everything okay?" he asked.

"The alarm went off at the cafe."

Since Logan had appointed himself her personal bodyguard, he stared for a long hard minute, probably to see how she was taking it.

To put his mind at ease, Amy shrugged. "It's probably nothing. Just the wind."

Logan nodded, but didn't look convinced.

Chapter Three

Amy crawled off the barstool to leave.

"Are you going straight home?" Logan asked as though he knew she wouldn't.

He was right. She wanted to stop by the cafe, but knew if she didn't tell him and he found out later, a lecture would be in order.

"I'm going by the cafe to bring in the shovel."

"Wait," Logan said. "Let me get Connie to cover and I'll go too."

It's a shovel! Not a desperate man in a ski mask.

When she insisted she'd be fine, Logan shook his head like he disagreed but said, "Call me, if you need me."

Knowing he meant well, Amy smiled and said, "Thanks Logan."

"For what?" he asked.

"Just thanks." She left the bar and hurried to her car. After crawling behind the wheel, she glanced into the back seat because some habits were hard to break.

Cranking the engine, she thought about Logan. He was everything she could want in a man and she couldn't for the life of her figure out why she hadn't taken him off the market. Yes, she could. Since the attack, the thought of an intimate relationship, sent her into a full-blown panic.

The night terrors had stopped four years ago, shortly after she moved to Sawyer Creek, but the memory of the purse snatcher's rough hands, was still very much alive.

****

Amy drove down Main Street, passing street lamps that looked like giant candy canes and turned into the alley behind the cafe. It was dark, almost sinister. Why had the one and only security light blown tonight? She illuminated the back door with the car's high beams. The shovel was still leaning against the building, where the sheriff had left it. Nothing looked out of place, yet the fine hairs on the back of her neck refused to lay flat.

With the engine idling, Amy opened the door and stepped into a light mist, ignoring the plastic bag flapping on a nearby post. She approached the back door and wiped cobwebs from the rusty lock. She forced the key in and gave it a quick twist. It clicked. She reached inside and flipped on a light.

Eager to get home, her heels rapped against the storage room's concrete flooring as she set the shovel by another door leading into the cafe.

Amy turned and squealed when she saw the silhouette of a man was in the doorway framed by the fog. Slowly, he lifted his head. She recognized him as the man she'd seen earlier in front of the cafe getting out of the truck. Up close, he appeared taller. Thicker, too.

Fight or flight came to mind. Obviously, flight was a no-brainer but with him blocking the only way out and the door going into the cafe locked, it wasn't an option.

The man lifted his hand and said, "I'm not here to hurt you."

Her brain screamed, *But trespassing is okay?* In a shaky voice, she managed to ask, "What do you want?"

"I need your help."

"If you need a place to stay, there's a motel a few miles south of town."

"My truck is broken. I hitched a ride here."

The longer he stayed between her and freedom, the more desperate she became. She blurted, "Take my car. But I have to warn you, it spits black smoke in the morning when it's cold."

"I don't want your car, lady."

Tears welled in her eyes. *Oh God! What then?* Her bottom lip quivered as she bit down and expected to taste blood. Part of her wanted to plead. Beg even. Only nothing would come out, as if he'd somehow magically stolen her voice. Cold reality began to set in. Whatever he intended to do, she didn't know if she could stop him.

Sure. To collaborate her story, she could collect his DNA by scoring his face with her nails or sinking her teeth into his arm.

Amy shielded her body with her arms while studying the man's face, memorizing details. Like the eagle tattoo peeking above the denim collar of his jacket and the faint scar above his right eye.

Once again falling prey to a stranger— no, a monster—was terrifying. She vowed if she lived, she'd make a career out of putting him behind bars and disposing of the key.

As if having a mind of their own, her feet shuffled backward until her spine collided with the wall. Fear fueled her hands into action. She reached for the shovel. The same one Matt used to bury the cat that had died on the doorstep two days prior.

Pivoting on the balls of her feet, she grabbed the handle with both hands, spun and shook it at him like a mighty Samurai warrior.

She said, "Don't come any closer."

Unfortunately, his reaction wasn't the one she'd hoped for.

The man chuckled, then doubled over, holding his side. When he straightened up again, blood seeped out from between his fingers.

"Oh God," Amy said. "You're hurt."

His hand dropped to his side, exposing what looked like a hole in his shirt. It was quickly turning fire-engine red. Blood dripped from his fingertips onto the floor near his boot.

"You need a doctor," Amy said, reaching for her phone and hissing when she remembered leaving it on the front seat of the car. "The nearest hospital is forty miles away."

"No hospital," he said.

She held her breath. "What then? Do you want to die?"

"I want *you*... to remove the bullet."

"Bullet?" Are you crazy?" It was an absurd request from a man who looked as though he might collapse at any given moment. "I own a cafe. I cook. I don't do bullets. *Sorry*."

"I'll walk you through it," he said like one crash course would be equivalent to years of valuable training. "But, I'm almost certain... I'll pass out before you're done. Now listen carefully—"

"No!" she shouted, throwing up her hands. "*You* listen. I won't be responsible if something goes wrong."

"Like what?"

"Like me inadvertently killing you."

"If you don't remove the bullet, I'll bleed out. None of it will matter."

"None of what?"

His knees gave way. He was going down. Amy tossed the shovel aside and lunged for him. Worst case scenario, she'd cushion his fall.

Then what?

Balancing on a knee, he let out a heart-wrenching groan as he re-applied pressure to his side. The bleeding seemed to slow down, but didn't stop.

Amy had to do something, and fast. But each time she reached for him, her attacker's face flashed in her mind and she pulled back.

On her last attempt, the man reached out, snagging her wrist. "Listen...to me," he said between clenched teeth. "We don't have much time."

"We?" she said, trying to pull free from his ironclad grip. His fingers only tightened, turning his knuckles white. "You said you'd pass out," she said. "I can't do this alone!"

Out of the blue, he asked, "What's...your name?"

"A-Amy," she replied. "What's yours in case you die and I have to call the police—"

"I said...*no police.*"

"It won't matter when you're dead."

Was he a fugitive? If so, what was he running from?

"Who are you?"

"I used to be a SEAL."

"The mammal?" Granted, it was ridiculous, but she wished he would say yes to prevent her from having a massive coronary.

The man chuckled then pinched his eyelids together. "Dammit, that hurt!"

"I'm sorry," she said. "Who did this to you?"

"I don't know."

"How could you not know?"

"I stopped at a bar outside of San Antonio. A man challenged me to a game of pool. I didn't want his money, but he wouldn't take no for an answer. When I ran the table, he accused me of cheating. He left and when I stepped outside, a truck blinded me with its headlights. By the time I saw the flash, it was too late."

Amy watched his eyelids drift shut and his body go limp and she helped him to the floor.

"No," she said kneeling over him. "You have to walk me through this, remember?"

His chest heaved and he appeared to be fading in and out of consciousness.

"Please," she said, fisting his jacket. "Wake up!"

His eyelids twitched and then opened into tiny slits. He asked, "Do you live nearby?"

"Yes," she said. "I have a house at the edge of town—"

"Take me there..."

Chapter Four

The street was lit up from the Christmas decorations that the city had put up the day after Thanksgiving. But Sawyer Creek always resembled a ghost town after seven o'clock on any given night. Except Saturdays, when bored teens congregated in Miller's parking lot to socialize and play loud music.

Amy drove slow, taking care to stay under the speed limit in case Deputy Barnes was out. How could she explain an ex-Navy SEAL bleeding profusely on her backseat?

She had never met a SEAL before but had heard they were extraordinary men who endured things normal people couldn't. They were fearless in risking their lives for others. She was sure anyone else would have expired by now and seeing him in this vulnerable state, was frightening.

Were his organs purposely shutting down to prolong the inevitable?

Amy glanced in the rearview mirror and whispered, "Don't die on me, SEAL..." as though somehow it would keep his heart pumping a little while longer.

She slowed down past a streetlight to keep from rolling him onto the floorboard as she made the turnoff to her house. She followed a gravel driveway into the forest. Century old oak trees lined both sides. It was the perfect cover to get him inside without being seen from the street.

She recalled back at the cafe, when she'd helped him into the car, his body felt heavy like flesh over concrete. When he stumbled and she had to catch him, she realized just how heavy he was. She doubted she could have loaded him into the car had he not come to. Hopefully, he would regain consciousness again to help get him to the guest room.

While watching tree branches cast shadows on the side of the house, Amy killed the engine. She calculated the easiest route. Front or back. Either way, getting him up a small flight of stairs would be a challenge. She chose the back because it was the shortest. Before getting him out, she needed a clear path. Lights had to be turned on inside. She couldn't have him tripping on throw rugs or banging into the walls.

"I'll be right back," she muttered over the back of the seat, and then added, "Don't move."

It was a wasted breath for someone so near death and she doubted he'd heard anyway.

She got out and quietly pushed the car door shut, until she heard it click. Then she ran to the back of the house. In a small town, people seldom locked their homes, and hers was no exception. She called it therapy in renewing her trust in mankind. Until now, it had been working.

Like a crazed animal, Amy charged through the house, flicking light switches and kicking rugs aside. When all potential booby-traps were eliminated, she rushed to the guest room and stripped the queen-sized bed of the comforter she'd made in a quilting class. She chose an older blanket that didn't have sentimental value. The decorative pillows, she tossed along the wall, but left the main bed pillows.

Amy jerked to attention when a car door slammed. She raced to the window to see a shadow dart across the yard. No other cars were in the driveway. It had to be him.

What if he didn't remember her or asking her to bring him there?

Either way, he needed her help. She rounded the corner and bounced off his chest which was akin to colliding with a wall.

Hissing, the SEAL splayed one hand on the wall, his eyes pinched shut and his chest heaving.

"I'm sorry," she said, eyeing the bloody handprint on the wall. "Are you okay?"

Despite a muscle flexing in his jaw, he nodded.

"Let's get you to bed." She looped an arm around his waist, ignoring the blood transferring from his shirt to hers.

Without protest, he draped his arm over her shoulders. Each step he took was slow, calculated, and seemed more difficult than the last.

With a few feet left to go, he asked, "Do you have a husband or boyfriend?"

Glaring sideways she said, "That's really none of your business."

"I don't like surprises."

"Oh," she said, feeling slightly disappointed and not knowing why. "I don't have either."

She still wondered what his name was, but dared to guess.

What do you call a superhero when all the best names are taken?

The SEAL groaned as she eased him onto the bed. Before lying back, he removed his shirt, exposing more blood and several tattoos. She had a feeling each of them told a unique story.

"When you got out of that truck, I saw you holding your side, but I never dreamed that you were shot."

Grinning, the SEAL appeared amused that she'd been watching him.

Feeling slightly embarrassed, she tried to explain. "It's just that.... *well*...you look like a regular man. Not a bad-ass SEAL."

Her insides quivered under his intense gaze.

Clearing her throat, which had become dry, she said, "I didn't catch your name."

He laid back onto the pillows and whispered, "Casanova. My real name is... Cass Alan Nova. My SEAL buddies called me Casanova. It stuck."

"Are you?"

"What?" he asked.

"A Casanova?"

"Get a pen and paper. You'll want to take notes."

Chapter Five

Amy raced around the kitchen, taking care not to knock over a fresh batch of Christmas cookies Matt had given her as she tossed household items into a basket and checked them off the list. Whiskey, dish towels, and a sharp paring knife. She ran to the bathroom to get a sewing needle, thread, gauze, cotton balls and a pair of tweezers.

Finding everything he said she'd need, she returned to the guest room which now doubled as a poor excuse for an operating room. Sweat broke out on her forehead at the thought of removing the bullet. Especially when she hated digging out a splinter. She didn't want to think of the consequences, should she deviate from the notes.

She whispered, "I have everything on the list." She set the basket on the nightstand. He didn't answer, but moaned with his eyes closed. If not for an occasional twitch, she could easily have mistaken him for dead.

The saltwater IV attached to a dark purple vein in his arm, was half empty. He was quite resourceful. Using a silicone glove, rubber tubing and a needle from a turkey injection kit, had been ingenious on his part.

Leaning over the bed, Amy whispered, "Cass."

He didn't move. Panic set in. Surely, he wasn't...

In a last-ditch effort to bring him to, she nudged his shoulder. "Cass, wake up. You can sleep after I remove the bullet. Sewing you up will be easy." She ran to the closet, fisted the quilt and shook it at him. "I stitched this. I'm good with a needle."

He still didn't respond.

Pacing the floor at the foot of the bed, she thought about calling the sheriff. He could dispatch an ambulance. They would rush him to a hospital where he would get the care he needed, from a real doctor in a sterile environment. Not in a dust-laden bedroom built in the sixties.

After feeling his face for a temperature and not finding one, she traced the stubble on his lower jaw and was surprised that it was soft.

She whispered, "Why me, Casanova?"

When he still didn't move, she grabbed the notes she'd taken on how to remove a bullet and begun reading them out aloud.

****

An hour later, the deed was done. Amy dropped the bloody bullet into a bowl on the nightstand and then stitched the hole up and applied a bandage and tape to hold it in place. With Cass still out, she rushed to her bedroom and replaced her blood-splattered shirt with a fresh one. Lastly, she scrubbed the handprint from the wall and was glad that it washed off easily.

She stopped by the guest room to check on Cass and frowned when she saw his complexion had taken on a grayish tint. He looked frail. She cupped his forehead then his cheek, and was glad that he was still warm, but not overly hot.

Once again, his eyelids twitched. Was he dreaming? She couldn't imagine what an ex-SEAL would dream about and vowed to ask him later, when the doorbell rang out.

Halfway to the doorway to see who it could be, Cass mumbled incoherently. She paused and he drifted back to sleep.

This time, someone knocked.

Surely it couldn't be Logan. The bar didn't close for another hour.

Amy tiptoed across the living room to peer out a small peephole in the door. Sheriff Martin was on the porch with his hand resting on his holster. *What was he doing here?* He wasn't on duty. Deputy Barnes was. *What had brought him back out?*

Knowing he wouldn't leave without making contact, she drew in a deep breath, exhaled slowly and swung open the door. "What's up, Sheriff?"

While massaging the back of his neck, the sheriff looked up and said, "Amy, I stopped by the cafe. The back door was open."

Damnit! She must have forgotten to secure it back after getting Cass into the car.

"It was me. I stopped to bring in the shovel. I guess I forgot to lock it again."

For a second, he stared as if weighing the possibility of someone holding her at gunpoint on the other side of the door. "Is everything okay?" he asked.

"Yeah," she said trying to sound more convincing then she felt. "It's been a long day. I was getting ready for bed."

"Amy, there's more. I saw what looked like blood inside the door."

"Oh that!" Amy said, waving her hand. "The lock was rusty. I nicked my finger. All I could think about was getting home to disinfect it."

"Sawyer Creek has good folks, Amy, but an open business door—"

"I know, Sheriff. I'll be more careful next time. Thanks for stopping by. Now, if you'll excuse me. I have water running in the tub."

"Sure," he said, backing down off the porch.

She waited to wave until he got in his patrol car and was pulling away. She stepped inside and from a thin sheer curtain, she watched the taillights on his patrol car disappear into the trees.

With the sheriff gone, she spun on her heels to check on Cass and squealed when his warm breath fanned her cheek.

"Jesus!" she said, stumbling backward. "You scared the crap out of me."

"I told you, I don't like surprises," he said.

"Well, that makes two of us," she scolded. "Now, stop sneaking around. This is my house. My rules."

"What did the sheriff want?"

"I forgot to lock the cafe when we left."

"You forgot?" he asked. "Or you did it on purpose knowing it would trigger a courtesy call?"

"Look, Casanova," Amy said, glaring. "I could have left your ass here while you were out. I didn't. You could be a little more appreciative."

Glancing down, she saw fresh blood seeping through his bandage. "Let's get you back to bed. If you tear those stitches out, I'm not sewing you up again."

She lied. She would have done it but didn't want him to know that. Not waiting for him to protest, she ducked under his arm and steered him down the hall.

"I'm sorry," he said so quietly she almost missed it.

"For what?" she muttered sarcastically. "For being an ungrateful asshole?"

"Yeah," he said and snickered. "That too," then tensed as if it hurt to laugh.

After getting him back into bed, she stopped in the doorway on her way out of the room. "Are you hungry?"

"You cooking, or am I?"

"Me, of course." She chuckled at his sense of humor, then paused. "Wait. You cook?"

"Yeah. Are you surprised?"

"How long do you plan on staying in Sawyer Creek?"

"Is this a verbal eviction?"

"Of course, not. You can stay as long as you need to. But, on two conditions."

"What's that?" he asked.

"No more sneaking around and I don't have to remove any more bullets. Deal?"

"Deal."

Chapter Six

Amy watched from the doorway as Cass slowly closed his eyes. She looked away from the blanket riding dangerously low on his hips, exposing perfectly shaped abs. After stepping into the hallway she quietly pulled the door shut so not to wake him.

On the way to the kitchen to fix something to eat, Amy flipped on the TV and stopped on a channel playing music videos. Knowing Cass would most likely be starving when he woke up, she got eggs and a package of bacon from the fridge.

One of her favorite songs came on and she swayed with the music while dropping strips of bacon into the hot skillet. She broke several eggshells and deposited the inside contents into a bowl. As she mixed them with a fork, her hips kept time with the beat.

Someone snickered, causing Amy to drop the fork and spin around with her butt pressed into the counter.

Cass sat on a barstool on the other side of the island counter, smiling.

Hissing, she rolled her eyes. "I thought we talked about this."

"About what?"

"You sneaking up on me."

While rubbing his eyes with the heels of his palms, he inhaled and exhaled deeply. "Damn, that smells good."

"I hope you're a fan of bacon and scrambled eggs."

He nodded and then once again high-jacked the conversation in another direction. "Have you ever been married?"

He asked such personal questions. Nothing like going for the jugular.

"Have you?" she blurted.

"Do you always answer a question with a question?"

Glancing up, she said, "Only when I'm under interrogation."

"Sorry." He flashed her a grin. "Some habits are hard to break."

She put the egg mixture into the microwave, set it for two minutes and then turned around. "What do SEALS dream about?"

"Excuse me?"

"Your eyelids. They were twitching. I just wondered what a man like you would dream about."

"Trust me," he said. "You don't want to know."

"It can't be that bad," she said, transferring crispy bacon strips onto a paper towel.

The microwave dinged and Amy removed the bowl.

"Yes. It can," he said, following her to a small glass table with four chairs by the window.

She set the eggs and bacon down. "Eat before it gets cold."

Smiling, she watched him pile some onto his plate and dig in like he hadn't eaten in days.

"It might help to talk," she said.

"It might not," he said between bites. After swallowing, he asked, "Have you always lived in Sawyer Creek?"

"Are you writing a book?" When he didn't answer, she sighed then continued, "No. I grew up in San Antonio. Four years ago, I went for a drive and ended up here. From the moment I rolled into town, it felt like home. I relocated for the peace and quiet."

The edge of his mouth lifted. "So much for that idea, huh?"

"I have to admit, Casanova, when I saw you in the doorway—"

"I didn't mean to scare you. But I wouldn't have made it through the night. It wasn't the way I pictured myself leaving this world."

Past memories reeled in her head of the night she was attacked. It was late. She had just parked her car and was walking to her apartment when rough hands grabbed her from behind. "Don't scream," a male voice had said to the side of her face.

Cass tilted his head as if he somehow knew he'd triggered a flashback. Judging by the look on his face, he knew it wasn't a fond one.

Blinking, Amy forced the horrible memory into the recesses of her brain. She cleared her throat and said, "I did what any decent human being would do under the circumstances."

"Would you have used it?"

"What?" she asked.

"The shovel?"

"Damn skippy, Casanova."

Deep laughter came from his throat echoing through the room like a trumpet.

Amy glanced at the microwave and noted the time. "Oh no!" she said rising up from the table, wiping her mouth with a paper towel. "I have to get ready for work."

"I thought you said you own the cafe. Don't you have employees?"

"Actually, four," she said. "But, my cook is leaving at the end of the week and I have a waitress with a faulty alarm clock."

"And, the others?"

"They're worth their weight in gold. But, I like being there in case they need me. If I don't show up, they'll worry something's wrong."

He arched a brow. "Is there?"

"What?"

"Something wrong."

"If you don't count an ex-Navy SEAL with an attitude in my house, no."

With her plate in her hand, Amy took a step toward the kitchen when Cass stood up and blocked her path. She instinctively stepped back. He was in what her shrink had described as her safe zone.

"I got this," he said reaching for her plate. "Go."

"Are you sure?"

"Yeah. I do dishes, too."

"You're a man of many talents, Casanova."

"So I've been told."

She hurried to the bedroom, took a quick shower and had changed when Cass shouted from somewhere within the house.

"Are you really going to leave me unsupervised?" he asked.

She snickered. "Are you going to steal anything?"

"No."

She grinned. "Good. Then I'll be back in a few hours to check on you."

Chapter Seven

The smell of cinnamon and bread pudding was heavy in the air when Amy arrived at the café. With the holidays approaching, Matt was constantly whipping up new desserts. She was surprised when he told her Sue Ellen had gotten there early.

"Well that's a first," Sue Ellen said while adding pinecones sprayed with cinnamon oil to the branches of an artificial Christmas tree in the corner.

While continuing to her office, Amy mumbled back at her. "Damn alarm clock."

Amy plopped down in the leather chair behind her desk and began thumbing through the rolodex for Percy's Meat House. After locating the number, she picked up the phone and froze when there was a knock on the office door.

"Come in," she said setting the receiver back into the cradle.

Matt peeked his head inside. "Is everything okay?"

"Yeah. Why?"

"You always beat everyone here," he said stepping into her office and setting a plate of sugar cookies with multi-colored sprinkles on top. "Not the other way around."

"Everything's great, Matt," she said eyeing the cookies. "Thanks for the concern."

Smiling, he gave her a one hand salute and after she thanked him for the cookies he left her office whistling.

Amy devoured a cookie then dialed Percy's number thinking, *someone has a lot of explaining to do.*

****

By 9:00 a.m., the morning rush had dispersed with the exception of a few stragglers. Eager to check on Cass, Amy was gathering her things when Sue Ellen showed up in the office's doorway. Just as well, she'd been wanting to speak to her anyway.

"Miss Olson, do you have a minute?" Sue Ellen asked.

"Sure, Sue Ellen. Come on in."

Sue Ellen meandered to a chair in front of her desk and began fidgeting with her hands. "I really need this job, Miss Olson," Sue Ellen said. "Maybe now, more than ever."

With her chin on her hands, Amy listened.

Sue Ellen blurted, "Miss Olson, I'm pregnant."

Amy heart dropped into her stomach at the thought of Sue Ellen raising a child. She was only nineteen. Since she didn't sleep around, the father had to be her good-for-nothing boyfriend who couldn't hold a job. It was the perfect recipe for disaster.

"I know what you're thinking, Miss Olson," Sue Ellen said, "How can I possibly care for a baby when I can't even take care of myself."

Not wanting to make matters worse, Amy said, "You made it to work on time. That's a start."

"Yeah. It felt good too," Sue Ellen said, grinning. "I didn't have to rush around to get ready for my shift.

Now that I'm going to be a mama, I need to set a good example."

"Does your mom know?"

"Not yet. She always said this would happen. I'm not ready for a lecture just yet."

"Well, your mama loves you and I'm sure she only wants what's best."

Sue Ellen grinned. "It's a shame *you* don't have kids, Miss Olson. I think you would make a terrific mom."

Amy ignored the statement and asked, "Does Mason know?"

"Yeah," Sue Ellen said looking down into her lap. "He took it hard. Last night he left and moved back in with his parents. He said he needed time to clear his head."

"What he needs, is a *job*," Amy said, shoving away from the desk. She winced at what she was about to suggest. "Can Mason cook?"

Sue Ellen's jaw dropped as she nodded. "Yeah. He can cook," she said then paused, and added, "When he's home, that is."

Amy stood up, walked around the desk. "Tell Mason to come see me. Tomorrow. 8:00 a.m. sharp. Not a minute less."

Sue Ellen jumped to her feet and threw her arms around Amy's neck.

"Calm down," Amy said, hugging her back. "He doesn't have the job yet. But, at least I'm willing to talk to him. First, we need to get a few things straight."

"I'll make sure he's here," Sue Ellen said, jogging off then pausing midway to the door. "Thank you, Miss Olson."

"You're welcome. Now, get back to work. Oh, and before I forget, I'm taking the rest of the day off."

"Are you sick?"

"No. There are a few things I need to tend to."

Sue Ellen pinned her shoulders back. "Well if you need anything, just let me know."

Amy nodded as the girl scurried out. Funny, how a baby could change some people overnight. And others, not so much. She thought about Mason and palmed her forehead.

What was she thinking.

If she agreed to hire Mason, he'd be a work in progress for who knew how long. Only somehow it seemed trivial in comparison to having Casanova occupying her guest room. After what she'd been through, letting any man into her home was a big improvement. Especially for someone who secretly feared the entire male population.

Right after the attack, Amy had taken leave from her job at Myron's Accounting Firm in downtown San Antonio. She had groceries delivered to her doorstep and only ventured out once a week to meet with her female shrink.

Moving to Sawyer Creek, was a new beginning. And it was a miracle that she trusted Logan enough to become friends. But even that wasn't fail-proof.

One night, while watching a movie, Logan leaned in for a kiss. It wasn't planned. It just happened. At the time, it didn't feel forced, until she broke into a cold sweat before his lips even touched hers, and ran to the bathroom, locking herself in.

The nightmares had stopped, but Billy Granger was still very much alive in her head. When she closed her eyes, she could still feel his hands snatching her purse strap from her body.

Her doctor had called it panic attacks, saying under the circumstances, it was a normal reaction. Since Amy was against taking anti-depressants, the doctor suggested counting to ten.

With her heart racing, Amy looked up at the ceiling and began to count. "One...two...three...four...five." She stopped to inhale and exhale slowly then continued. "Five...six...seven...eight...nine...*ten*." Almost instantly, her heart rate began to drop.

She needed to check on Cass. After taking another breath, she wiped her face with a tissue from the desk and then discarded it into the wastebasket on her way out.

CHAPTER EIGHT

Amy parked in her driveway, got out and approached the back of the house. When the door opened, machine gun blasts blared from a military documentary on TV. Cass was sound asleep with his head at one end of the couch and his heels on the other, breathing through his mouth but not snoring.

His hair was damp as though he'd just taken a shower within the last five or ten minutes. For a moment, his eyelids jerked then stopped. Her gaze took in the fresh bandage on his side which rose and fell with each breath.

Amy sat her cell phone on the counter and walked quietly past him and down the hallway to her bedroom. The hinges creaked as she shut the bedroom door. Her skin was clammy. A shower was in order. It had been years since she'd had a panic attack of that magnitude.

After slipping out of her clothes, grabbing a pair of wind shorts and a T-shirt, she rushed to the spacious bathroom Logan had added during the renovations. She was equally pleased that he'd figured in a walk-in closet.

For someone single, Logan seemed to know a lot about women.

Water pelted her shoulders, relieving the tension and washed lingering despair down the drain. While shampooing her hair, she took in the delicious scent of coconut. Just when she shut off the water and yanked back the curtain, a shadow moved from under the door. Grabbing a towel, she hugged it to her chest and waited.

There was a light rap on the other side.

"Yeah," she said.

"Your phone went off." Cass's voice sounded husky as though it had awoken him.

"I'm sorry," she said, surprised that he'd heard it over the TV. "I shouldn't have left it on the counter."

"Who's Logan?" he asked.

"My friend. Why?"

"He wants you to call him." Feet shuffled away from the door.

She dried off, got dressed and finger combed her hair. After draping the towel over the curtain rod, she reached for the doorknob, but stopped when her heart started to race. What if Cass was still in her bedroom? Gritting her teeth, she willed her mind to stop with the paranoid "what ifs" before it brought on another panic attack.

When she opened the door, Cass was nowhere in sight, so she continued down the hallway toward the kitchen. He was on the sofa with his feet propped on the coffee table and his head against the cushions. He glanced up. Why was he smiling?

"What?" she asked, noting a sparkle in his eyes.

"Nothing. You look...*different*."

She chuckled. "Is that good or bad?"

"Depends..."

"On what?"

"Nothing."

He did that a lot. Started a sentence and didn't finish it.

Amy rolled her eyes. "Are you hungry?"

"Yeah. What do you have in mind?"

"Chicken Dorito casserole."

Cass frowned. "Is it really made with Doritos?"

"Yeah. Next to my famous cheeseburgers, it's a lunch favorite. It also has cream of chicken, taco seasoning, and diced tomatoes."

"Whatever doesn't kill you, makes you stronger, right?" he teased.

"I suppose. How's your side?"

"I'm not ready to climb Mount Everest, but thanks to you, I'll survive."

Cass lunged for the window when someone knocked on the door. Staring through the thin sheers, he said, "It's a man. Why am I not surprised?"

Amy rose up on her toes to see out the door's peephole.

"Crap," she said, stepping back.

"You know him?" Cass asked.

"Yeah. It's Logan."

"You never called him back?"

"I got distracted... My car's in the driveway. Logan won't leave until I answer the door."

"Then, let him in."

Amy arched a brow. "Are you sure?"

"You said he was a friend, right?"

"Yeah."

"Then he shouldn't be upset when he sees me."

"What do you want me to tell him?" she asked. "I mean about you."

"Anything, but the truth."

"You're a big help," she said while opening the door and forcing a smile. "Hey, Logan."

"Hey," he said looking past her. "I went by the cafe. They said you left early. Is everything okay?"

"Yeah. Why?"

"You never leave early."

"I have company. A friend from San Antonio stopped by."

Logan looked past her, again and she stepped back for him to enter. Logan came in, shut the door behind him, and immediately caught sight of Cass. As the two men locked gazes, she could only imagine what was going through Logan's head.

"Logan, this is Cass. Cass, Logan."

Logan nodded.

Cass returned the gesture then glanced at her like he was expecting her to say more.

Logan lifted his chin, sniffing the air. "Is that chicken Dorito casserole I smell?"

Amy nodded. "Want some?"

"Yeah, if you have enough and providing your friend doesn't mind."

"There's plenty. Cass doesn't care, right Cass?"

"The more, the merrier," Cass said. "But if you'll excuse me, I need to wash up."

Cass left the room.

Logan whispered, "Did I interrupt anything?"

"No," Amy mouthed. "It's fine."

Cass reappeared wearing a T-shirt with his jeans. It looked wrinkled as though it had been balled up for months. He sat down, studying Logan from across the table while Amy set the casserole dish in the center.

She went back to the kitchen for plates and utensils. "Paper okay?" she asked.

"Yeah. Less to wash," Cass said and Logan agreed.

Amy joined them at the table. While spooning casserole onto her plate she turned to Logan. "Do you have to work tonight?"

Logan nodded while shoveling casserole into his mouth and packing it to one side like an over-sized chipmunk. "I have to be there at 5:00 p.m. If you and Cass don't have plans, you should come by."

"I don't know. Cass had..." Not knowing what to say, Amy glanced at Cass. When he didn't chime in she said, "*An accident.*"

"I saw that," Logan said raising an eyebrow. "What happened?"

Cass shrugged like it was no big deal and Amy waited to see what kind of story the ex-Navy SEAL would fabricate. She doubted it would be anything close to the truth.

Wrong.

Cass said, "It happened outside a bar."

Glaring sideways at Cass, Amy covered her mouth to keep casserole from spewing across the table.

Logan said, "I hope the other guy left on a stretcher."

Cass chuckled but didn't say one way or the other.

For the rest of the evening, Cass dominated the conversation. Logan bombarded him with questions after learning he'd been a SEAL. Nearly all of Cass's stories were fascinating. Others pulled at her heartstrings, like when he carried a wounded SEAL mate to safety. As terrifying as some of them were, she was certain he withheld the horrifying details.

Logan was especially amused about Cass's nickname, Casanova.

Soon Logan had to leave. He got up, shoved his chair in and stared down at Cass. "I'm serious, man. Stop by. I'll buy you a beer."

Cass shrugged. "I might just take you up on that."

Chapter Nine

Amy turned into the bar's parking lot and parked near the front door. Multi-colored Christmas lights flashed from the outer edge of the roof. She turned to Cass. "Are you sure you want to do this?" she asked, shutting off the car.

"I'm fine."

She got out. "What?" she asked when Cass stopped by the passenger's side door.

"Aren't you gonna to lock it?" he asked.

She laughed. "You're not in Kansas anymore, Casanova. The residents of Sawyer Creek don't lock their doors. Relax."

When they stepped inside, the jukebox was blaring as usual. Amy chuckled when Logan had on a red and white Santa hat and waved from the bar. They passed Connie balancing a serving tray loaded down with drinks, also wearing a Santa hat identical to Logan's. Amy gave her a nod as they made their way to the counter and sat down on a pair of barstools.

Logan snickered then asked, "What will it be, Casanova?"

Hearing Logan call Cass by his nickname, made Amy blush and she wasn't sure why, but at least it was dim, so hopefully no one would notice.

"Do you have Bud Light?" Cass asked eyeing his hat.

"Sure do," Logan said pulling an ice-cold bottle from a cooler, popping the top off and setting it down on a cardboard disk in front of him.

Logan turned to her. "Rum and Coke?"

Cass raised an eyebrow at her while chugging his beer.

"Nah. Not tonight," Amy said, turning a darker shade of pink. "I'll take what he's having."

Logan removed the cap from another Bud Light, set it down in front of her and then went to the other end of the counter to take another customer's order.

Staring at a couple engaged in a slow dance near the jukebox, Cass said, "I had you pegged as a fruity kind of girl with a cute bamboo umbrella."

"I like those too," Amy said, and then sipped her beer.

The song ended and a slow song began.

Cass got up and held out his hand. "Do you want to dance?"

"No," Amy said shaking her head. "I have two left feet. Trust me, you'll thank me later."

Cass reached for her hand anyway as though he wouldn't take no for an answer. "I have two right feet," he said. "It'll make us even."

He began pulling her toward the dance floor.

Panic set in. Suddenly, she wasn't seeing Cass. It was him, her attacker, staring through a black ski mask. She blinked several times to make him disappear and when he didn't, she pulled free and ran to the bathroom, trembling.

Once inside, Amy braced against the wall, staring up at the ceiling wondering if she would ever be able to live a normal life again. She was tired of seeing her attacker's face at every turn.

The door opened. Logan walked in like it was no big deal coming into the ladie's room. He tilted her chin up and gazed into her tear-filled eyes. "It's okay, Amy. It'll take time."

"How much time, Logan? Don't I deserve to be happy?"

"Yes. You do," he said, brushing a tear away from her cheek. "I wish I could get my hands on the bastard that did this to you."

Listening to him made her realize the incident hadn't only screwed her up. People close to her were affected by it as well. It had a snowball effect and for that, she was sorry.

Trembling, she stared up at Logan. "I can beat this, right?"

Logan shut his eyes, paused, then reopened them again. "What do you want me to do, Amy? Just say the words." The concern in his voice resonated in his eyes. "I'll do anything."

She whispered, "Kiss me."

Licking his lips, Logan fixated on her mouth. "Are you sure?" he asked.

"Please, Logan...I need you to *kiss me*." When he leaned in, she whispered, "You're Logan. You're not him."

Logan slowly drew back. "Yes. I'm Logan."

Amy reopened her eyes to see Logan staring at the ceiling. "What's wrong?" she asked.

"Do you know how long I've wanted to do this?"

She shook her head even though she had a good idea.

In a low husky voice, Logan said, "Ever since you moved to Sawyer Creek, I convinced myself that if all we could ever be was friends, it would be enough. I was wrong. I want *more*."

Her heart raced. "More?"

With one hand on the wall beside her head, Logan nodded a few inches from her face. "I said I would do anything. But, please...don't ask me to take part in some kind of an experiment. If you want a *real* kiss, I'm your man. If not, don't ask me to do this."

Amy was speechless. She knew Logan cared, but she didn't realize how much, until now.

The door opened. Music filtered inside the bathroom. Candice waltzed in, singing Christmas carols. When she glanced up and saw Logan she squealed. "What the hell are you doing here, Logan?" Candice's voice was several octaves higher than normal. "I got a good mind to call your mama."

"I'm leaving," Logan said, heading toward the door. But then he stopped, turned back to Amy and caressed her chin. "Think about what I said."

Amy nodded.

On his way out, Logan pointed at Candice. "Call her, if you want. I'll deny it." He flashed her his famous 'bat shit crazy' grin before disappearing into the bar.

Giggling, Candice sauntered to the mirror waving a tube of lip gloss that she'd dug out of her pocket. "'Bout time you came to your senses, girlie."

"Excuse me?" Amy asked.

"That man has been in love with you from day one."

"It's not what you think, Candice."

"Still in denial, huh?"

"I'm not in denial about anything. I'm—"

The door flew open once more.

Logan poked his head in. "Come quick. It's Casanova."

Amy lunged with Candice at her back, mumbling, "Did he say Casanova?"

Chapter Ten

Amy followed Logan to the parking lot where Cass leaned against the building, holding his side.

"What are you doing?" she whispered so Logan, Candice and the crowd gathering wouldn't overhear.

Glaring, Cass said, "He was here, Amy."

"Who?"

"The man that accused me of cheating. The same one who—

"Are you sure?"

"Yes!" he snapped. "He was driving the same red truck." He stopped talking when Logan stepped up with his arms folded.

Glaring, Logan asked, "You want to tell me what's going on?"

Amy cringed at his tone.

Cass doubled over. Hopefully, he hadn't reopened the wound. She wanted to lift his shirt and check, but couldn't with everyone watching.

Knowing Logan deserved answers, she grasped his arm. "Come by my house tomorrow before work. We'll talk then."

Logan had a 'deer in the headlights look' as she turned back to Cass and draped his arm over her shoulders to help get him to her car.

Seeing her struggle, Logan ran ahead, opened the passenger's side door, then helped get him onto the front seat.

Logan opened his mouth to speak but Amy silenced him with a finger, whispering, "We'll talk later."

Logan rubbed the back of his neck and nodded.

****

"Shouldn't we call the sheriff?" Amy asked letting off the gas pedal when she saw she was going over the speed limit.

Cass replied, "I said no police."

"What is it with you and police?" she asked. "Are you in trouble?"

"Trouble has a way of following me."

"Oh God, Cass," she said staring through the windshield. "You're upsetting my karma. I don't need this. I have my own problems to deal with."

"Like what, Amy? Logan?"

Frowning, but not taking her eyes off the road she mouthed, "What?"

"I was worried when you ran off. I was outside when that blonde went in. I saw you and Logan."

"What exactly did you see?"

"I can read body language, remember?"

"Good! Then read this!" She turned to him with narrow lips and big eyes.

Cass reached for the dash and shouted, "Look out!"

Amy slammed on the brakes to keep from ramming a car in front of her who was making a right-hand turn.

Cass reached into his jacket and pulled his hand out covered in blood.

"Oh God, you're bleeding again," she said making a turn and racing down the driveway to her home.

She slid the car to a stop, shut the engine off and then rushed around to his door.

Once inside the house, she guided him past the guest room to the bathroom. As he eased down on the commode lid, he removed his shirt and she gasped at the sight of the cherry red bandage.

Neither of them spoke as she dropped his bloody shirt into the sink to wash later. After he peeled the bandage away, she handed him a paper towel doused with peroxide and he applied it to his side. With the wound wiped clean, she could see that the stitches were still intact. After applying more antiseptic gel, she covered it with fresh gauze and tape.

"I'm sorry," he said.

"For what?" she asked.

He blinked away. "For the way I talked to Logan."

"It's okay," she said not wanting to discuss it any longer. "Let's get you to bed."

"I don't want to go to bed."

She snickered at his childlike response which was so un-SEAL-like.

"How about a movie?" he suggested.

"On one condition," she said.

"What's that?"

"I get to pick it out."

Smiling, he nodded.

****

Amy stared at the TV screen as the camera panned to the woman's legs treading water under a silvery moon. It wasn't the first time she'd seen *Jaws*, but it didn't matter. The famous '*do-do... do-do*' music still made her heart race.

Leaning over, Cass whispered, "Get ready..."

"Stop!" she said drawing her knees up and pinning them to her chest.

Cass grinned. "I thought you said you saw this before?"

"I have," she blurted. "But it's a great white for crying out loud!"

Cass shrugged. "They normally won't bother you if you leave them alone."

"Normally?" Her head jerked sideways. "Are you talking from experience?"

"I've been on a few missions that required swimming through shark-infested water to reach a destination."

"Have you ever been...um...*bitten*?"

One edge of his mouth lifted. "Not by a shark..."

Amy blinked away. A warm sensation gushed through her. But not from a panic attack brought on by her attacker.

What kind of woman would Cass be interested in, blonde or brunette? Would she be curvy or slim? she wondered.

Suddenly Cass asked, "What did he do to you?"

Amy scooted to the edge of the sofa, staring at Cass who was now gazing back at her.

"Excuse me?" she asked.

"Why are you afraid of men?"

How did he know?

"Did Logan tell you?"

"He didn't have to. I read body language, remember?"

A lump the size of a golf ball, rose in her throat and she needed something to wash it down. She charged to the kitchen. "I need a beer. Want one?"

"Sure," he replied.

She barely knew Cass. How dare he pry into her personal life, even if he was right?

Carrying two beers back, she shoved one at him. He glanced up, but didn't take it right away. When he did, his fingers raked hers and she snatched her hand back so fast, beer sloshed onto the cushions.

Cass wasted no time in wiping it up with the paper towel that his empty bottle had been resting on. "It might help to get it off your chest," he said.

How could he say that? He was one to talk!

Using a phrase out of his playbook, she snapped back, "It might not!"

Even as she blinked tears away that were threatening to spill onto her check, she knew he was right. Was it possible he knew her better than she knew herself? Maybe she did need to talk to someone other than a beady-eyed woman from behind a mahogany desk who insisted that the root of all her problems came from childhood.

Cass was easy to talk to. Maybe if she told him...she could put it behind her.

Chapter Eleven

Amy cleared her throat, searching for the right words. Talking about that horrible night, was always hard. Even with her therapist, the words hadn't come easy. Amy took a breath and exhaled slowly...the words began spilling out.

"I went to a club with my friends. It was a little after 3:00 a.m. when I drove back to my apartment. While walking across the parking lot, a man grabbed me from behind. He covered my mouth so I couldn't call out." She hesitated.

Giving her hand a gentle squeeze, Cass eased her down beside him on the sofa. "It's okay. Take your time and if you don't want to talk about it—"

"No," she said, wiping a stray tear off her cheek. "You wanted to know."

Cass squeezed her hand tighter and she drew strength from him to go on. "He grabbed my purse. But the strap was across my body and wouldn't break. I tried to scream. He shoved me. I hit a parked car, busting my lip." More tears flowed. "Someone yelled. The man ran off."

"Did you call the police?"

Her jaw dropped. *Coming from a man who said no police, to hear him say it was comical.*

"Yes. But, the man's face was covered. I couldn't give them a description other than a black ski mask."

Cass flexed his jaw like he regretted making her recall the experience. "Do you trust me?" he asked.

Staring behind a thin veil of tears, she nodded.

Cass extended his arms. "Let me hold you."

Her first instinct was to bury up in his chest, but something held her back. She shook her head. "I can't—"

"Don't let that son-of-a-bitch win, Amy."

Cass was right. If she lived in fear for the rest of her life, her assailant would be the victor.

She whispered, "Promise me...if I tell you to let go... *you will*."

"I promise..." he said, inviting her into his embrace.

Pinning her fists under her chin and shielding her body with her arms, Amy leaned forward, her face barely grazing his chest. With her eyes pinched shut, she waited to feel the weight of his arms. When she didn't, she whispered, "What's wrong."

"You're in control," he said. "Tell *me* what you want."

"You mean like...put your arms around me?"

He nodded.

"Do it, Cass..."

He slipped his arms around her, applying the slightest of pressure. It was when his palms rested at the small of her back, she tensed.

"It's okay," he whispered. "I got you."

Despite wanting to flee, she nodded.

"Now, slip your arms around my waist."

He sounded like an experienced negotiator coaxing her off a ledge.

Holding her breath, Amy eased her arms around his waist.

He whispered, "Lock your fingers."

When she tried, they barely touched. Each forced exhale came as shallow bursts of energy.

"Shh," he said resting his chin on the top of her head. "Breathe with me."

Taking his lead, she filled her lungs until his chest retracted and mimicked his actions. "Good," he said. "Again."

This time his grip tightened, sending another rush of adrenaline racing through her. She trembled like a dog that had never been shown an act of kindness.

He leaned slowly into the cushions, taking her with him.

They sat like that for minutes with neither of them saying a word. His hands made a pass up and down her back. It was working. She felt her body soften until someone knocked and she jerked to attention.

Cass darted to the window. Staring through the sheer white curtain, he said, "It's a young blonde girl."

The only person Amy knew matching that description, was Sue Ellen. She ran to the door.

Staring out the small peephole, she mumbled, "It's Sue Ellen. She's going through a tough time. Can you give us a minute?"

Cass gave her a compassionate nod. "I'll be in my room if you need me."

Blushing, she recalled how safe she'd felt in his grasp earlier. But it wasn't personal. It was therapy.

After Cass padded off to the guest room, Amy opened the door. Sue Ellen glanced up with tears in her eyes and more on each cheek.

"What's wrong, Sue Ellen?" Amy asked, pulling her inside.

"It's Mason," Sue Ellen said between sobs. "We had a terrible fight. He said the baby isn't his..."

Amy guided her to the sofa. "What happened?"

"He said he wanted to talk. I've never seen him so angry. He said his mother told him a childhood illness had left him sterile. I tried to tell him, she was wrong."

Amy squeezed the girl's trembling hand. "Surely, he'll come around. Maybe he just needs time."

Sue Ellen gave her head a violent shake. "No," she said. "He's leaving tomorrow to live with a relative up north." Her bottom lip quavered. "I haven't slept with anyone else. The child is his, Miss Olson."

"Of course it is," Amy said, giving her hand a gentle squeeze.

Sue Ellen was a lot of things. A cheater, wasn't one of them. Mason was a fool to think otherwise.

"Would it help if I talked to him?"

Sue Ellen blinked. "You would do that?"

"Yes. I'll tell him that I believe you and that he should too. Whether it will do any good or not, that's up to him. Tell him to come by tomorrow at 4:00 p.m."

"Here?" Sue Ellen asked.

Amy nodded.

Sue Ellen pulled her into a tight hug. "Thank you, Miss Olson."

While getting up off the couch, the girl stopped midway. She pointed at the floor. "Whose are those?"

Amy knew she couldn't pass Cass's boots off as hers. They were too big. Forcing a laugh, she gave her the same story she'd given Logan, that Cass was visiting from San Antonio. Sue Ellen glanced at a nearby chair.

"Isn't that the same jacket the man was wearing who got out of that truck in front of the cafe?"

Amy bared her teeth and shrugged. "Yeah."

"Why didn't you say you knew him?"

"I haven't seen him since he joined the Navy and became a SEAL. His truck broke down just outside of town. He hitched a ride." Sue Ellen's eyes lit up like Cass was some kind of celebrity and Amy cringed, wishing she'd left the SEAL part out, but it was too late.

"Oh wow!" Sue Ellen said bubbling over with excitement. "A Navy SEAL in Sawyer Creek!"

"Ex-Navy SEAL," Amy corrected, downplaying his status so Sue Ellen wouldn't plaster it all over town.

"Where is he?" Sue Ellen asked, staring over her shoulder toward the hallway. "I'd love to meet him."

"He's resting."

Judging by Sue Ellen's shocked expression, Amy guessed that Cass was standing behind her.

Sue Ellen stepped around her. "Sir, it's an honor having you in Sawyer Creek."

Grinning, Cass gave her a nod and said, "Thank you."

"Can I get your autograph?" she asked beaming like a shiny lighthouse beacon.

"Sure," Cass said. "Amy, do you have something I can write on?"

Shaking her head, Amy scurried off to the kitchen to get a pen and paper from a spiral notebook she normally used to jot down last-minute recipes ideas.

Cass scribbled a short message, signed it and handed it back to the nineteen-year-old.

After reading it, Sue Ellen glanced up with eyes the size of tiny saucers. "Your name is Casanova?"

"It's what my SEAL buddies called me."

Amy chuckled as Sue Ellen jogged out of the house and off the porch to her car like Cass was the coolest thing since sliced bread.

Chapter Twelve

Amy watched from the porch as Sue Ellen pulled out of the driveway. Hopefully, she hadn't bit off more than she could chew by saying she'd talk to Mason. It wasn't her place, but someone needed to talk sense into the boy. Too bad his father died in a car crash when he was five.

Amy opened the door and stepped back into the house.

Cass was looking out the window. "Do you believe her?" he asked.

"About not sleeping around? Yes, I do."

"How old is this Mason?"

"Twenty-four. Maybe twenty-five. Why?"

"If you think it would do any good, I could talk to him. I can be very persuasive when I have to."

Amy chuckled as she recalled how easily Cass had coaxed her into his embrace. It felt good to trust again. If she were a shrink, she would say she was well on her way to putting the past behind her.

Glancing at the clock and seeing that it was 10:30, Amy scrubbed her weary face. "I don't know about you, but I'm exhausted."

"Too much excitement for one day?"

"You could say that," she said, smacking her lips and going to the kitchen for a glass of water before bed.

****

Amy shot up, screaming, "No!"

With her chest heaving, she looked around the bedroom expecting any minute to see her attacker in the shadows. Her head jerked toward the feet pounding the hardwood in the hallway.

Within seconds, Cass was at her bedside in a pair of spandex boxers. "Are you okay?" he asked looking around the room.

Peering over the comforter tucked under her chin, she nodded and mumbled, "Yes."

"No. You're not," he said, towering over the bed, obviously not convinced.

"Cass?"

"Yeah," he said.

"I know this is going to sound crazy..." She paused while gathering up the courage to ask the unthinkable but he spoke before she could get it out.

"Yes. I will," he said as if reading her mind.

To make sure they were on the same page, she asked, "You will what?"

"Hold you until you fall asleep."

Sitting in the chair beside her bed would have been sufficient. But, holding her? That was even better.

After feeling incredibly safe in his arms earlier, she wanted—no, *needed*—to feel it again.

Cass stretched out on top of the comforter and drew her into his arms while she took in his clean fresh scent after taking a shower. The overhead fan spun in a lopsided motion causing the tiny chains to gently tap together. As he cradled her in a cocoon-like fashion, her body softened while she drifted to sleep in his arms.

Shivering, Amy opened her eyes and was surprised to see her breath fanning out around her mouth.

She wasn't sure how long she'd been asleep, but, with Cass trembling beside to her, she lifted her head.

He tightened his grip. "I got you," he mumbled, groggily, sounding as if he was clenching his teeth.

Amy raised on her elbows. "It's freezing. The propane must have run out."

Cass lifted his head shooting two streams of vapor out from his nostrils.

Knowing the gas company didn't open until 8:00 a.m., Amy said, "Come get under the covers."

Cold and dazed, Cass rolled out of bed, peeled back the bedding and crawled in. "Roll over," he said, then pinned his chest to her back.

His skin was chilly as though he'd been outside. When she shivered, he drew her deeper into his arms while skirting his hands up and down her back to generate added warmth.

With his breath at the back of her neck, she drifted to sleep, smiling. Apparently, they lay that way the rest of the night, because when she woke up, they were still in the same exact position.

Sunlight poured in through the blinds as Amy lifted her head from his forearm, trying to focus on the digital clock on the nightstand. It was nearly 9:00 and she pulled out of his arms, crawled to the edge of the bed to check her phone and gasped. She had five missed calls. Seeing that she was always at work by 7:00 a.m., it didn't come as a surprise.

Grasping her phone, she hurried to the closet for clothes and then tiptoed past Cass so as not to wake him and darted to the bathroom.

After getting dressed she dialed the cafe's number and waited for someone to pick up.

Matt said, "Amy's Cafe."

"Hey. It's me," she whispered into the phone.

Matt chuckled. "Is everything okay?"

"Yeah. I ran out of propane last night. It's freezing. I burrowed up in the covers to stay warm and just woke up."

"This wouldn't have anything to do with the SEAL, Casanova, would it?"

"Ex-SEAL," she corrected. "And no, it doesn't." She rolled her eyes, knowing by noon everyone in Sawyer Creek would know she was housing a military hero.

"Are you coming to the cafe?" Matt asked.

"Is everyone there?"

"Yeah," he said then snickered. "You'll be glad to know Sue Ellen was thirty minutes early."

"That's great. I need to call the gas company. You can reach me on my cell phone if you need me."

"Can't they deliver and bill you?" Matt asked. "It's not like you're leaving town or anything..." Matt paused. "Oh. I get it. It's the SEAL, huh?"

"Zip it, Matt!"

Amy ended the call but not before hearing Matt chuckle into the phone.

Just when she went back into the bedroom, she froze. Cass was stretched out on his back with his fingers laced behind his head, smiling.

"Congratulations," she said pinning her hair to the top of her head with a clip.

"For what?" he asked.

"For being the best thing that's hit Sawyer Creek since electricity."

Chapter Thirteen

From the porch, Amy waved as the propane driver left her driveway. Just as she turned to go inside she gasped when Logan's truck pulled in behind her car.

He got out, slammed the door and approached the front porch. "I decided to come early," he said. "Wasn't sure how long this would take."

"Logan, I'm sorry for not being truthful about Cass."

"How long have you known him, Amy?"

Amy dropped her head, but refused to lie. "A few days."

Logan raised his sunglasses and rested them at the top of his head. "And, just like that, you invite him to sleep in your house?"

Cass stepped out of the house, pulled a chair around backward and straddled it. "She didn't ask me, Logan, I invited myself."

For a second, Logan glared while flexing his jaw and then he turned his attention back to her.

Amy went to the porch swing. "Have a seat, Logan."

Logan sat down on the steps.

Cass told him about getting shot in the bar's parking lot and him approaching her in the storage room.

Logan shook his head when he heard that Cass had coaxed her into removing a bullet. He clenched his teeth. "Are you two—"

Knowing what he was going to say, Amy jutted her chin. "We aren't sleeping together, if that's what you're asking. You and I are friends, Logan. Why are you acting this way?"

Logan made a fist like he wanted to punch something. Anything. "You don't know?" he shouted.

"No," she replied.

"I can't pretend anymore, Amy. Last night, when I said I wouldn't kiss you for the sake of an experiment, I meant it."

Cass got up and went inside.

Logan got up too and headed for his truck, but before walking off, he turned around like he had something to say. But when nothing came out, he turned to leave.

Amy shouted, "Logan!" at his back.

His feet froze as if they were embedded in quicksand.

Amy ran to him but when he didn't turn around, she stepped around him. Staring into his face, she said, "Logan, you're my best friend."

His gaze was glassy as he raked his fingers through his hair. "I can't be your friend anymore, Amy."

"Why?" she asked.

He exhaled hard and then said, "I eat, drink and sleep...*you*."

Hearing how deep his feelings went, Amy blinked. She had no idea.

Logan's gaze drifted to her lips. He dipped his head. Inches from her mouth, he paused.

She whispered, "I wasn't altogether honest when I said Cass and I haven't slept together."

Logan pulled back, clenching his jaw.

"It's not what you think," she said. "Last night, I had a bad dream. Cass rushed to my side. I told him everything. He held me. I needed that to put that terrible night behind me."

"Did you—?"

"No! He was a perfect gentleman."

Logan turned and headed back to her house. "I need to talk to him."

She grasped his arm. "What are you going to say?"

The front door opened. Cass stepped out with his backpack over one shoulder.

The two men locked gazes.

Logan asked, "Where are you going?"

Cass shrugged. "I hear there's a hotel on the south end of town. Thought I would check it out."

Amy stepped forward. "Cass, I lied. There's no hotel. I was scared and only said that so you would go."

Looking toward the driveway, Cass shook his head. "Then I'll find somewhere else to stay."

Amy lunged for the porch steps waving her hand. "I have an idea. Matt's leaving in a few days. I need a cook." Looking up at Cass, she asked, "Are you interested?"

Cass shrugged. "I guess I could take the job, but only until my truck is ready."

Amy said, "I have another idea... You could stay at the cafe."

Cass lifted an eyebrow.

"Before you say anything, hear me out. We can turn the storage room into an apartment." She whirled around to Logan. "It's air-conditioned and has a full bathroom." When Logan didn't protest, she turned back to Cass. "With a few coats of paint, a bed, and a dresser, it'll make the perfect bachelor pad."

Logan stepped closer. "She's got a point. You wouldn't have far to go to work."

Nodding, Cass agreed then added, "You can deduct the rent from my pay."

"No rent," Amy said, shaking her head. "Consider it a benefits package. Besides, you'd be doing me a favor."

Chapter Fourteen

That night, Amy watched Cass turn up a glass of water in front of the sink with his jeans low on his hips exposing six well-defined abs. She hadn't studied a man's anatomy since the attack. And now here she was admiring his chest and arms with brazen interest.

His wound had scabbed over and he refused to wear a bandage, saying the air would do it good.

She was happy, yet somewhat nervous, that he had agreed to stay until the storage room renovations were done. But then again, where else could he go when Sawyer Creek didn't have a hotel?

After Logan left for the bar last night, they'd barely spoken. The air was so thick she was sure she could slice it with a butter knife. She wanted to talk, but couldn't find the right words. Apparently, neither could he.

When he got out of the shower, she blurted, "Do you want to watch TV? Or are you ready to turn in?"

Without looking up, Cass rinsed the glass he'd been drinking from and placed it in the sink, upside down. "TV is fine," he said but didn't sound overjoyed.

The response was so unlike the intimidating man who had surprised her in the storage room, full of confidence, cutting through the chase and saying exactly what was on his mind. Why was he distant now? More importantly, why did she care?

Amy didn't have time for a relationship even if she wanted one. He had already made it clear he was leaving

Sawyer Creek when his truck was fixed. If ever she wanted to read minds, it was now.

The silence was deafening. Amy couldn't take it any longer. She grabbed the remote off the coffee table and tapped the On key. Cass plopped on the sofa with his elbow propped on the sofa's arm and his chin in his hand.

"You pick something this time," Amy said sliding the remote across the cushions.

Still refusing to speak, Cass picked it up, flipped through the channels and settled on a wildlife documentary about a pride of lions in South Africa. "How's that?" he asked.

Amy turned sideways at the other end of the sofa. "Have I done or said something to offend you?"

"No," he snapped sharply. His gaze remained glued on the TV as though he was recording every detail to memory.

"You're just not...yourself."

He forced a laugh which was the only indication that he'd been listening. "You haven't known me a week," he said. "How do you know what 'myself' is?"

"Good point," Amy said, relaxing against the cushions watching a lioness teaching four young cubs to hunt. Cringing, she drew her feet up when the creature masterfully singled out an injured antelope.

Animals had to survive but she didn't care to watch the slaughter in progress.

Chuckling, Cass said, "I take it you don't hunt."

"My dad took me once," Amy said, glad that he'd finally spoken. "We spent the morning tracking a deer. My father raised his gun but when he saw me tearing up, he couldn't pull the trigger."

"What about the meat in a grocery store? Where do you think it comes from?"

"That's different."

Cass tilted his head in her direction and made a face.

She blinked away. "I try not to think about how it got to be in the wrapper."

"Do you tell yourself wrapped ground beef grows on trees?"

Amy shrugged. But, sadly he was spot-on. She mumbled, "Maybe."

Shaking his head, Cass focused back on the lioness and her cubs.

Not wanting to watch the mother and her babies feast, she said, "Cass, I want to thank you."

"I should be the one thanking you," he said. "I can't image what you'd be thanking me for."

Once again, she turned sideways to explain. "For the therapy session," she said. "You did more in five minutes than my therapist has done for me in six months."

"Wait until you get my bill," he teased, then patted the cushion like it was an invitation to move closer. Just when she'd contemplated doing it, her heart rate went from zero to sixty.

There was barely enough oxygen in her lungs to manage a high-pitched, "Fine."

Jutting her chin, she got up and sat down with her hip adjacent to his and her thigh, touching his thigh. Amy tensed when he slid his arm around her shoulders.

"Relax," he said. "I got you."

The sensation of his mouth inches from the side of her face, made her heart pound. Licking her lips, she fought to regain composure and dismissed wanting to know what his lips would feel like against her mouth.

As if reading her mind, he turned sideways until her body was between his legs and patted his chest. Amy turned to face him and noticed that he was gazing at her lips.

Out of the blue, he asked, "Can I kiss you?"

Her head nodded like a clueless bobble head doll. Still gazing at her mouth, he cupped the back of her neck, leaned forward and then pressed his lips ever so lightly against her lips. Her breasts heaved against the contours of his chest.

Like a masterful kisser, he slipped his tongue between her lips. Gently at first and then with more conviction. A burst of energy released somewhere inside her core like years of pent-up passion exploding all at once, sending oxygen out to all her extremities.

Amy blushed when she realized her fingers were digging into his shoulders with an urgency so unlike her. Pulling back, each breath came out ragged, yet in tempo with his as his scent swirled inside her head.

Without warning, Cass broke the kiss.

Amy locked on his half-hooded gaze. There was a hunger in his eyes, an insatiable need and she longed for him to kiss her again even if it was wrong. She needed it, *deserved* it...

Before her brain could coordinate with her mouth, a smile pulled at one edge of his mouth.

"You don't want this," he said tucking a strand of her hair behind one ear.

Her brain shouted, *No! You're wrong! It's exactly what I want.*

She tried to say the words out loud, but he silenced her with a finger, rose and then disappeared down the hallway. She wanted to go after him. But her legs wouldn't comply.

Was the kiss just a therapy session? No. It went way beyond that.

She barely heard the guest room door shut over the pounding of her heart.

Chapter Fifteen

Amy slowed down in front of Sawyer Creek's Sheriff Department and was relieved to see Sheriff Martin's patrol car parked near the door.

She silenced the engine and turned to Cass. "You're doing the right thing. Whoever shot you, could still be in Sawyer Creek."

Cass frowned like he was having a change of heart about talking to the sheriff. "I'm not used to asking for help."

Amy pulled the keys out of the ignition and shot him a sideways glance. "That's not true. You asked me."

"I was dying, Amy. That was different."

Amy reached for the door handle. "Let's get this over with."

When they stepped into the lobby, Christmas music was playing softly.

Mary looked through the dispatch window. "Hey, Amy."

"Hey, Mary. Is the sheriff free?"

Mary glanced at a blinking red light on her console and then back up. "He's on the phone..." she said and then paused when the light went off. She grabbed the receiver. Pressing the same button, she blurted, "Sheriff, Amy's here. She needs to see you." Mary nodded and pressed the buzzer to let them inside. "Sheriff said to go on back."

Amy paused when Cass hesitated like they were in school and had been summoned to the principal's office. Amy grasped his arm and pulled him inside.

The dispatch door latched and they followed a narrow hallway to a door with a gold nameplate engraved with the sheriff's name.

"Is everything all right?" the Sheriff asked, rising from his desk while adjusting his body armor and a bulky belt weighed down with tactical gear.

Not knowing where to start, Amy glanced at Cass to see if he might help. He offered no assistance, so she said, "Sheriff, Cass has something to tell you."

The sheriff sat down, eyeing Cass from behind his desk while Cass told him about leaving San Antonio and stopping for a beer, getting shot in the parking lot and asking Amy for help.

When he had finished, the sheriff kicked back in his chair. "The red vehicle you're describing matches Henry Cobb's truck."

Amy glanced down. "Where do I know that name...?" Then it hit her. "Isn't that the guy that moved in next to Logan?"

The sheriff nodded.

Amy mumbled, "To think I almost called him in for an interview. Thankfully, I hired Mason instead."

"Mr. Cobb isn't his real name," the sheriff stated then roared into his phone, "Mary, call the Bexar County Sheriff's Department. Have Detective Marshall call me ASAP. I think we've located Henry Turner."

"Will do, Sheriff," Mary replied.

"Turner?" Amy asked, wondering what that had to do with Cobb.

The sheriff nodded. "I think Henry Cobb is an alias Turner uses and if I'm right, he's wanted for robbery out of Bextar County." He looked at Cass. "And now, attempted murder. I'll need to get a statement from you." Frowning, the sheriff turned back to Amy. "You're a nurse now?"

"No," Amy said, shaking her head. "I'm not."

Cass covered his mouth and chuckled behind his hand. "I didn't leave her much choice, Sheriff," he said. "She saved my life."

The sheriff scrunched up his tanned forehead. "I knew something was up when I saw blood on the storeroom floor. I just never figured..." He hesitated like he knew it was a waste of time to ramble, then turned to Cass once more. "Just for the record, you might want to seek professional help next time."

"Hopefully, there won't be a next time," Cass answered.

The sheriff asked, "Has Mayor McNeil contacted you yet?"

Cass shook his head.

"He wants you to ride on the veterans float this year in our annual Christmas parade."

Cass shook his head again. Amy remembered he'd clearly said no police or hospitals. Apparently, he didn't like parades either.

"I think you should do it," Amy said. "The kids would love it."

Cass gave her an eye roll.

The sheriff told Cass not to leave town as he walked them out into to the lobby where Mary announced that he had an incoming call from Bextar

County. Immediately, he excused himself and darted back inside.

Cass opened the door and sighed when Mayor McNeil met them on the sidewalk.

Blocking the sun with his hand, the mayor shouted, "Cass! I've been meaning to get with you."

Cass raised his hand. "If this is about riding on the Christmas float, that's not me, Mayor. I prefer watching from the sidelines."

"Nonsense, Mr. Nova. You deserve the VIP treatment. I'm just the man to deliver."

"Thanks," Cass said, glancing at Amy and smiling. "But I already have plans."

The frustrated Mayor McNeil ran his hand over his thin gray hair. "Fine," he said. "But the offer stands in case you change your mind."

"I appreciate that, Mayor, but I don't see that happening."

Mumbling incoherently, the mayor limped to his black BMV idling at the curb.

Chapter Sixteen

Two weeks flew by and Amy spun on the newly tiled floor, admiring the storage room's fresh coat of paint. All the supplies had been moved to another room inside the cafe. The renovation took longer than expected because Logan had insisted on adding a dividing wall, leaving a hallway from the back of the cafe to the alley. The remainder of the space was sectioned into a spacious apartment for Cass.

For the last two weeks, Cass had continued to sleep at her house. They all chipped in with the renovations until Logan had to leave for the bar. Matt agreed to stay on for a few more weeks.

In the evenings when they drove back to her house, they would shower then watch TV for a few hours and would go straight to bed so they could do it all over again the next day.

Amy jumped out of the way as Logan and Cass brought in a queen-sized mattress still wrapped in plastic. They laid it on the dark mahogany bed frame they'd gotten the previous week at Sawyer Creek's Flea Market. Next, they hauled in a dresser and two matching nightstands.

"This really turned out nice," Amy said gazing around the room.

Logan clamped down on Cass's shoulder. "Only the best for *Casanova*."

Cass shook his head, but didn't object to Logan calling him by his nickname.

Logan went back outside to bring in the last of the things Amy had picked out to give the room a homey feel— pictures, bedding, towels, an artificial Christmas tree and a few decorations.

Cass said, "Thank you."

"For what?" she asked.

"This." He gave the room a sweeping motion with his hand.

"It's for my benefit, as well as yours," she said, downplaying her generosity. "I have a temporary cook to replace Matt. You have a place to stay. I just wish you'd reconsider leaving Sawyer Creek. It really is a peaceful place to live."

"Yeah," Cass said, grinning. "Until a stranger shows up bleeding on your doorstep."

Logan returned carrying a shopping bag on each arm and a painting in each hand.

Cass turned and went outside. She recalled while watching television one night, Cass talked about his childhood and how he'd grown up unsupervised with a drug addicted mom and a drunk dad. At seventeen, he enlisted in the Navy. Once turning eighteen he hopped on a bus to boot camp. Four years later, he joined the SEALS and never looked back until an IUD exploded by his boot, nearly sending him to an early grave.

One night after a few beers, Cass told her about metal he still had embedded in his body and no way to get it out short of running him through a sifter. As the slivers worked their way to the surface, one could easily pierce an organ, so the government thanked him for his service and gave him an honorable discharge.

When she asked him where he intended to go when his truck was fixed, he said, "Wherever it takes me."

Upon hearing his mother had over-dosed on meth while he was in Afghanistan and his father drank himself to death, Amy ran to the bathroom. It was the saddest thing she'd ever heard and she didn't want him to see her cry. Leaning against the bathroom door, she forced tears back, and fought the urge to comfort him the way that he had comforted her.

Now that the storage room was done, he would be moving out. Granted, she would still see him at the cafe, but at least it wouldn't be in the privacy of her home. There was a chemistry between them that seemed to lie just below the surface and slowly coming to a boiling point.

Logan leaned the pictures against the wall and tossed the bags onto the mattress.

"You've done a good job," Amy said after swallowing the lump in her throat from thinking about Cass.

"We're going to get Cass's things. You want to come?"

"No," Amy said. "I need to make a fresh batch of Chicken Dorito Casserole for the lunch rush. "You go on."

She blinked away, as Cass entered the room and she saw a muscle flex in his jaw.

"Okay," Logan said, oblivious to the turmoil going on inside her. "Be back in a few."

She nodded, ignoring the stab in her heart at the thought of Cass moving out.

"Are you okay?" Logan said.

"Yeah. I'm fine," she said. "Go. I'm sure Cass is eager to get settled in."

Cass scrubbed his face and she got the uncanny feeling he wasn't as eager as she thought. In the short time she'd known him, she found he was a master at hiding his feelings. Her eyes bored into his back as he followed Logan outside.

Was he falling for her?

If so, her mother was right, you don't choose love...it chooses you.

Chapter Seventeen

Four days had passed and Logan begged her to take the day off because he had something that he wanted to ask her that couldn't wait. The more she tried convincing herself that Logan was a good catch, the more her heart resisted.

"You ready?" Logan asked drawing her back to the present.

"Yeah," Amy said handing him a red and white checkered blanket and a picnic basket containing finger foods.

Outside, Logan strapped the basket to a cooler on the ATV's luggage rack, then crawled aboard. Amy slipped in behind him.

The four-wheeler hummed along a path in the direction of the lake at the back of her property. For December, it was exceptionally warm. The sun beat down from a cloudless sky. A flock of geese took flight when they neared the lake's edge. Logan shut off the engine and helped her down. He handed her the basket and two beers from the iced down cooler.

After spreading the blanket out, Amy removed the lid from the container of cheese, crackers and pepperoni slices she'd prepared before leaving the house.

"To us," Logan said, holding up his beer for a toast.

"To us," she said tapping his bottle gently with hers.

Logan took a drink of his beer, swallowed hard and then leaned in like he was going to kiss her. When he didn't aim for her cheek, she turned her head and offered him a cheese and pepperoni cracker.

He didn't seem upset by it and asked, "What do you want for Christmas?"

Amy shrugged. To tell him she wanted Cass, wasn't an option, so she asked, "What about you?"

"You," Logan said leaning his back against a tree trunk and staring out over the lake. "We should do this more often," he said.

"It'll be cold soon. I'm surprised it isn't already—"

"That's not what I meant," he interrupted her.

"What then?"

"City Hall is looking for a heavy equipment operator. I thought I'd apply. It would mean I wouldn't have to work nights anymore. We could spend more time together."

"I thought you loved working at the bar?"

"I do," he said gazing into her eyes. "But, I've been thinking..." The grin he was wearing, faded. Afraid to know why, Amy held her breath. Logan cupped her cheek, "Marry me, Amy."

Feeling as if the breath had been knocked out of her, Amy stared at him all the while forcing herself to breathe. She knew Logan cared about her, but *marriage?*

"I think we should go slow," she said.

"We've known each other over four years."

"Logan. I—"

He silenced her with a finger. "Just think about it."

The next few hours flew by. They talked about the cafe and Matt leaving. They discussed Sue Ellen and how much she'd changed with a baby on the way. Logan didn't mention Cass. Neither did she.

"I need to get back. It's almost time to open the bar."

Amy nodded. They packed everything up and drove back in silence. Logan parked near the back door, handed her the basket, unloaded the cooler and set it just inside the back door. When he came out, he unexpectedly pulled her into his arms.

Dipping his head, he kissed her so hard that it nearly stole her breath away, but sadly, didn't make her heart flutter.

Cradling her face in his hands, Logan whispered, "I love you Amy. I always have."

Amy opened her mouth, but nothing would come out.

Logan didn't seem upset that she couldn't say anything. Smiling, he rested his forehead to hers and then ran off to his truck and fled down the driveway. For a moment, she could see her and Logan growing old together. But when she closed her eyes and pictured them entangled in the sheets, she saw Cass.

Shaking her head, she went inside to the kitchen to empty the basket and put everything away. Cass was leaving. Somehow, she had to get him out of her mind. In a few days, or maybe sooner, the station would call saying his truck was ready. Maybe then she could focus on Logan.

A shower seemed to be in order. The water felt good pulsating against her skin and it wasn't until it ran cold that she realized how long she'd been in there. She turned the tap off, dried herself and slipped an over-sized T-shirt over her head. As she padded to the living room, she flipped on the TV.

With the holidays a few weeks away, she chose a Christmas musical and stretched out on the sofa.

****

The movie was over and Amy stretched her arms up, yawning, as the TV screen turned into a fuzzy mass of snow. Wondering at the time, she glanced at the microwave clock. It was well after midnight.

After silencing the TV she was on her way to bed when there was a sudden knock on the front door. She ran to the window and froze when she saw Cass standing on the front porch with his hands tucked in his pockets and his breath fanning out around his mouth. Gasping, she looked down at her T-shirt that barely covered her thighs. She needed to change, but he knocked again.

What if something happened at the cafe?

Taking a deep breath, she flipped the porch light on and flung open the door. "Is everything okay?" she asked hugging her T-shirt.

Cass raised his head and gave it a slight shake. Her gaze wavered to his chest. How odd that he wasn't wearing a shirt under his denim jacket as if he'd thrown it on at the last minute.

"What's wrong?" she asked.

"We need to talk, Amy."

Feeling self-conscious standing before him wearing only a T-shirt, she replied, "It's late, Cass. Can't it wait until tomorrow?"

"No," he said. "It can't."

Chapter Eighteen

Amy stepped back and waved Cass into the living room. Before she could say anything, he had her face in his hands, fanning her with warm puffs of air.

Knowing he didn't have a vehicle and the cafe was a few miles away, she asked, "How did you get here?

"The station called. My truck was ready. I picked it up after closing the cafe."

There was a wild look in his eyes. She trembled. "Cass, you're scaring me."

"That makes two of us. Let me put it another way..." Her chest heaved as he dipped his head, his lips hovering over hers as if he might kiss her. At first, he was gentle, but then the tip of his tongue slipped past her lips to explore her mouth. He pulled back, leaving her weak and dazed. "If you tell me to go, I will," he said in a deep voice. "But, it better be soon."

"What about Logan?"

"It sucks to be him because I'm crazy about his girl."

"I'm not his girl," Amy corrected.

"I'm sure he doesn't see it that way."

Her heart swelled at hearing Cass say he was crazy about her. After the attack, she never dreamed it was possible to feel this way again.

Amy whispered, "I thought it was *me* that had fallen for *you*."

"I fell for you the moment I approached you in the storage room."

Was she dreaming? If so, she didn't want to wake up.

With his head buried in the side of her neck, Cass lifted her up and carried her to the kitchen. Wave after wave of bliss consumed every fiber of her being as her legs curled around his waist. If there were consequences to her actions, she'd deal with them later. Logic and reasoning were the farthest thing from her mind.

The drop down counter creaked as Cass placed her on the edge. He groaned and whispered huskily, "Do you want me to go?"

Hypnotized by his manly scent, she shook her head and was leaning in to kiss him, when the front door flew open. Through a hazy fog, she saw Logan in the doorway clenching his fists at his sides. Cass saw him too and went around the counter toward him.

Amy jumped down and wedged herself between them, splaying a hand on each of their chests. Shoving with all her might, she shouted, "Stop!" Cass was the first to back down and return to the kitchen, so she concentrated on Logan. "What are you doing here?"

"Connie's watching the bar. I wanted to say goodnight."

"Logan, you can't barge into my house like this."

"What about him?" Logan said, jabbing an angry finger at Cass.

"Look," Amy said, grasping his arm and lowering it. "He knocked. I let him in."

Logan looked hurt, deflated, as if he'd just caught her cheating. How was it possible to cheat on someone that she hadn't yet committed to?

It didn't matter. What did matter though, was that she had to defuse the situation. And fast.

"Logan, don't do this. We've been friends a long time—"

Glaring, Logan cut her off. "Amy, friends don't ask friends to marry them."

She cringed because she hadn't told Cass that Logan had asked her to marry him.

To her surprise, Cass chuckled, seemingly not surprised. "You're right, Logan," he said stepping forward. Cass reached for her hand. "Amy, marry *me*."

Amy pulled out of Cass's grip, waving her hands. "You guys are making me crazy."

Logan followed her to the living room, blocking her path. "Amy, you don't know Cass like you know me."

Staring into Logan's eyes, she said, "You're right, Logan. But in the short time I have, he makes my heart skip. My mom was right. She said you don't choose love...it chooses you. I never understood that..." She turned to Cass. "Until now."

Cass walked toward her, took her by the hand and pulled her into his space. Holding her tight, he raked his chin over the top of her head.

Logan turned away, obviously frustrated and headed toward the door. Within seconds, the front door opened and slammed.

Amy ran out on the porch after him, shouting, "Logan, wait!"

Poor Logan. He never looked back. He continued to his truck and tore out of the driveway leading a cloud of dust. Amy watched his taillights disappear into the trees. Her heart ached. But, sadly, it wasn't for the reasons Logan would have wanted.

Would he ever talk to her again? Could she blame him if he didn't?

From behind, Cass wrapped his arms around her while whispering to the side of her face, "That could have just as easily been me."

Amy whirled in his arms. She wanted to tell him that she could never send him away, but his lips rained down on hers, halting all logical thought.

When she trembled, Cass pulled back. "It's cold. You need to go back inside where it's warm."

Was he leaving?

"What? You're not staying?"

He shook his head. "Not because I don't want to. But, after everything you've been though, if I stay, I may not be able to control my actions. I won't rush you into something you're not ready for."

Her heart pounded. She had to make a choice. Let him go or convince him to stay? She chose to go with her gut and brushed her lips over his until his hand at the back of her head, drew her closer.

Pressing against the bulge at the front his jeans, Amy moaned and her knees felt weak.

Within seconds their sounds came together as one as they stumbled back into the house and slammed the door. Her inner walls constricted at the thought of what they were about to do.

Cass began fumbling with his belt, his button and finally his zipper.

Amy eyed the dark patch in the front and wasn't surprised that he wasn't wearing anything underneath. A delightful throb ached between her thighs and she pinned her legs together.

Cupping a butt cheek in each hand, Cass lifted her up and carried her to the kitchen. His lips left her mouth then traced a path to her neck and back as he sat her back on the counter and aligned himself between her legs. With one hard thrust he filled her, stretching her moist lining like nothing she'd ever felt. They rocked in harmony, twisting and grinding until they were a mass of sweating flesh rising to a magical place that only lovers could go. As she cried out Cass's name, her release came swift, fast, and hard, and was insanely gratifying.

His heat-filled eyes watched her as he plunged deeper into her cavity. She convulsed again. A husky moan emitted from somewhere within his throat, confirming that his release was just as incredible.

Pinning her to his chest they fought to replenish every ounce of air that they'd lost during what had to be the most mind-blowing orgasm ever.

Chapter Nineteen

Amy stood outside Logan's trailer with her knuckles inches from his door, summoning the courage to knock. It had been days since Logan had stormed out, upset, and she hadn't seen or spoken to him since. He hadn't come by the cafe for his favorite chicken Dorito casserole either. It was as though he'd dropped off the face of the Earth. Even if he didn't want to see her, she needed to know that he was okay.

On the drive to the trailer park, she'd rehearsed what she would say and how she would say it, but standing outside his door, she couldn't remember where to start.

Just do it, a voice echoed from somewhere inside her head. She gave the door a light rap.

Within seconds, it flew open. Logan eyed her from the doorway with a lazy grin, wearing jeans and squinting into the sun.

"This has gone on long enough, Logan. We need to talk."

Wiping his face like he'd just woken up, Logan shook his head.

Amy said, "Logan, I still want to be friends."

Logan pinched his eyes shut and gave the door a few hard raps with his fist. After a short pause, he whispered, "Amy, please go. This is not a good time."

"Since you won't take my calls, it's the only way." Not waiting for him to slam the door in her face,

Amy darted under his arm. He had barged into her house. The least she could do was return the favor.

Narrowing his lips, Logan looked away and asked, "What do you want from me?"

"You're my best friend."

Logan threw his head back and laughed. When he was through, he glared at her. "Don't you get it?"

"Get what? I feel like I'm losing you."

"No, Amy. You're not losing me. I have voluntarily moved on."

Someone cleared their throat from inside the trailer.

Amy whirled around and was surprised to find they weren't alone. From the hallway, Connie had the same weary-eyed look Logan had when answering the door. Judging by the sheet tightly wrapped around her body and disheveled hair, she'd been up all night and perhaps had just fallen asleep.

Amy had always suspected Connie had a thing for Logan and now she regretted barging in.

The blonde goddess asked in a wee voice, "Logan do you want me to go?"

Amy wanted to explain why she was there. "I'm sorry, Connie. Please, don't go on my account. *I... It's* just that..." Sighing heavily, Amy strolled past Logan to the door, patting his tattooed shoulder lightly. "You're right. This is not a good time."

****

When Amy got home, she was surprised to see Sue Ellen's maroon Honda Civic parked in her driveway. After shutting the engine off, she palmed her forehead, remembering she had told Sue Ellen to bring Mason by for a heart to heart talk.

Sue Ellen met her at the top of the porch steps. Amy looked around for Mason. He wasn't anywhere in sight. *Had he refused to come?*

Sue Ellen pointed to the back yard. "Cass is with Mason."

"That's wonderful," Amy replied. "If anyone can get through to him, Cass can."

Amy lost her train of thought when Cass and Mason walked toward them, laughing as though they were long-lost friends.

Mason stopped in front of Sue Ellen. Tears flowed from her eyes as he pulled her into his arms and kissed the top of her head. He turned to Amy. "I hear you need a cook."

Amy nodded. "You interested?"

"Yeah," he said. "We have a baby coming. When can I start?"

"Don't you want to know how much it pays?" Amy asked ignoring the issues she'd initially wanted to address.

Mason shrugged. "The way I see it, it's more than I'm making now."

It was a good answer which earned him another dollar on top of what she was going to offer him.

Cass gave her shoulders a squeeze with his arm.

"Are you hungry?" Amy asked.

"Let me guess," Cass said. "CDC."

Mason raised an eyebrow. "Center of Disease Control?"

Sue Ellen chuckled and then whispered, "Chicken Dorito casserole, silly."

Mason's face lit up. "Sure," he said. "Sue Ellen swears it's as amazing as my mom's fried chicken.

"I don't know about that," Amy said. "But's it's pretty darn good."

Amy herded them inside and immediately she went to the kitchen. Sue Ellen grinned from ear to ear as she helped set the table with the plates and silverware Amy had laid out. Cass and Mason went to the living room and Mason bombarded him with military questions.

Sue Ellen said, "I haven't seen Mason this happy in a long time."

"Well why wouldn't he be happy?" Amy replied. "He's gonna be a daddy and has a job."

"We are blessed, Miss Olson, to have you in our life."

Amy gave her a wave of her hand. "Aww, it was nothing."

Chapter Twenty

After dropping Cass off where the Christmas floats were lining up, Amy turned into the fairgrounds parking lot. Jason, Sandy Morrison's teenage son, motioned with an orange flag for her to go right. Amy took the next available spot beside a white pickup and cut off the engine. As she hurried to the passenger's side to get her dish, she heard Christmas carols playing through the fairground speakers.

There were two classes for the cook-off. Main dish and mouth-watering desserts. Since baking had never been Amy's strong suit, she stuck with what she knew. Last year, she entered ribs and took second place. Today, it was her famous chicken Dorito casserole.

Donna pulled up next to her in a blue, four-door sedan. "Hey Amy!" Donna said getting out and hurrying to the passenger's side in a flowered jumpsuit and sandals.

Amy waved to her while studying the large round container she got out of the car, wondering if it was Donna's award-winning chicken spaghetti.

Why wouldn't she enter it? It had gotten first place for three consecutive years. Together, they walked to the security guard standing beside an opening in the chain link fence.

Halfway there, Donna glanced down at Amy's aluminum foil-covered dish. "Chicken Dorito casserole?" she asked.

"Yeah," Amy said, glancing sideways at her bowl. "Chicken spaghetti?"

Donna's hair was pinned up with the exception of two long blonde curls that framed her face and fanned her cheeks as she gave her head several confident nods. "Where's Cass?" the woman asked.

"I dropped him off up front," Amy told her. "Mayor McNeil talked him into riding on the military float this year."

"My brother can be relentless," Carol said, staring ahead.

Someone shouted, "Hey! Wait up!" Gripping her dish, Amy spun around. Sue Ellen and Mason were a welcome sight hurrying toward her hand in hand.

While waiting for them to catch up, Carol said, "I'm going inside. See you at the booth."

Amy wished the mayor's sister good luck. Carol did the same then slipped past the guard since the food contestants had paid in advance when registering.

"Was that Carol I saw you talking to?" Sue Ellen asked.

"Yeah," Amy replied.

"Let me guess," Sue Ellen said. "Chicken spaghetti again?"

Amy nodded.

Sue Ellen wrinkled her nose. "I have a gut feeling you're gonna take first place this year."

"Second is fine," Amy said, lifting her chin.

"Not according to Ricky Bobbie," Mason replied craning his neck around Sue Ellen. "He swears if you aren't first, you're last."

"You need a new action hero Mason," Amy said, chuckling. Mason had turned out to be an excellent cook, but sometimes said the strangest things. It was okay, though. He was never late and since Sue Ellen rode to work with him, she was on time too.

Amy nodded to the security guard. He nodded back, checked her name off, and she slipped through the fence. Just inside, she waited while Mason handed him ten dollars for and him and Sue Ellen to enter.

Gravel crunched under heavy boots as Sheriff Martin and Deputy Barnes raced in front of craft booths displaying homemade Christmas decorations, to the other end of the fairgrounds.

"What's going on?" Sue Ellen asked, stepping up beside her.

Amy shrugged. "I don't know."

Logan appeared from nowhere, shouting "Amy, come quick. It's Cass."

Instantly, Amy's heart dropped to her stomach. "What is it?" she asked.

"He had a run-in with Henry Cobb."

Knowing she only had five minutes to check-in her casserole dish before being disqualified, Amy handed Mason her dish and asked if he would see that it got there on time. Mason nodded, grabbed Sue Ellen's hand and off they went.

With her heart pounding against her ribcage, Amy followed Logan to the other end of the fairgrounds. Her foot slipped in the gravel and Logan grasped her hand as they pushed through the gathering crowd. In the center, Cass was talking to Sheriff Martin while Deputy Barnes stood over a man on his belly with his hands cuffed behind his back. Blood trickled from one of his nostrils as he slowly began to come to.

"Is that Henry Cobb?" she asked.

"Yeah," Logan replied as they made their way to Cass.

Cass looked up and smiled. As she approached, he drew her to his chest. Staring up at a small cut on his lip, Amy asked, "What happened?"

"Henry jumped me when I came out of the men's room."

Sheriff Martin tapped Cass's shoulder. "Hey, I'm going to headquarters to add this to Henry's long list of offenses. Stop by tomorrow. It should be ready for you to sign." The sheriff shook Cass's hand. "I'll contact Bextar County to see when they can arrange to transport him back to San Antonio. The sooner he's out of my town, the better."

Sue Ellen and Mason ran up, winded and gasping. "Did you...hear?" Sue Ellen asked, forcing air into her lungs.

"Hear what?" Amy asked.

"The judges announced the winners of the cook-off. Your...chicken Dorito casserole...won...first place!"

Amy covered her mouth. With everything going on, she had almost forgotten about the contest.

"You mean *we* won," Amy said giving Sue Ellen and Mason a group hug because if they hadn't gotten her entry to the judges in time, she would have been disqualified.

"There's more," Cass said, taking her hand. "I was going to save this for after the parade, but I've changed my mind."

Amy gasped when he got down on one knee.

"Will you marry me, Amy?" he asked extending a tiny gold present with a shiny white bow on top. She didn't need to see what was inside to respond.

"Yes," she said wiping a tear from her cheek while more took its place.

"Open it!" Sue Ellen shouted, bubbling over with excitement.

Cass stood up as she tore the paper off and lifted the lid. A diamond ring sparkled up at her. Cass removed it and slipped it on her ring finger.

Sue Ellen, Mason, Logan, and Connie cheered in the background along with a growing crowd. Cass kissed her then gathered her into his arms and made a tight circle while the Christmas carol, 'Do You See What I See' blared from the fairground speakers.

Amy felt her heart swell. This was going to be the best Christmas ever. It was the new beginning that she'd hoped for, but could never find. She had won all right. In more ways than one...

Chicken Dorito Casserole Recipe

Ingredients:

3 cans of Cream of Celery soup

3 boneless chicken breasts or 1 bag of diced chicken strips already cooked

1 can of diced tomatoes

1 large bag of Doritos

1 package of taco seasoning

3 cups of shredded cheese

- Boil chicken and cut into small chunks (or use precooked diced chicken)
- Crunch Doritos (place a couple handfuls aside for topping)
- Mix diced tomatoes, crunched Doritos, 3 cans of Celery, Taco seasoning, shredded cheese and diced chicken in a casserole dish.
- Top with remaining Doritos and sprinkle with shredded cheese

Bake in oven on 350 for approx. 45 mins (50 minutes for crispy topping)

Margie's Magic Christmas Bars

Laura Strickland

Chapter One

"It's absolutely the most magical time of the year," Margie told her best friend, Liz, as she used white icing to cement the wall of a gingerbread house to its base. "Think about it: flying reindeer, elves and letters to Santa. And mistletoe. Don't forget the mistletoe!"

"Who could?" Liz returned with considerable amusement. She sat at the table in Margie's tiny apartment kitchen, eating a broken section of gingerbread roof. "But, sweetie, all that stuff's just for fun. You can't really believe in it."

"Not believe?" Margie looked up from her task and froze; she couldn't even imagine such a thing. She widened her eyes and puffed out a breath, which stirred the fringe of bangs above her eyebrows. "Liz, the worst mistake of all is to stop believing."

Magic, as Margie knew very well, was the ingredient that sweetened life the way sugar sweetened a recipe. What happened when you left the sugar out? Nothing tasted right.

Without magic, without belief in it, nothing *went* right. Margie, who'd had her share of that and then some, determined this year would be different.

She used her knife to scoop another dab of icing and said, "It's *believing* that makes dreams come true. My mom taught me that."

Liz's expression softened. "I know. You must miss her something fierce."

Margie nodded and her pony tail bobbed. "Every day, but especially now when I start Christmas baking."

Margie's mom had succumbed to cancer nearly two years ago, right after Christmas. Baking cookies with her over the years was one of Margie's favorite memories—the laughter, silliness and the stories Mom shared while they worked together. Even now, just thinking about it made her ache.

"Mom got me started baking and I still follow most of her recipes."

"You're an amazing baker. I keep telling you, you should audition for that show, *Home Bakers Turn Up the Heat*. Then you'd become famous and could quit your job at Campbells."

Margie wrinkled her nose and scooped more icing. A graphic artist when she wasn't baking, she'd joined Campbell's design firm soon after her mother died, but creating layouts for the backs of cereal boxes didn't exactly satisfy her creative urges.

Campbell's did have one attraction though—Trent Ross. Since the day she started there, she'd had a major crush on him. But Trent didn't seem to see her, at least not unless she came armed with baked goodies.

This year would be different, though. This would be *her year*.

"Campbell's isn't so bad," she said.

"You have to be kidding! You never stop complaining about the place."

Neither did anybody else who worked there, and turnover was brisk. No one seemed to stay long—except Trent, thank goodness.

She paused in her work and stared Liz in the face. "At least I get to see Trent every day."

Liz snorted. "Trent sounds like a first class wienie."

"Hey! Don't say that." Margie swiftly defended the object of her affections, who had sandy blond hair, a charming grin and blue-gray eyes that never failed to send a thrill down her spine.

"He ignores you unless you feed him, and from what you've said he acts like a hound."

"He just hasn't noticed me yet." She might not be Trent's usual type. Among other members of the staff, he seemed to admire leggy women with cutting-edge fashion sense.

Margie had been described as cute, sweet—even elven. Never leggy. She wanted very much to be beautiful—if only in one man's eyes.

She told Liz earnestly, "All that's going to change. I have a plan."

"Oh? Is it a daring plan?"

"Very."

"And what does this daring plan involve?"

"Baking, of course." And magic.

Liz waved the hand not holding gingerbread. "Pontificate."

"This year Mrs. Campbell decided we should have a Christmas party with a Secret Santa exchange." Loretta Campbell, who'd founded the graphic design firm, ran it with an autocratic fist.

"So?"

"Well, I rigged things so I'm in charge of the Secret Santa thing." In truth, no one else seemed interested. Margie had seized the assignment with ease. "And I pulled Trent's name *before* I passed the other names around."

"So?" Liz said again.

"So I'm Trent's Secret Santa."

"O-kay," Liz drew the word out doubtfully.

"You're not getting the whole picture. He'll receive a gift from me and only me. I intend to bake him something that will knock his socks off and make him notice me—really notice me."

Liz's gaze dropped to the table. "You're making him a gingerbread house?"

"No, these are for the children's hospital. I'm dropping off half a dozen. The Secret Santa exchange isn't till next week."

"I see. And what will you bake in an effort to win Trent's heart?"

"I'm pulling out the big guns and making him the cranberry-chocolate Christmas bars."

"Yum," Liz said .

"I know, right?"

"If that doesn't win him over, nothing ever will."

"I agree. Anyway, I believe it'll work." This was going to be her year, her Christmas. Plus she had her secret weapon—magic.

"Good scheme. I can, however, see a couple 'what ifs.'"

"Yes?"

"What if Trent doesn't eat the bars?"

"Can't happen. He always scarfs down my baking the way a coyote scarfs a prairie dog."

"Er—right. And what if somebody else eats them before he can?"

"Equally impossible. The man's a hog—he never shares."

"You're not painting a terribly attractive picture of the guy, Margie."

"Oh, he's attractive." Margie's eyes went dreamy. "Just my type."

"Well, I like your confidence. But what gave you this idea?"

"Mom."

"Huh?"

"What I mean is, I remembered something Mom said. It was that last Christmas we had together, when we were baking." More precisely, Margie had baked while her mom, terribly weak, mostly watched. "She said one day my baking would bring me my true love." She widened her eyes again. "And there'd be magic."

"Oh, sweetie…" Liz told her. "I don't doubt that. Your baking's chock-full of magic."

Chapter Two

"I sure hope I'm doing the right thing, Mom," Margie whispered as she dumped sweetened condensed milk into a bowl and added a measure of almond extract. "Not about the recipe—I know the recipe's great—but about Trent Ross."

Margie heard no reply. If her mom—or rather her spirit—hovered in the warm kitchen, she stayed silent. Margie swore, though, that when she baked she could feel her mom so close, it didn't seem strange talking to her.

"The thing is, I'm tired of waiting. It's time to act. And you did say my baking would bring me my true love."

Promised.

"Yes, you promised." Margie paused with her spoon in the air and listened hard. This time she had heard something...No; it had to be her imagination.

With swift, sure hands she set about assembling the magic Christmas bars. If she felt confident about anything, it was her baking skills.

She wished she felt quite as confident about tweaking the Secret Santa draw. Nothing could go wrong, correct? It better not; the party at Campbell's was tomorrow and she was ready—more than ready—for her Christmas wish to come true.

She patted graham cracker crumbs onto the melted margarine in the pan and scattered on the coconut. Dried cranberries and dark chocolate morsels followed before she poured on the sweetened condensed milk and scattered slivered almonds on top.

Then she paused, lips parted and eyes wide. The last ingredient was the most important. She held out her hands, scooped together in front of her, and imagined them full of magic dust.

What was it Mom always said? Believing in something made it happen.

She knew very well, though, wishing wasn't enough—she'd wished so hard for her mom to get better that last Christmas and it hadn't done a bit of good. Mom slipped away not two weeks later.

Believe. The whisper came again.

Margie squeezed her eyes tight shut. "I believe this measure of Christmas magic will bring my true love to me. As soon as he tastes my baking, he'll know I'm the one."

She blew on the invisible dust and sprinkled it liberally over the bars just before she slid them into the oven.

****

Bryan Kulwicki climbed into his car in front of Wanda's Rental Shop and slowly lowered his head until it rested against the steering wheel. How did he get into these situations? And why did he get the feeling life was taking pot shots at him for the sheer fun of it?

With a groan, he turned and looked at the garment he'd dragged into the car behind him. Large and bulky, most of it draped across the passenger seat, but the head, which came separately, seemed to have a mind of its own. In fact, the branching antlers barely fit into his subcompact.

A reindeer, of all things. He had to attend tomorrow's Christmas party at Campbell's as a freaking reindeer. Could it get any worse? He understood that as the new guy on staff, he stood at the head of the line for crappy assignments. And he tried to be a good sport about whatever he was asked to do.

But this went above and beyond.

Damn, and he'd been looking forward to this party. Not because he particularly liked social events—he didn't—or loved hanging out with his coworkers, whom he barely knew as yet. But because she'd be there.

And it had seemed like such a miracle when he drew her name in the Secret Santa pool. His first chance to get close to her—meant to be.

How the hell was he supposed to attract the object of his attentions while hidden inside a reindeer suit?

"Man, Bryan," he said to himself bitterly as he started the car. "You sure know how to blow an opportunity." Not that Margie MacGillivray ever glanced in his direction, anyway. Any fool could see she only had eyes for Trent Ross.

She seemed like such a smart woman, bubbly and full of enthusiasm. Couldn't she see what a tool Ross was? Or was she so blinded by the idiot's good looks she never noticed the way he used people or that he had a laugh like a braying mule?

"Sour grapes, Bryan," he spoke to himself again, further supporting his private conviction that he'd become unhinged ever since his first day at Campbell's, when he met Margie and saw her wide brown eyes, glossy dark brown hair and perfect smile.

She looked like a Christmas elf—the very best kind. Too bad she wasn't. One of Santa's elves might actually take an interest in a reindeer.

****

"Perfect." Margie pulled the Christmas bars from the oven and inhaled deeply of their aroma before setting the pan on the cooling rack. She'd need to let them cool completely before she cut them and packed them in the special bag she'd bought—one decorated with a silly picture of Santa on the outside.

Santa, who made impossible wishes come true.

"Believe," she whispered to herself. And what should she wear to the party tomorrow? Should she go with seasonal? Elegant?

In a perfect world, she'd prefer to dress like an elf. But she couldn't see that impressing Trent Ross much. Maybe her good black leggings and that sparkly new red top she'd bought. She had those strappy red shoes, too, and they made her legs look great.

Whatever she chose, it had to be perfect. If all went according to plan, this would be the most important party of her life.

Chapter Three

Margie hurried into the elevator, balancing carefully and carrying not only her Secret Santa gift for Trent, but a bowl of dip she'd brought for the party. Wouldn't you know, she complained to herself, it would snow today—the first real snow of the season, two full weeks before Christmas. Usually she found the first snow enchanting. Today, it had snarled traffic and made her hopelessly late.

When the elevator door opened on the fourth floor, which housed Campbell's suite of offices, she saw with relief, the hallway lay empty. She could sprint down to their suite, shed her coat and join the festivities, which she could hear already in progress.

Good thing no one would see her wobbling down the corridor on her heels, much higher than she usually wore. She had her goal in sight when the door of the men's room, right beside her, opened and something large and very tan hurtled out.

That couldn't be…a reindeer?

Whatever it was, it barreled into Margie and sent her flying. She felt the bowl and bag shoot from her hands as she went one way and they went the other. Margie landed inelegantly on her butt and slid a foot or so on the highly-polished tiles. When she looked up she saw…

Definitely a reindeer, all plushy tan and brown fur, with an absolutely enormous head and a set of antlers that would make Blitzen proud. It stood upright on its hind legs, staring at her wildly with big, plastic eyes, before it reached up and plucked off its own head.

"My God, I'm sorry! Are you all right?"

Margie, gazing up at the strange juxtaposition of a deer's body with a man's head, made no reply. She recognized the head: he was the new guy from the copy department .

At the moment he looked disheveled, sweaty and more horrified than seemed reasonably possible. His dark brown hair had followed the deer's head when he hauled it off and now stood on end. His eyes stretched wide with dismay.

"Margie? Are you hurt?"

He knew her name. She certainly didn't know his—if she ever had, she'd forgotten it. New hires usually got dragged around by HR for introductions, but for the life of her, Margie's mind stayed blank.

He knelt on the floor beside her, furry knees against the tiles, and reached out.

"I'm so sorry," he repeated and started babbling. "I'm playing reindeer. For the party. They sent me into the men's room to change and when I came out—well, I didn't see you. I can't see much with the head on. I think I caught you with an antler. They're way too big."

"You hit me like a linebacker."

"I apologize. Really. Are you hurt?" he asked yet again.

"I don't think so." She'd be bruised, that was for sure, especially her butt. And she must look like a fool sprawled here—good thing no one but the reindeer had witnessed her slide. The bowl of dip, which had flown from her hands, had to be a dead loss though and…

"No!" She let out a wail worthy of a fire siren and peered down the hallway in dismay.

Her magic bars!

Sure enough, the bowl of dip had landed upside down at a considerable distance. Good thing she'd chosen a plastic bowl. But the cling wrap had flown off during the flight and spinach-cream cheese blobs splashed the tiles liberally. Margie barely noticed because the Secret Santa package had landed still farther away.

The bag must have attained considerable velocity because it had split on impact. Squares lay spewed everywhere. All her dreams, in ruins.

She moaned like a woman in pain, maneuvered onto her knees and scrabbled down the hallway. "No, no, no—"

"What's wrong? Is that your gift? For the Secret Santa thing?" The reindeer, pursuing her down the corridor, sounded demented. "Here, let me."

Leaping forward, he reached the main landing site ahead of Margie and gathered up the split bag with plushy hands. "Umm, cookie bars! Look, they're all right. Most of 'em didn't actually break, see? Only the ones that flew the farthest. I can get those for you."

"Don't—" Margie began but the reindeer failed to listen. Stripping the furry mitts from his hands, he tossed them down before pursuing the far-flung goodies.

"Please don't bother." Margie climbed to her feet and stood surveying the destruction of her daring plan. Damn it, she'd had such high hopes. She'd believed in her mom's promise. "It's all spoiled."

The reindeer stared up at her in consternation. "No, really—it's okay. I'll bet even these broken ones still taste great." He stared reflectively at the chunk in his hand. "They sure smell good. See?"

Before Margie could protest, he popped the broken bar into his mouth. Dismay promptly closed her throat.

He'd eaten a magic bar. Off the floor, no less. What kind of person did that? And what effect would it have on him?

She struggled to breathe. Calm down, she ordered herself. The spell she'd whispered when she sprinkled on the magic guaranteed that only her *true love* would be affected. That meant Trent. This guy should feel nothing.

But his eyes widened. His face went blank for a moment before becoming transfigured by an expression of bliss. "My. God. That's the best thing I've ever tasted."

"You ate my Secret Santa gift! What am I supposed to do now?"

"I only ate one. I think you can still use the rest. Look, these are all still good. You'll just need a new bag or box. Anyway, it's only a present, right? You can tell the person you pulled, there was an accident. Who are they for, anyway?" He looked at the tag still stuck to the ruins of the bag. "Oh."

He shot Margie a strangely intense look, one she had no hope of interpreting.

The bars weren't just a present. But even if she tried to explain that to this reindeer, he'd never understand.

****

Well, Bryan thought bitterly, *he'd blown that big time. Before he even got a chance to win Margie*

MacGillivray over with his Secret Santa present, he'd completely alienated her. He cursed himself for a clumsy fool.

And after he'd spent most of yesterday evening choosing the perfect gift for her—had agonized over it. He'd hoped when the Secret Santas were revealed, the present would make her look at him and really see him. Now though, all he glimpsed in her eyes was distress.

"Look," he said. "I brought a gift for Mrs. Campbell, a bottle of wine. You can use that as your Secret Santa gift—just switch the tags."

"What about the bars?" she wailed.

"They won't go to waste. I'll keep 'em. I don't mind that some of them hit the floor. Really, they're delicious." He sounded like a demented idiot. How could he hope to attract this woman when he wore half a reindeer costume and behaved like a lunatic?

"I don't want to give him a bottle of wine." She said the words, *bottle of wine* the way she might utter *bottle of poison.* "Those bars were special."

They sure were; given a choice, Bryan would gladly sit down and eat the whole bagful on the spot. He licked the residual chocolate off his fingers and Margie stiffened.

"I'm sure the guy would appreciate a bottle of wine." Bryan judged Trent Ross no stranger to the pleasures of alcohol.

"He really, really likes my baking."

"Then give these to him anyway. Only about half a dozen smashed. Mind if I eat those?"

"Yes, I mind." She marched up and snatched the torn bag from his hands. "I'll go with your suggestion and put what's left in a new package."

"Okay." Given the advantage of close range, Bryan stared into her face. She had the most beautiful eyes he'd ever seen—deep and dark, tipped up just a bit at the corners, with long lashes. Gorgeous, just gorgeous. "Hey, I'm really sorry about the collision."

"Not your fault." She seemed to have calmed down now that she had the goodies back in her hands. "As you said, it's hard to see in that costume."

"Yeah."

Farther down the hall, the door of the office suite opened. Mrs. Campbell's head appeared.

"Where's my cavorting reindeer?" she called.

"Here, Mrs. Campbell." With resignation, Bryan picked up the enormous head and gave Margie a smile. "Gotta go. Don't worry about the rest of this mess. I'll come back and clean it up."

She sighed.

He fitted the head over his own. "Oh, and Margie? Merry Christmas."

Chapter Four

What did I expect? Margie asked herself that question some two hours later as she stood alone by the buffet table. Any party that had started as disastrously as this one could only continue on a downward spiral.

So far, everything about the gathering had proved as painful as her bruised butt. The Secret Santa gifts had been passed out early by the big, tan reindeer. Trent barely glanced at his, now in a box Margie had managed to bum off a coworker. Leaving it abandoned on a table, he'd stood around talking to other people, mainly Mrs. Campbell, and said not so much as a word to Margie.

Of course, he'd need to eat one of the bars in order for the magic to take hold and for him to see her as his true love.

Fat chance of that. So far, he'd eaten only nacho chips, with a drink always in his hand. Margie had one last hope—the moment when the identities of the Secret Santas were revealed. Mrs. Campbell, who had very definite ideas about most things, had asked them not to identify themselves on the tags. Instead, they were supposed to walk up and say, "I was your Secret Santa."

Of course, in Margie's head, she'd imagined Trent would know. He'd take one bite of a magic bar and turn his eyes to her. After all, he knew she brought in treats all the time.

She spared a thought for her own Secret Santa gift, also unopened and tucked into her pocket. It was very small, wrapped in pretty blue-and-silver paper.

"Having a good time?" asked a voice beside her.

Ah, the reindeer—now devoid of his costume and with his hair neatly combed. He it was who'd placed the gift from under the tree in her hands, at Mrs. Campbell's direction.

She shrugged.

"I went back out to clean up the mess in the hallway as soon as I got rid of the suit. It was all clean. You do that?"

"I couldn't leave it. Someone might slip on the way to the restroom."

"Yeah. Listen, I'd like to apologize again."

"Forget it." The afternoon was coming apart around her, nothing working out the way she'd imagined.

He tipped his head toward hers. Not a particularly tall man, he nevertheless topped her five-foot nothing—five-foot three in the red shoes—by quite a bit. "Have you opened your Secret Santa present yet?"

"No."

"I'll bet it's something special. Something picked just for you."

That made her look at him in surprise—really look at him for the first time. He had blue eyes which contrasted nicely with his nearly black hair and a wicked, Eastern-European sort of nose. Not exactly her type, but he had a great smile.

"Maybe," he suggested, "you should open it now."

"Well," she smiled back at him, "maybe I should."

"May I hold your drink for you?"

She handed it to him and drew the diminutive package from her pocket. "Pretty," she said. "I almost hate to spoil it."

"Presents exist to be opened."

That made her smile again. She tugged the ends of the silver ribbon and the bow came apart in her hands. Inside the paper, she found a white box and inside that...

"Oh!" Despite herself she gasped in delight. For the first time all afternoon she forgot the existence of Trent Ross.

"You like?"

"Oh my, it's—it's magical." Nestled inside the box, lay a glass ornament. Margie lifted it out with care. Inside the spun glass globe, someone had created a miniature scene—Santa's workshop complete with elves making tiny toys.

"It's exquisite." She switched her gaze to the face of the man beside her. "Are you, by any chance, my Secret Santa?"

"Might be. Are there prizes for guessing correctly?"

"I don't know." She wrinkled her brows, desperately wishing she could remember his name. "But this must have cost way over the dollar limit Mrs. Campbell set."

"Didn't your mother teach you not to ask the price of a gift? Anyway, I was shopping and it just screamed Margie."

"How thoughtful. I'll treasure it, really. It's just the sort of thing I love."

He smiled into her eyes. "I'm glad to hear that."

A sudden outburst of laughter drew Margie's attention back to the group that included Trent and Mrs.

Campbell. Trent now virtually leaned on his boss's shoulder while giving her his most charming smile.

The reindeer jerked his head toward the group. "Did he like your present?"

"I don't think he's opened it yet." Margie nodded at the neglected gift, alone on a table.

"Hmm. Think he'd notice if I stole another of those bars? I've been craving one all afternoon."

Margie sighed. She might just as well give them to the reindeer—Trent certainly didn't appear to want them.

But then what about her Christmas wish? What about the magic?

"Tell you what," she said on impulse. "I'll bake you a batch as a thank you for the wonderful ornament. I'll bring them in for you on Monday, okay?"

"That would be great, but I'm not sure I can wait till Monday." The reindeer turned to face her. "Maybe we could meet for coffee or something over the weekend."

"Uh—" Margie's heart fell in dismay. Sure, the reindeer seemed like a nice guy, but what he suggested sounded a little too much like a date. And she planned on dating Trent.

No doubt reading her expression, the reindeer said quickly, "Just coffee as friends, I mean. So you can pass along the bars."

"Well…"

"Do you do a lot of baking?"

"I do, actually."

"Just at Christmas or all the time? My grandma used to bake up a storm at Christmastime, and would be in the kitchen late into the night. My sister and I would hang out with her, lick the spoons and generally get in the way."

Margie smiled. "Great memories, right?"

"The best."

"I do bake year-round. I guess you could say it's my hobby. But like your grandma, I make a special effort for Christmas."

"Well, I'm glad to have bumped into you, Margie MacGillivray." He held out his hand. Margie had no choice but to shake it.

"Likewise," she said. "Welcome again to Campbell's."

He drew his phone from his pocket. "Want to give me your number? I'll call with a time for coffee."

Margie did, kicking herself for still failing to remember his name.

He said, "I have to skedaddle. Need to return the reindeer costume tonight or they'll charge me for another full day."

"You had to pay for your own costume? That stinks."

He smiled at her. "I suspect it was worth it."

"Okay. Thanks again, Secret Santa, for the lovely gift."

Another burst of laughter from Trent's group kept her from hearing the reindeer's reply as he stepped away.

The group containing Trent had started to break up; maybe she could intercept him. Surely she'd be able to snag one minute with the man.

Sure enough, Trent headed toward the table where he'd left Margie's gift and picked it up. Before Margie could lose her courage, she joined him there.

"Hi. Did you like your gift?"

He looked at her in surprise and juggled the box lightly. "You mean this? I haven't had a chance to look inside." He cracked the lid and his face lit up. "Hey, those look—and smell—great."

Margie drew a breath. The heck with Mrs. Campbell's instructions. "I'm your Secret Santa. I baked those for you—they're special."

Trent's heavenly blue-gray eyes zeroed in on her. "That's right. You're the girl who brings in all the treats, right? Mary."

"Margie," she corrected, her heart starting to race.

"Well thanks. Thanks a bunch. I'll enjoy 'em."

"I hope so." And she hoped he'd be sure and eat at least one. She needn't tell him they'd been on the floor.

"Sure." With a smile, he reached into the box and popped a piece into his mouth. His eyes crinkled in bliss. "Wow, delicious."

Margie exhaled. He'd tasted the magic. Now everything would change.

As if to prove the fact, Trent leaned forward and deposited a kiss on her cheek. She received a sudden wave of his scent—fresh soap, aftershave and a generous dose of alcohol. "Thanks again, Margie. Merry Christmas."

He sauntered off with a swagger. Margie stood like a poleaxed steer, cheeks flaming, till she realized someone else stood at her side. Loretta Campbell, of all people.

Mrs. Campbell followed the direction of Margie's gaze before she spoke.

"You can do better, Margie."

"What?" Margie stared. She couldn't possibly have heard the woman correctly.

But Mrs. Campbell gave her a knowing look. "That young man's a rogue."

"Oh, Mrs. Campbell, I really don't think—

"He's been busy hitting on me all afternoon. Thinks it will help him advance his career. He's wrong."

"Oh!"

"Let me tell you something, Margie MacGillivray—just consider it my Christmas gift to you: Trent Ross is the sort of man with whom a woman amuses herself. But he's no keeper."

Chapter Five

"I've got to make this work, Sam," Bryan said to the Jack Russell mix who sat on the bathroom floor near his feet. I figure I'll only get one chance with Margie MacGillivray."

Sam vibrated in response, as Sam frequently tended to do. Bryan had rescued the little dog a year and a half ago after seeing an online appeal from the rescue organization that had removed him from an abusive situation.

Despite the mistreatment he'd received, Sam seemed to hold no grudges and loved nearly everybody.

"The question is," Bryan went on as he scrutinized himself critically in the mirror, "how do I turn coffee into something more? I'm pretty sure it's just pity coffee at this point. She isn't interested in anybody except that jerk."

He thought again of how he'd seen Margie in conversation with Trent Ross while he was leaving the Christmas party, and the way she'd looked at Trent.

Like he'd hung the moon, as Grandma used to say.

"Grruff," said Sam in reply.

"You're right; I can't lose heart. You never did, did you boy?"

"Rup!" Sam replied, which Bryan interpreted as meaning, "Treat!" Most of what Sam said could be translated as, "Treat!"

Bryan turned to him. "This shirt all right?"

"Yap!" This time, Bryan hoped, it meant yes.

"I figure if I get her on my own, out of sight of that tool, maybe she'll really see me."

"Yap."

"All right, I'll give you a treat but then I gotta go. I'm meeting her at three o'clock."

He thought back to last night when he'd called Margie, how awkward it felt. For an instant he'd been sure she meant to cancel their coffee date.

Instead she'd said, "I have your gift all ready."

Gift? Oh, she meant the Christmas bars. Thank God for them—probably the only reason she still agreed to meet.

"Wish me luck," he told Sam as he snatched up his coat and dashed out.

A Saturday afternoon just two weeks before Christmas, meant he found the streets packed with shoppers and traffic in a snarl. Bryan drove around the block three times before he found a parking place and hurried into the coffee house five minutes late.

There he panicked, thinking Margie had changed her mind after all, because he couldn't see her at any of the tables. Then he caught sight of her in a long line and joined her.

"Hi," he said, and smiled.

"Hey," said the guy standing behind Margie. "You can't just cut in line."

"I'm with her," Bryan told him, hoping it might come true.

"And I've been waiting ten minutes for a double-double."

Margie turned around. "Don't be rude. Have you no Christmas spirit?"

The guy glowered but shut up.

"Sorry I'm late," Bryan told Margie. "The traffic—"

"Awful, I know." She passed a Christmas bag into his hands. "Here you go."

"Thanks. I see you found a reindeer bag. Ha!"

She smiled and, gazing into her eyes, Bryan forgot for a minute where he was. He forgot *who* he was.

"Hey, buddy," said the guy behind them. "Want to at least move up with the rest of the line?"

Bryan turned around. "Give me a break, will you? I'm trying to…"

"Yeah, yeah I can see what you're trying to do. Just move up."

Bryan and Margie negotiated the rest of the line in silence, picked up their orders and stood like two marooned castaways.

"No tables," Bryan observed.

"That's okay." Margie nodded to the bag in his hand. "At least you've got your Christmas treats."

"No, wait." Bryan felt his afternoon slipping away from him. "You can't leave."

"But…"

"I was hoping we could talk a while, get better acquainted. I don't really know anybody at Campbell's yet."

"This place is jam-packed. I don't think we'll find a table for a while."

"Let's walk down the street to Santa's Village. It isn't far. There are benches, right? And the sun's out."

She smiled slowly. "Okay."

They walked along the sidewalk, buffeted by shoppers and balancing their coffees with care. The village, set up in a tiny park, boasted displays of everything from animated trains to Christmas trees as well as a raised dais where Santa perched on his big chair receiving children. Several benches had been placed at intervals, probably for the convenience of waiting parents.

They chose one next to a large wooden Rudolph.

"Here," Margie said. "You'll be in familiar company. So, Bryan, how did you get the job of playing reindeer for the party, anyway?"

"Low man on the totem pole, I guess. I was ordered, more than chosen."

"Other than being forced to wear antlers, how do you like Campbell's?"

It's great because you're there. Gazing once more into Margie's eyes, Bryan knew that for the truth, but didn't suppose he should say the words out loud. God, how pretty she looked sitting there in the winter sunshine with a fuzzy red hat on her hair and a red scarf bringing out the color in her cheeks.

"Bryan?" she prompted when he didn't answer.

"Oh, Campbell's is okay."

"Don't know if you've had time to notice, but the rate of turnover is pretty fierce. You won't be low man on the totem pole for long—if you stay, that is."

"Oh, I'm not going anywhere." Even if it meant watching her chase that jerk, Trent Ross. "Why do you think turnover's so high?"

"A combination of things. As you've already discovered, Mrs. Campbell's pretty dictatorial. The pay is low and most people find the work soul-destroying."

"I can see that." Already, coming up with fresh ideas for boring copy taxed Bryan's patience to the limit.

"So far I've been stuck in a vortex of plumbing supplies. Ever try to write scintillating copy for a sump pump?"

Margie laughed and countered, "I'm stuck on cereal boxes. Ever try to make an illustration of wholesome ingredients look riveting?"

"So what's your dream?" he asked.

"I'm sorry?"

"Everybody has one, right? If yours isn't illustrating bran flakes, what is it?"

She looked at him—really looked—and for the first time that afternoon he felt as if they connected. "I love to bake. I guess I'd like to do that full time if I could."

"You mean, be a pastry chef in a big kitchen somewhere?"

"Maybe."

"So how did you end up a graphic artist instead?"

"I had to choose which road to pursue, way back in high school. Back then, baking seemed like just a hobby, something I did with my mom. Since her death, it's become so much more."

"You lost your mom? I'm sorry."

Margie's amazing eyes flooded with tears. "Cancer."

"When?"

"It'll be two years next month. She's the one who taught me how to bake. From the time I could stand up next to the kitchen table, we spent so much time laughing and just being close. I—I don't suppose I'm handling losing her very well. And when I bake, well that's when I still feel closest to her."

"Hey, it's hard. Losing somebody like that leaves a big hole in your life." Bryan hoped Margie wasn't trying to fill that hole with Trent Ross. Ross, a real user, would only hurt her again and Bryan could barely stand that thought.

He said quickly, while Margie blinked away the tears, "My grandma was the baker in our family. I felt pretty close to her, too. Her Linzer cookies were to die for—almost as good as your Christmas bars."

"So, Bryan, what's your dream if it's not writing copy for hardware?"

He laughed self-consciously. "The great American novel, of course."

"Wow! Have you started it?"

"I scribble in my spare time."

"Mystery? Adventure?" She leaned her head toward him, face bright with interest. "Don't keep me in suspense."

He laughed, looked into her eyes again and went breathless. "Fantasy. I seem to be a natural at that."

Chapter Six

"Something should have happened by now," Margie muttered to herself as Trent Ross walked past her cubicle without sparing her so much as a sideways glance. It had been nearly a week since the Secret Santa party and the weekend swiftly approached once again. Trent must have eaten at least a few more of the magic bars and should be displaying the effects.

Yet so far, he'd failed to seek her out, neglected to gaze at her longingly or pant for her company. In fact, at the moment, he appeared to be panting after the new girl from accounting—Jenny—and had just followed her toward the breakroom.

Margie wondered if it would be too obvious if she got up and followed him in turn. She could use a cup of tea.

"Hi." Bryan Kulwicki popped up at the side of her desk like a jack-in-the-box. She seemed to bump into him often enough, which was nice, but she'd begun to wonder if she should worry about it. He had eaten part of a magic bar, after all—off the floor no less. But no—the spell she'd cast had been meant to work on her true love and no one else.

"Hi," she returned, genuinely glad to see him. Maybe his appearance at this moment had saved her from making a fool of herself with Trent.

"How go the cereal boxes?"

"Mind-numbing. How about the plumbing copy?"

"Soul-destroying. I think I need some downtime, Margie. How about dinner tonight?"

"Oh, I don't know. The weather's supposed to turn bad. I just want to get home and snuggle up."

"Want some company? I could stop by with a take-out, save you from cooking when you get home."

"I wouldn't want to put you to any trouble."

"No trouble at all."

Margie stole a look at Trent who'd trapped Jenny just outside the door of the breakroom and now leaned against the wall beside her, oozing charm.

That charm should be directed at me, she thought—harnessed by Christmas magic.

She sighed. "You know, Bryan, that sounds like fun. We can watch a movie if you like."

He grinned. "I like. Only thing is, I should swing by my place first and take care of Sam."

"Sam?"

"My dog. I don't like to neglect him after he's been alone all day."

"Bring him along. I love dogs." And that would make it less like a date, more like a visit from a friend. She scribbled her address on a card and handed it to him. "Thanks, Bryan, that's very thoughtful of you."

He pocketed the card and went off happily. Nothing wrong with spending time with a friend, Margie assured herself, while waiting for Trent to come to his senses.

****

It started snowing when Margie left work, and traffic once more snarled in the busy streets, the weather adding to the congestion. Margie grew concerned about Bryan and Sam even before she reached home.

Hurriedly, she tidied the tiny apartment, half expecting a phone call saying Bryan had decided not to come.

Instead, she heard a knock on the door and opened it to find Bryan with a take-out bag in one hand and a small bundle of canine energy tucked into the other arm. Snowflakes decorated his dark hair and the shoulders of his coat.

"Please come in," she invited. "Oh, Bryan, I'm so sorry; it's getting bad out there. Maybe you shouldn't have come."

"Hey, I'm not scared of a little snow."

"Looks like this might turn into more than a little. Well, hello!" Margie went on as Bryan passed the small dog into her arms in order to remove his coat. "You must be Sam."

"The incomparable Sam," Bryan agreed, hanging his coat from the doorknob. "As you can see, he has only one eye but that doesn't stop him getting into enough mischief for a dog five times his size."

Sam wriggled in Margie's arms and licked her chin. She melted and relaxed for what seemed like the first time in days.

"I'm glad you didn't leave him home alone. Here, come on in. Just put the bag on the table."

"Nice apartment. Great tree!"

"You can see what has pride of place." Margie walked to the tree and pointed out the spun-glass ornament, front and center.

"Looks good. Do you know, I live only a few blocks away from here? Sam and I sometimes pass this building on our walks."

"Small world."

"Yeah. I picked up the food at the deli on the corner."

"Please make yourself comfortable. I dug out some movies—what would you like to watch?"

"Feels like a perfect night for a Christmas movie."

Margie smiled. "I just happen to have a few."

"Somehow, I thought you would."

****

If his heart hadn't already been lost, Bran thought some time later, it would have been stolen by the picture Margie MacGillivray made cuddling Sam in her arms. The feisty little Jack Russell mix, who seldom kept still for long, seemed content there and unusually docile.

He already loves her. As much as I do? Impossible.

Bryan knew that thought should scare him a little. After all, he'd reached the age of twenty-eight pretty much unscathed in the love department, after years of casual dating.

Now nothing about Margie felt casual—not how right it seemed being here with her this evening, or the way his heart sped up every time he so much as looked at her. Certainly not how bemused he became when she smiled at him or how breathless he got at the thought of kissing her.

They never did watch a movie. Instead, they shared the food he'd brought and then talked about everything from childhood to life at Campbell's. The tiny living room became a cozy haven full of warmth and laughter while, outside, the snow piled up and the world grew quiet under a blanket of white.

Sheer happiness, so Bryan decided, lay in Margie's company. He wouldn't ask much more except maybe to switch places with Sam, still in her arms, or to steal that kiss.

And the best part—the very best part—was that Margie proved to be everything he'd imagined: warm and funny, smart and adorable. Her eyes filled with ready tears when he told her how he'd first seen Sam's picture on the site of a rescue organization and read about his history of past abuse.

"You'd never know it now," she said, tickling the little dog under his chin. "Bryan, you've done a wonderful job with him."

"All I did was give him some security."

"And love."

"And love. He's spunky, that's for sure." Bryan laughed. "I don't think he's going to want to leave here tonight." *Just like me.*

"What made you decide to take on a rescue, anyway? Most guys wouldn't want to be tied down."

"He'd been in rescue for eleven months. I guess most potential adopters were put off by the whole eye thing. I just knew eleven months was too long for any dog to wait for a home and if I could take him, I should."

"I'm so glad. And, Sam, you're welcome to visit any time, right along with Bryan. In fact if he shows up without you, I'll be disappointed."

At last Bryan rose and stretched. "Much as I hate to say it, we'd better get going for home. Work tomorrow."

Margie got up too and went to the window. "Oh, you should see all the snow. I hope you can get home safely."

"It isn't far." Bryan came up behind her and peered out over her shoulder. Instead of the scene outside, he saw Margie reflected in the windowpane with him standing close enough to wrap her in his arms, the lights from her Christmas tree glittering all around the image.

Longing seized him. If only that image might be his future—dared he make it his Christmas wish?

"Margie, thanks for a great evening."

She turned around, virtually in his arms. "It was fun. We'll have to do it again, only actually watch the movie next time."

"This weekend?"

"Maybe. You know, it's nice knowing I have a friend at Campbell's."

Friend? Oh, but he wanted to be much more than that. How could he convince her?

"Margie," he whispered. "Margie, you're magic."

All at once, he did have her in his arms. Had she taken that extra half step, or had he? Impossible to tell, because it felt so natural, so right, as did the moment he placed his mouth on hers—natural, thrilling and momentous.

She tasted sweet and tangy, like those Christmas bars she'd made. Just like the bars, he knew one taste would never be enough.

But she broke the kiss hastily, much sooner than Bryan liked, and placed both hands on his chest. When she raised her eyes to him, they looked enormous.

"Bryan—not a good idea."

"I think it's the best idea I've ever had." Should he tell her he loved her? No, that would send her running for sure.

She shook her head. "This isn't a line we should cross. It's too nice, us being just friends."

"Just friends." God, she still didn't see him as anything more. What would it take?

How could he become her Christmas wish?

Chapter Seven

"Hey, um—Margie, right? Could I talk to you a minute?"

Sunk into a miasma of inexplicable gloom, Margie started when someone spoke at her elbow.

Two days had passed since the evening she'd spent with Bryan and Sam, and she couldn't stop thinking about it—how comfortable she'd felt with the three of them cozied up together. To be honest, she couldn't stop thinking about the kiss that ended the evening. She'd relived that moment again and again till she could barely concentrate on anything else.

Not a good idea. She sure didn't want to mess up what looked like a really promising friendship. And anyway, she was interested in…

Trent. That was who stood beside her cubicle now, speaking to her.

She stared at him with wide, disbelieving eyes but he failed to dematerialize. That looked like Trent all right—fair, wavy hair, six feet of lean muscle and a smile that could reduce a woman to a puddle of goo at thirty paces.

Maybe her sprinkling of Christmas magic had finally taken effect.

"Oh, hi," she returned.

"Hi. Can you spare a minute? In the break room?"

"Yes, sure." Margie's thoughts raced as she got up and followed Trent to that haven. Loretta Campbell, aware she employed a stable of creative types, set no hard-and-fast rules about break times but encouraged them to take a breather when they needed it. That occasioned a fair bit of coming and going, as well as socializing. The breakroom, large and nicely-appointed, contained comfortable chairs, a gourmet coffee maker and a microwave.

At the moment, Margie found it occupied only by Mark from the copy department, who sat with his feet up and earbuds plugged into his ears.

She ignored him and focused entirely on Trent, who turned to her with an eager look in his eyes.

"I wanted to ask you about those Christmas bars you made me."

Margie's heart started to pound and she flushed with heat. This was it. The spell had taken a while to work, that was all.

"Yes?"

"You did make those, right? They're really good."

"I'm so glad you liked them, Trent."

"Amazing, simply amazing."

How long had she waited for him to look at her this way, with enthusiasm in his eyes? Oh, thank you, Mom.

Trent went on, the charm oozing off him, "And I remembered you're always baking something, bringing in treats. Right?"

"Yes, baking's my hobby. Well, it's more than a hobby really."

"Great hobby. Your boyfriend's a lucky guy."

Margie reeled. "Well, I don't actually…I'm not seeing anyone at the moment."

"That's good."

"Is it?"

"Then there's no one to get mad if you attend a party with me."

"A party?" Aware that her conversation failed to be even remotely scintillating, Margie felt too overwhelmed to care. It was happening. Trent Ross was asking her out.

"It's a Christmas thing with family. It's also my grandparents' fiftieth anniversary so I can't get out of it."

A family gathering. Surely that had to be significant?

"So, are you busy this weekend?"

"Well…" She'd made tentative plans to see Bryan and Sam again, watch that Christmas movie. But they hadn't set a specific time and surely, being a friend, Bryan would understand. This was Trent Ross asking her out.

"Which day's the party?"

"Saturday, unfortunately. Family stuff always seems to take up the best day of the weekend, doesn't it?"

Maybe she could still see Bryan on Sunday.

"I'd love to come to the party with you, Trent."

The way his face lit up made her breathless. "Oh, that's great. I can't tell you. You've saved me from a real bind."

Did he want her to believe he had trouble getting a date even for a family function? Could this truly be her magic spell kicking in?

"I'll look forward to it. Is your grandparents' anniversary celebration Christmas-themed?"

"Yeah. In fact everybody's supposed to bring a Christmas dish. I thought maybe you could make those bars." He smiled persuasively. "They sure were good."

"Well yes, I could do that. No trouble."

"Since you like to bake so much."

"I do love to bake. I also love Christmas parties."

"Great! And my sister asked me to bring some *hors d'oeuvres*. I don't suppose you could bake those too?"

"Most *hors d'oeuvres* aren't baked but I do have a few recipes—"

"You're a lifesaver, Margie. I really appreciate it. Here's my number." He pulled a card from his shirt pocket and passed it to her. "Text me your address and I'll pick you up around three o'clock. Okay?"

"That will be perfect, Trent."

"Perfect!" he repeated and granted her another smile before he hurried out of the breakroom.

Margie found herself staring at Mark who stared back at her over his coffee for a long minute till she retired to her cubicle.

****

"Another conquest for our man Trent," Mark muttered as he slid into his chair at the desk opposite Bryan's.

Bryan looked up from his copy without much interest. He'd been thinking about plans for this weekend—now that there was so much snow on the ground, maybe Margie would like to go sledding on Saturday. And Trent Ross's dating habits meant little to him.

They could visit the park and then go back to his place after, where she'd have a chance to see Sam. Bryan could swear the little dog had been moping for her.

Bryan knew *he* had.

He raised an eyebrow at Mark in inquiry. "Oh? Who's he hitting on now?"

"That cute little girl with the brown hair over in layout."

Bryan shot up in his chair. For an instant his heart seized in his chest. "Who?"

"I think her name's Maggie or something."

"Margie, you mean."

"That's it. He just hit her up in the breakroom for a date. On Saturday."

"You're kidding." Bryan wondered in alarm whether he was having a heart attack. His brain screamed, *That's the girl I love.*

"Yeah, he's smooth, I have to admit. Makes it look so darned easy."

"She said she'd go out with him?" Of course she did—it was what she'd been waiting for.

"Sure did. Almost fell over herself."

Oh God, Ross had made a move and he, Bryan, had lost her. Not that he'd ever really had her. Except as a friend. Aw hell, who was he kidding? Had he really thought he could compete with someone like Ross?

Damn straight he had. He did. Because he and Margie MacGillivray were meant to be together. He knew it right down to his bones. And he wasn't going to give up so easily.

Striving desperately to sound casual, he asked, "Where's he taking her, do you know?"

Mark shrugged. "Some party. Even asked her to bring the food."

Ah, playing on Margie's soft spot, was he? Well, he, Bryan, could do that too and he happened to know when it came to soft spots, Margie had more than one.

He managed to be in the right place at the right time when five o'clock rolled around and made sure they rode down in the elevator together. Margie looked radiant—she fairly glowed— which worried Bryan a little. Did it make her so happy, having a date with Ross? And why couldn't she look at him like that?

"So, Margie," he asked as jovially as he could manage, "are we still on for Saturday?"

Her face fell almost comically. "Actually, Bryan, I was going to—"

He didn't give her a chance to finish. "'Cause Sam is really looking forward to seeing you. He's even moping a little."

"Is he?" Her gorgeous brown eyes became wide with distress. "Oh, what a sweet boy. But—"

"I was thinking we could take him out for a romp in the park. Or go sledding. You choose."

"Both ideas sound great. Could we switch it to Sunday though? I have a date. On Saturday. With Trent."

Funny how hearing her say it felt like a knife to the chest even though he'd been forewarned.

"Trent Ross?"

"Yes. A family Christmas thing."

And Bryan could just see her all dressed up in some holiday outfit, looking too pretty for words. All at once, he didn't know what to say. He'd meant to make a game of this, goad her a little. But it no longer felt funny.

He lowered his voice even though, against all likelihood, they were alone in the elevator. "Margie, you'll be careful around that—around him, right?"

"You mean Trent?"

"Yeah."

"Why?"

"The guy's got a reputation. Something of a charmer."

"He's charming all right."

"A hound."

"I don't think that's a very nice thing to say. You barely know him, do you?"

"I hear things. And see things."

She stiffened. "I think I can look after myself, thanks, Bryan."

"Can you?" He wanted to look after her. With his every male instinct, he longed to protect her—for life.

"Of course. You must take me for a fool."

"Not a bit." He took Ross for a jerk and a user. "I just wish—"

The elevator dinged and the door opened. They stepped out into the busy lobby.

Bryan reached out for her. "Look, Margie—"

"I need to go, Bryan. I have some baking to do tonight."

"Sure. I'll call you on Sunday. Hope you have a good time tomorrow."

And that, he admitted to himself as he watched her hurry away, made one whopper of a lie.

Chapter Eight

Margie blew out a long breath in an effort to control her nervous excitement. She'd barely slept last night, anxious that nothing should go wrong with her plans. She'd tried on no less than six outfits and agonized over the one she chose. By the time Trent showed up at her door, she could barely think straight.

Because it was working. The magic she'd employed—and her mom's promise—was coming true. How much more thrilling could things be?

Trent showed up looking handsome and just a bit impatient. "All ready?" he asked when she answered the door. "You have the food?"

"Sure."

"You look nice," he said belatedly.

So did he, clad in a dressy coat worn over a nice pair of slacks and a Christmas sweater.

"Well," he said, "I guess we'd better get this thing over with."

Not the best sentiment to begin a date, Margie thought, *especially one she'd looked forward to so long.* But he explained when they got in the car.

"I hate these family things. Always awkward. But this one's unavoidable."

"I'm sure it'll be fun."

He flashed her a smile. "Keep that thought."

By the time they reached their destination, a large handsome house on the west side of the city, Margie felt alive with expectation. This date would start it all—her relationship with Trent and their potential future together.

Her first clue that things might be going terribly wrong came when they arrived at the house and Trent introduced her to his aunt, who answered the door, as *Mary*.

"Hi, Aunt Carol. Please show Mary, here, to the kitchen. She has the food you requested."

"It's Margie, actually."

Trent flashed an apologetic smile. "Oh, sure. Sorry! Auntie"—he waved a hand—"just tell Margie what you need her to do."

Margie's stomach clenched in doubt and apprehension. But..."

"Come along, dear." Aunt Carol led her away into a large kitchen, never pausing to introduce her to anyone. They passed groups of people, some of whom appeared to be the guests of honor, but none of them so much as glanced at Margie.

In the kitchen, several other women bustled around preparing platters of food. They looked at Margie without much interest.

"What did you bring?" Aunt Carol indicated the plate and tray Margie juggled. "Put those on the table. We're just getting ready to take the *hors d'oeuvres* around."

"But..."

"You can take off your coat and hang it in the little closet off this hallway. Oh good—I see Trent asked you to dress appropriately for the holiday. Now, girls, it's going to be busy out there. I don't want to see any of our guests without a drink or a plate in hand."

Margie, who'd shrugged out of her coat, glanced doubtfully at the other girls in the kitchen—no less than four of them. She certainly didn't mind helping out, especially at a family party, but this felt all wrong.

"Excuse me," she said more firmly, "but there seems to be some mistake. Do you think I'm waitstaff? I'm here as Trent's date."

They all stared at her. Two of the girls exchanged looks. Aunt Carol gave a tight smile.

"Is that what he told you? I swear that boy needs a good slap."

Margie's cheeks flamed. "Are you saying I'm not here as a guest?"

Now the women looked sympathetic. Aunt Carol shook her head and left the kitchen. The other girls picked up various trays and followed—all but one. She lingered and gave Margie a kindly smile.

"My aunt's right—Trent needs a good talking to. He's my cousin, but I can't say anyone in the family approves of how he's living his life. Honestly, you're probably better off without him."

"You think so?" Margie choked back tears of humiliation and disappointment. How could she have gotten things so wrong?

"He plays women," the girl said. "You're not the first and probably won't be the last."

Anger rushed to Margie's defense. "Well if he thinks I'm staying here to serve food like his maid, he's mistaken."

"Good girl. You go tell him."

"I will!"

Margie shrugged back into her coat and picked up the items she'd prepared with such care—a platter of shrimp puffs and the bars which, in this case, certainly contained no magic. She marched back out of the kitchen with her supporter on her heels.

Margie hated scenes—usually. She went out of her way to avoid them and certainly shunned being the center of them. Now though, her anger carried her straight to Trent's side.

He stood with a small group of other men and already had a drink in his hand. He stared at Margie when she popped up next to him, as if he'd never seen her before.

"Trent?" she asked loudly and clearly. "Do you mind telling me exactly why I'm here?"

"Huh?" His expression—which moved from astonishment to rueful chagrin—might have looked comical in another situation.

"Why did you ask me to come here with you this afternoon? Was it a date?"

The room, which had been full of merry noise, fell abruptly silent.

"Well, uh—it's a party. Everybody enjoys a party, right? Hey, Mary, lighten up. Don't take yourself so seriously."

"No, Trent," she told him firmly, "Taking myself seriously isn't my mistake—it was taking you seriously. You heard the word *food* and thought of me, right? That's the only reason you thought of me."

"Hey, come on."

"Well, here's your food. I hope you enjoy it."

Margie tore the foil off the shrimp puffs over which she'd labored so long last evening and smashed the tray into Trent's chest. Bits of shrimp filling stuck to his sweater, accompanied by several gasps around the room.

Trent's expression changed again. His face darkened with rage and he no longer looked even remotely handsome.

"You little bitch."

The words were soft, but just as ugly as his expression. Margie recoiled and dumped the Christmas bars at his feet.

"That's what I think of you," she said, and headed for the door.

She heard Trent follow her, and heard the other guests begin whispering to one another in his wake. Trent caught her at the door and seized her arm in a bruising grip.

"Let go of me."

"You stupid girl. How could you embarrass me that way?"

She glared into his eyes. What had ever made her think him attractive?

"You used me," she accused. "Let me think this was an actual date…"

His lips curled in a cruel smile. "Well, how dumb are you? Did you really think I was interested in anything besides your cooking?"

Yes. She'd pinned her hopes on the possibility he'd been interested, and woven a Christmas spell to that end. Now fury made her say, "I must have been crazy."

"Yeah, you must."

"You're not nearly good enough for me." She reached for the doorknob.

"Yeah well," Trent sputtered. "If you walk out of here, don't expect me to ask for your help again."

"I can't run fast enough!"

Not till she stood out on the street, still suffused with anger and humiliation, did Margie realize she had no way to get home. The street, a sea of cars, seemed worlds away from her little apartment.

She dug her cell phone from her pocket and made a call. "Liz? Can you come get me?"

"Sure, honey. Where are you? And what's wrong?"

"I'll tell you when you get here." Margie gave Liz the address. "But I'll be down on the corner." She couldn't get far away from Trent Ross fast enough.

Chapter Nine

By the time Liz arrived, the tears had started, but they were still mostly tears of anger. Margie shed them the whole way home while telling Liz the tale.

"That creep," Liz said indignantly. "Want me to stop for some ice cream?"

"He isn't worthy of ice cream. After all, it isn't a break-up." Except of her long-held dreams about the man.

Fool, fool, fool.

"Liz," she wailed. "What's wrong with me that I could be taken in so easily? Am I really that naive?"

"Margie, you're sweet and warm, and you tend to think the best of people. That's what makes you *you*. Since there isn't a mean bone in your body, you don't expect others to be mean either. That's a good thing."

"It isn't. I need to grow a thicker skin. You'd think I'd have learned a few things after losing Mom. I put all my hope in her getting well, trusted in the magic of how much I loved her. That failed too." Margie wept in earnest now, Trent nearly forgotten in the larger pain.

"Oh, sweetie, you've never really got over losing her, have you? But, Margie, maybe the magic's its own reward. It's a gift to be able to believe the way you do—a beautiful thing your mom taught you, right?"

"Right."

"Don't let Trent Ross steal that from you. I think you need to keep believing. 'Cause you deserve something—someone—so much better than him."

"I know."

"The guy's a piece of work, a total loser. I'd hate to see you waste another thought on him."

"But, Liz, it's not just that. What about the magic Christmas bars?"

"What about them? I thought you dumped them on his shoes?"

"Not those bars—the original batch. They were supposed to bring Trent to me."

Liz shuddered. "Thank God they didn't."

****

Bryan woke nose to nose with Sam, who stood on his chest. The little terrier mix had a singular way of letting him know when he'd slept long enough.

A sick feeling churned in his gut when he realized it was Sunday. He lay flat on his back in the bed, wondering what had happened between Margie and Trent Ross yesterday.

Had Margie been swept off her feet? Did she now believe she loved that ass? Did she think all her dreams had come true? Damn it all, why did Ross have to ask her out anyway?

'Cause Margie was magic, that was why. She was like nobody else, funny and warm, so beautiful... Even a half-assed idiot like Ross had to see that eventually.

But she's supposed to be with me.

Sam licked his chin and whined.

"Sure," Bryan told him. "The world could end, civilizations rise and fall, universes die and you'd still want your breakfast."

Sam huffed at him excitedly. *If only*, Bryan thought as he obediently got out of bed, *his life could be so uncomplicated.*

He fed the dog and took him for a long walk through the snowy morning, thinking how much nicer it would be if Margie were with them. But she might be lost to him. He'd promised to call her later today, but would she even want to hear from him?

Before he took Sam home, he made his own Christmas wish—a big one.

****

Margie woke with the mother of all headaches and no immediate memory of what had happened the day before. Then it returned to her in pieces that made her want to pull the blankets over her head.

Idiot!

She and Liz had shared a couple glasses of wine after she got home but that didn't explain the way she felt now. Like a woman emerging from a bad dream.

Liz was right, she thought, pulling herself together. She'd wasted enough time and energy on Trent Ross. Better she found out now, what he was really like.

She jumped into the shower and stood under the pelting water, wondering why her disappointment refused to fade. Maybe Liz was right about that too— maybe it had little to do with Trent. She still grieved for her mom.

And was that so hard to accept? she wondered as she toweled herself off. She and her mom had been best friends, had laughed and worked in the kitchen together. The promise of magic wrought by those Christmas bars had seemed like her mom's last gift to her.

Now, nearly two years after her death, Margie had believed her mom's last promise would come true.

Your baking will bring you your true love.

She stood staring at herself in the steamy bathroom mirror, arrested.

But wait, *wait.*

Trent Ross couldn't be her true love. He'd proved to be a first class creep, a user and a cad, just like everyone warned.

But someone else had sampled her magic Christmas bars—off the floor, no less.

Bingo! It seemed as if she heard Mom's voice, filled with laughter, in her ear. *It took you long enough.*

Still only half-clothed, Margie hurried from the bathroom to her Christmas tree in the living room. The spun glass ornament hung front and center, winking at her, waiting for her. Just the way love waited?

She cupped the delicate bauble in her hand and remembered a number of things all in a rush—the way Bryan had looked at her after he sampled that broken Christmas bar, the comfortable evening they'd shared and the kiss after.

She'd nearly missed the real gift, nearly tossed away the substance for the glitzy package.

And any damn fool knew it was what you found inside that mattered.

But had she left it too long? Did the magic still hold?

Would Bryan give her another chance?

****

"Okay, so we're agreed I'm going to call her," Bryan said to the dog that sat beside him, nearly vibrating with energy. "Or should I text? Mention real casually the plans we made for today? Which do you think would be best?"

Sam whined. He seemed impatient with the way Bryan had been dragging his feet since their early morning walk.

"You're right; whatever I decide to do I should just get on with it. But, see, here's the thing: if I'm honest, I'm afraid that ass Trent laid on the charm so thick yesterday, he swept her off her feet and made her forget I exist. Maybe she's gone over to the dark side with him, made plans to see him again today. God knows, I'd happily spend all my time with her if I had the chance. Why wouldn't he?"

Sam yipped in apparent agreement

"And here's an awful thought: what if she spent the night with him? What does that do to our chances?"

Sam vibrated harder.

"I agree. It doesn't seem like something she'd do. But it is something he'd do and it's obvious she can't see through the guy."

Sam did a little dance in place, displaying his eagerness.

"Yeah, all right—all right. It's better to know. And there's no room in this situation for cowardice."

He picked up his phone and had just located Margie's number when the doorbell of his apartment rang. Sam took off for the door, feet scrabbling.

Phone still in hand, Bryan followed him, swung open the door and saw...

Margie.

She wore her red knitted hat and a fluffy white jacket, and had her arms full of bundles. Her brown eyes sparkled and her whole face lit up when she saw him.

"Margie," he said involuntarily, his heart leaping in his chest alarmingly. "What—uh—I was just going to call you."

She bent to pat Sam with one mittened hand before shooting Bryan a look he couldn't quite read. "I hope you don't mind me stopping by."

"I don't mind."

"We did have a date for today, right? You, me and Sam."

"A date." His heart somersaulted again. Maybe he needed to see a doctor. If so, now definitely wasn't the time, not when a miracle had just appeared at his door.

He smiled broadly. "Come on, Sam, let the lady in." He took some of the packages from Margie's arms. "What's all this?"

"I stopped by the grocery on the way and bought a few things. Thought we might take Sam sledding and then come back here. I'll make dinner and bake you a dessert for after."

Ah, Margie in a new mood—positive, engaged, a woman who knew what she wanted. If only she wanted him.

Suddenly, he ached to fold her in his arms, draw her close and kiss her senseless. But he sensed they might be at the beginning of something—something important—and a man with any wits didn't rush a magic spell.

Instead, he invited her in with a gesture. "Welcome, Margie MacGillivray.

Welcome to my heart.

Chapter Ten

A perfect day, Margie had to admit. They'd taken Sam to the park, hauling Bryan's old sled behind amid showers of snowflakes. The three of them had ridden down the hill more times than Margie could count and she'd laughed till her sides ached in the most delightful way. In fact, Margie couldn't remember when she'd laughed so much.

Back at Bryan's apartment, he'd dug out some Christmas CDs and they'd cooked a meal together, complete with dessert—one of her mom's recipes, of course.

Now they sat on the sofa together, the lights from Bryan's tabletop tree, the only illumination in the room. Sam, completely tuckered out, snored near Margie's feet and Margie, examining her heart, found nothing there but contentment.

She felt so close to this man—as if she could say anything and be understood. Only one thing would make it better.

As if he heard her thoughts, Bryan put his arm around her shoulder and drew her in. Her head found the crook of his shoulder as if made to fit.

"Margie, do you believe in Christmas wishes?"

She closed her eyes and smiled. "Sure do."

"Would it surprise you to know I made one? And I think—hope—it might be coming true."

She turned and looked into his face—a good face, a kind face, one she might delight in seeing her whole life long.

"The thing about wishes is," she whispered, "you need to believe in them. Making the wish is the easy part. Keeping the faith is harder."

"I agree."

"My mom used to say—" Margie broke off and laughed sadly. "Well, she used to say a lot of things. She shared a heart full of wisdom when we worked in the kitchen together."

Bryan's eyes grew compassionate. "You miss her."

"I don't think I ever realized how much, till I met you."

"Me?"

"There was such ease in her company, a sense of comfort and belonging. I think—hope—I've found that with you."

"Margie, you couldn't say anything that makes me happier. I've never felt the way I do about you, not toward anyone."

He leaned forward, reaching for her lips with his. Much as Margie longed for his kiss, she stopped him with a gentle touch.

"Wait. Bryan, I have a confession to make."

"Eh?"

"Those bars you ate the day of the Secret Santa party? The ones that landed on the floor? They had a magic spell on them."

"Did they?"

"Yes. You see, my mom told me that last Christmas we had together, my baking would bring my true love to me."

"Your true love, eh?"

"Yes. And so when I made those bars, I sprinkled on some Christmas magic—the very best kind."

"I see."

"So I want you to be aware what you're feeling for me right now—what are you feeling?"

"You can't imagine." His eyes turned dark.

"Well, it might be partly to blame on those darned Christmas bars."

"Tell me what I'm feeling for you," he said and pressed his lips to hers.

Ah! She tasted warmth and sweetness, an underlying flavor of passion. Love—so much love—and yes, a definite glimmer of magic.

He broke the kiss and smiled into her eyes; it warmed Margie to her toes.

"I, too, have a confession to make, Margie MacGillivray."

"You do?"

He nodded. "Your mom was, no doubt, a very wise woman. I love the things she taught you and I most sincerely believe in Christmas magic. But it wasn't the Christmas bars."

"What?"

"They're not responsible, Margie. Not for the way my heart speeds up when I see you or the way I feel when I look into your eyes—or the fact I'm convinced you're the most beautiful woman I've ever seen."

"Beautiful? Me?"

"So very beautiful. Amazing, warm and talented—I do believe you should shake the dust of Campbell's off your feet and try out for that cooking show."

"You do?"

"Most definitely. My point is, I was in love with you before I ever tasted the Christmas bars."

Margie's eyes widened. *Well, Mom—I guess I was the one who needed the magic to see what was right in front of me. Either way, you were right.*

She caught Bryan's face between her hands and bestowed a kiss that, she hoped, made her feelings more than clear.

"Merry Christmas, my darling," she told him. Oh yes, this was definitely going to be her year.

Margie's Magic Christmas Bars Recipe

Ingredients:
1/3 cup melted margarine
1-1/4 cup Graham cracker crumbs
1 cup coconut
1 cup dried cranberries
2/3 cup dark chocolate morsels
1 can sweetened condensed milk
1 teaspoon almond extract
1/3 cup slivered almonds
1 generous sprinkle Christmas magic

Preheat oven to 350 degrees

Melt margarine in bottom of 8X8 or 9X9 inch baking pan. Distribute graham crackers evenly over margarine and pat down gently. Layer on coconut, cranberries and chocolate morsels.

Empty sweetened condensed milk into small bowl. Add almond extract and mix well. Pour milk mixture over other ingredients in pan and scatter slivered almonds on top.

Lastly, don't forget to sprinkle on a generous measure of magic while making your Christmas wish!

Bake 30 minutes or till lightly browned.

For a 9X13 inch pan, double all ingredients. Be sure to add a little extra magic and allow a little extra baking time.

May all your Christmas wishes come true!

ABOUT THE AUTHOR
SHARON KLEVE

Sharon Kleve was born and raised in Washington and currently lives on the Olympic Peninsula with her husband.

Sharon is a multi-published author of contemporary romance. She loves romance. She loves reading romance, living romance, and especially loves writing about romance. She gets no greater feeling than watching her characters come alive in each other's arms. Most of all, she loves giving her characters the happily ever after they deserve—with a few bumps and bruises along the way.

One of her favorite things to do is pick up a new book and sink into the story, immersing herself in the emotions between the characters. She hopes to inspire her readers the same way her favorite authors have inspired her.

When not writing, she can usually be found either curled up in her recliner with her cat and a good book, or in the kitchen baking sourdough bread or bagels.

Email: sharon.kleve@gmail.com
Blog: http://authorsharonkleve.blogspot.com/
Facebook
Page: http://www.facebook.com/sharonrkleve
Facebook
Timeline: https://www.facebook.com/#!/sharonkleve
TSU: https://www.tsu.co/SRKLEVE
Twitter: https://twitter.com/SharonKleve
Pinterest: http://www.pinterest.com/srkleve/boards/
Goodreads:
 http://www.goodreads.com/author/show/5399389.Sharo
 n_Kleve
Linkedin: http://www.linkedin.com/pub/sharon-
 kleve/56/ab/691/
Library
Thing: http://www.librarything.com/profile/SRKLEVE
Newsletter: http://eepurl.com/btSoS1
Google
 https://plus.google.com/u/0/+SharonKleveAuthor/posts

ABOUT THE AUTHOR
JENNIFER CONNER

Jennifer Conner is a best-selling Northwest author who has seventy short stories, books, and audiobooks. She writes in Christmas Romance, Contemporary Romance, Paranormal Romance, Historical Romance, and Erotica.

She has hit Amazon's top fifty authors ranking and her books have been #1 in sales.

Her novel Shot in the Dark was a finalist in the Emerald City Opener, Cleveland, and Toronto RWA contests.

Jennifer is an Associate Publisher for the indie e-book publisher, Books to Go Now who resides in the Seattle area. They pride themselves in helping new authors get their foot in the door with well-edited manuscripts, professional covers, and platforms uploads.

She lives in a hundred year old house that she grew up in. Her semi-small town holds an interesting mix of resident hillbillies, yuppies and Navy Seals. And of course, Seattle, only a few miles away, is the birthplace of Starbucks so coffee is always on the check list. She blows glass beads with a blowtorch, (which relieves a lot of stress and people don't bother you) and is a huge fan of musicals.

She loves to hear from her readers.
Please email her at jenniferconnerwriter@gmail.com
  Website: http://jenniferconnerbooks.com/
  Email: jenniferconnerwriter@gmail.com
  Publisher:

Bookstogonow@gmail.com www.bookstogonow.com
BLOG: http://jenniferconnerwriter.blogspot.com/
Facebook: https://www.facebook.com/jennifer.conner2

For Updates about new releases as well as exclusive promotions, visit Jennifer's website and sign up for the VIP mailing list.
http://www.jenniferconnerbooks.com/

ABOUT THE AUTHOR
ANGELA FORD

Angela Ford originates from Nova Scotia...Canada's Ocean Playground! Her love of the ocean and sunsets are always in her heart and give her inspiration. Her love for words keeps her turning the page. She is never without a book, whether she's reading or writing. Her dedication to volunteer and involvement with cyber safety seminars gave her an Award of Distinction and sparked the idea for her first book *Closure* - Best Selling Action/Adventure/Crime/Suspense. Ms. Ford continued her FBI series with *Forbidden* and *Obsessed.* Now available in a boxed set – *Cyber Crime Series.* In between mysteries, Ms. Ford writes short contemporary romance...sometimes with a dash of suspense! Visit her website Romantic Escapes at http://www.angelafordauthor.com to connect with her on social media. She loves to hear from her readers – they keep her smiling!

ABOUT THE AUTHOR
TAMMY TATE

Tammy Tate was born and raised in Hollywood, Florida but has lived most of her adult life in Texas. Her passion to write began in high school. It follows her everywhere she goes...creating a world where anything is possible. She's been married to the same wonderful man for over thirty years. Her secret to a long marriage? It's easy when you marry your best friend. In her world, Friday night is still date night.

Before she became a full-time author, she was an Executive Secretary, a Computer Consultant/Technician, and a Communications Officer (Police Dispatcher). She doesn't mind a challenge which has allowed her to race a late-model in a women's powder puff race, run barrels and poles in a play-day rodeo and drive an 18-wheeler. Somewhere in between, she and her husband raised three wonderful children. When she's not breathing life into her characters or jotting down ideas for a new book, she is most likely spending quality time with her husband or curled up with a good book.

Since she believes reading is the next best thing to writing, she enjoys romance, fantasy, science fiction and thrillers. In December of 2013, she signed her first book contract with a traditional publisher. Her books have made Amazon's Best Seller list.

Email me:
authortammytate@aol.com
Like my author
Facebook
page: https://www.facebook.com/tammytateauthor
Follow me
on Twitter: https://twitter.com/authortammytate
Check out
my blog: http://authortammytate.blogspot.com
Publisher: http://bookstogonow.com

ABOUT THE AUTHOR
LAURA STRICKLAND

Award-winning author Laura Strickland, born and raised in Western New York, has pursued lifelong interests in lore, legend, magic and music, all reflected in her writing. Although she enjoys travel, she's usually happiest at home not far from Lake Ontario, with her husband and her "fur" child, a rescue dog. Author of numerous Historical and Contemporary Romances, she is the creator of the Buffalo Steampunk Adventure series set in her native city. *Margie's Magic Christmas Bars* is her second title with Books To Go Now.

Books to Go Now

You can find more stories such as this at www.bookstogonow.com

If you enjoy this Books to Go Now story please leave a review for the author on a review site which you purchased the eBook. Thanks!

We pride ourselves with representing great stories at low prices. We want to take you into the digital age offering a market that will allow you to grow along with us in our journey through the new frontier of digital publishing.
Some of our favorite award-winning authors have now joined us. We welcome readers and writers into our community.

We want to make sure that as a reader you are supplied with never-ending great stories. As a company, Books to Go Now, wants its readers and writers supplied with positive experience and encouragement so they will return again and again.

We want to hear from you. Our readers and writers are the cornerstone of our company. If there is something you would like to say or a genre that you would like to see, please email us at inquiry@bookstogonow.com

Made in the USA
Middletown, DE
11 November 2017